False Friends

Grace Thompson is a much-loved Welsh author of saga and romance novels, and a mainstay of libraries throughout the United Kingdom and beyond.

Born and raised in South Wales, she is the author of numerous series, including the Valley series, the Pendragon Island series, and the Badger's Brook series. She published her 42nd novel shortly after celebrating her 80th birthday, and continues to live in Swansea.

D0994380

Also by Grace Thompson

Holidays at Home

Wait Till Summer
Swingboats on the Sand
Waiting for Yesterday
Day Trippers
Unwise Promises
Street Parties

A Badgers Brook Saga

The House by the Brook
A Girl Called Hope
A New Beginning
The Heart of the Home
False Friends

A Pendragon Island Saga

Corner of a Small Town
The Weston Girls
Unlocking the Past
Maisie's Way
A Shop in the High Street
Sophie Street

The Valley Sagas

A Welcome in the Valley
Valley Affairs
The Changing Valley
Valley in Bloom

GRACE THOMPSON
False Friends

CANELO

First published in the United Kingdom in 2007 by Severn House Publishers
Ltd

This edition published in the United Kingdom in 2021 by

Canelo
31 Helen Road
Oxford OX2 0DF
United Kingdom

A CIP catalogue record for this book is available from the British Library.

Print ISBN 978 1 78863 385 7
Ebook ISBN 978 1 91085 931 5

Look for more great books at www.canelo.co

Printed and bound in Great Britain by Clays Ltd, Elcograf S.p.A.

One

Lowri Vaughan ran down the road with her friend Marion Lewis close behind. They were going to collect the library books from Mrs Saunders to take back to the library and choose new ones for her. 'She loves romances, historical or modern, so it's easy to find something to suit.'

'As long as it won't take too long,' Marion said. 'The picture starts at two o'clock and we don't want to waste your half-day.'

The house where Mrs Saunders lived was one of a pair of cottages not far from the one rented by Lowri and her mother. She had been doing this service for the old lady for several months, so it was a surprise when she was told that she no longer needed her help.

'It's no trouble,' Lowri said, as dread filled her heart. 'If I haven't chosen well this time I'll try again, no bother.'

'Best you *don't* bother.' The woman's voice was sharp and she began closing the door as Lowri stared at her in disbelief.

'Why, Mrs Saunders?' she demanded, knowing the reason without needing to be told. 'Is it because my father is in prison? And like the rest you believe him guilty? Is that why, Mrs Saunders?' Hands on hips she stood as Mrs Saunders lowered her head and wordlessly closed the door.

'Come on, Lowri, let's forget her and those like her and go and have a laugh at the pictures, is it? Silly woman is what she is.'

'Yes, silly woman, following the opinion of the rest without a thought in her head! Her son was my father's friend, they used to go fishing together.'

'But he's a policeman so now she automatically believes your father's sentence was deserved.'

'Well she's wrong and one day I'll prove it!'

Lowri followed her friend and sat in the dark picture house, forcing smiles as the laughter of others told her when. She was aware of little that was happening on the screen.

They walked home and from Marion's comments, Lowri gleaned something of what the film contained. She would share the best moments with her mother. Laughter and a cheerful attitude, they were what would help them through the next few months, and years, while people stared and treated them like criminals because of her father's arrest and imprisonment.

The next morning she went early to the post office where she had worked since leaving school. Smiling cheerfully she waved to Mrs Potter, the postmistress, as she went in through the side door and straight into the shop to lift the blinds as usual. She waved to the two women standing outside waiting for the door to open. Since the arrest and sentencing of her father she had been afraid of becoming one of those people who expect endless sympathy when they were in trouble. She knew that even the kindest people soon became tired of a moaner and she was determined not to become one. Laughter and a cheerful attitude, she reminded herself.

'I stopped at the bakery and bought us a couple of cakes for our elevenses. Lovely morning, Mrs Potter. Beautiful walking through the park, fuchsias and geraniums still flowering a treat. You want me to start on the window, don't you? Shall I wait until the first rush is over?' She hung up her coat as she chatted away. 'Right then, what colour crepe paper are we using this week? Greens and browns with a touch of yellow, might be nice for a change, what d'you think?'

She turned to look at Mrs Potter who hadn't responded to her cheerful remarks and she wondered why. 'Is something wrong?' she asked in concern. 'There's me chattering on. Don't you feel well? Can I do anything?'

'I'm sorry, Lowri, but I have to ask you to leave.'

'Leave? You mean take the day off? But why?'

'No dear. I have to give you notice and instead of working the week, I think you should leave at once. I'll pay you for the week, and a bit extra, of course.'

Lowri frowned. 'What have I done wrong? Tell me and I'll put it right now this minute.'

'You... you just don't fit any more. I'm sorry. I'll give you an excellent reference, of course.'

Lowri's face hardened. 'It's because of my father, isn't it? But he's innocent! He would never steal from his own firm, and how can anyone suspect him of murder? Jimmy Vaughan, a criminal? You can't believe that, Mrs Potter, you can't! And besides, how does that affect me? I do my job and I've never caused you a moment's worry, so why...?'

'Your father, Jimmy Vaughan, was found guilty of fraud, and the rumours persist in blaming him for Ellis Owen's death. They aren't trivial charges and he is in prison, sentenced for fraud.' She looked away to where a

3

customer was knocking irritably on the glass door. 'Lowri, you must have noticed that people are refusing to be served by you. That's why I've asked you to leave the counter and clear the stockroom, do the weekly accounts, and the window display – jobs I usually do myself. I'm so sorry, my dear. I wish people were more tolerant, but I have my living to make, you must see that?'

'My father is innocent!'

'I hope you find a way to prove it. If I can help in some way...' Mrs Potter finished lamely.

Taking down the coat she had just hung up on the hall stand, Lowri left without another word. She went home, wondering how she could explain her unexpected return from work. Should she tell her mother now? Or wait until she'd found another job. She took the long way home, trying to decide how best to break the news to her already distressed mother. She went in, chanting: laughter and a cheerful attitude, to herself as a way to deal with trouble, to find her mother Emily sitting staring at a letter, the page shaking in her hand.

'Mam? What is it?' She snatched the letter from her mother's hand and read a politely worded request for them to vacate the premises by the end of October 1950.

'So this is it! Dad accused of fraud and suspected of a murder he didn't commit, and the rest of us are punished for no reason at all. The sentences the judges hand out aren't supposed to include the family, are they? So why have we been thrown out of our home and why have I lost my job?' All her plans of the best way of announcing this were forgotten.

'You've lost your job?'

'Yes, and for no reason at all! Just a couple of gossipy women complaining about being served by the daughter

4

of a convict and Mrs Potter tells me to leave. How fair is that? That Mrs Saunders is my guess! So important she is since her Harold joined the police force. How can she do that?'

Her mother didn't reply.

Later, they discussed the situation and Emily decided she would find a flat near the prison, where she could see Jimmy as often as she was allowed and wait for evidence that would prove his innocence.

'I want to get away too,' Lowri said, 'but I want to go further away, where no one knows me, and start again.'

'After all the publicity the case has been given you can't run far enough,' Emily told her daughter sadly.

'I still need to get away from these people who are treating us so badly. Dad doesn't deserve to be locked up in a prison cell and we don't deserve the treatment our one-time friends are handing out. It's so unfair, Mam.'

'We've been so lucky until now, luckier than many. We survived the war, except your Henry, and I suppose we can't expect to live a lifetime without some tragedy.'

'Nonsense! This isn't a tragedy. This is injustice. How can anyone say Ellis Owen was killed by my father when his body has never been found? Mam, I know it's foolish, but I look around as I walk the streets, expecting to see his face. I just know Ellis Owen isn't dead and he'll turn up one day.'

'Wishful thinking, love. Although his body was never found, the police have implied that Jimmy was suspected of manslaughter without even finding the body. I know it sounds crazy, but it could have been much worse. If there'd been the slightest evidence of pre-meditation, your father would have been charged with murder. You know there were rumours of a knife attack when they were in the water.'

'Dad wouldn't use a knife on someone! How can they think it?'

'Rumours spread and change and sometimes the impossible becomes just a little bit more believable with every telling,' Emily replied.

They gathered boxes and started packing their home into them, wondering when or where they would see their belongings again.

Harold Saunders, the local policeman, called that evening and, having been told they were moving, he offered to help if he could. 'Perhaps I can clear the unwanted stuff. It's a problem without a car and maybe I can take what you need to your new address.' Emily frowned and looked at him. 'You've never believed Jimmy guilty, have you?'

'I can't say. But I will tell you that Jimmy and Ellis Owen, and Jimmy's partner Jack Morris, enjoyed many a day fishing or out in Ellis's boat, and putting Jimmy in the role of cheat and possible murderer is impossible.'

They accepted his help, which seemed a relief to him, and arranged for him to help move the heaviest furniture when they were ready to leave.

'See,' Lowri said. 'Not everyone believes Dad is guilty.'

'Yet his partner, the man who helped him build their business, still does. I don't think I can ever forgive Jack Morris for accusing him of fraud.'

Suddenly, there was a crash of breaking glass and they hugged each other in fright. In the silence that followed, Lowri stepped from the hall into the kitchen. 'Mam,' she said, forcing her voice to sound calm. 'Just look at this!'

'This' was a shattered window and a scattering of stones and half bricks spread across the kitchen floor.

'I'm calling the police. We don't deserve this, Lowri.'

'No, Mam, don't let's bother. You have the address of that flat near the prison and I... well, I might join you later, but first, I'm going on that little holiday. I need to get away so I can decide what I'm going to do. Come on, you make us some tea and I'll clear up this mess, then let's finish packing, shall we? Later on I'll go and ask Mr Franks if he'll repair the window. Surely he won't refuse a few hours' work?'

It was early in November 1950 when they closed the door on their previous life and turned to face a new start. Tearfully, Lowri watched her mother step on to a bus to start her journey, heading for a small flat near the prison where her father was incarcerated.

'Mam, please try and persuade Dad to let me visit,' she pleaded.

Emily turned and gave a sad smile. 'He insists he won't let you see him in that awful place and you must wait until he's been given his pardon.'

Lowri gathered her small suitcase, handbag and thick winter coat, and went to stay with Mrs Potter, who had kindly agreed to allow her to stay for one week, as long as she kept away from the post office. Her bicycle and the rest of her things were already there and everything was set for Marion and her to leave early the following morning.

'No big send off, then,' Lowri said the next morning with an attempt at a smile. 'I thought they'd all be out to cheer and hope I'd never come back.' She glanced at her

7

friend and added, 'Thanks, Marion. I don't know what I'd have done without you.'

Marion had only been a casual friend, and Lowri had never been introduced to Marion's family. They had met occasionally to go to the pictures or for a walk, but when her father had been arrested, Marion had been the only one to remain her friend. She was grateful for the support and vowed to make sure Marion enjoyed the holiday with no reminders of her own unhappiness. Laughter and a cheerful attitude, she reminded herself.

Now they were going on holiday, having booked at a small guest house and were planning to explore the countryside around a small town called Cwm Derw – Valley of Oaks. The guest house where they were to stay was run by Elsie and Ed Connors. Ed Connors opened the door but apologetically explained that his wife Elsie was unwell and needed to rest in the afternoon. 'If you could come back nearer five o'clock she'll be here to greet you,' he promised.

They left their bicycles and pannier bags and Ed directed them to The Ship and Compass. 'My sister Betty Connors owns it and she'll give you a cup of tea while you wait.'

Betty Connors provided a few bar snacks and as the place was about to close after the lunchtime session, she made them a plateful of sandwiches and, having been told they were staying at her brother's guest house, invited them into her sitting room to eat them. In between serving her customers she told them a little about the area and suggested places for them to visit.

A barman called frequently and she dashed in and outbetween serving customers. She pulled a face. 'Will

Summers he's called but the regulars call him "Willing-But-Won't"! I can't get a decent barman and everyone I do get is worse than the one before.' The voice called again and she groaned and replied, 'All right, Will, I'm coming. Useless creature,' she whispered as she disappeared.

The air was chill, but once they had deposited their luggage and handed the landlady their temporary ration cards, they set out to explore. Walking along the hedge-lined lanes there was little to disturb the quiet. No traffic, only the occasional ticker-tick of a robin, the alarm call of a blackbird warning of their approach, a guard dog doing his duty.

'I wonder what the people are like in this place,' Lowri mused. 'Would they consider my family evil because of what happened to my father?'

'I suppose people are the same wherever they live, although, I can't imagine anyone in a lovely area like this being as horrible to you as those you've just left,' Marion answered.

'I think you're right and my only hope is to find a place far away from home and hope no one finds out.'

They walked along a lane and turned left, down a little used, overgrown track beside a wood, where branches from both sides met overhead to form a tunnel. Then as the track meandered alongside a steep drop into fields, they went into the trees. Fallen leaves were carpeting the ground and there was that exciting scent of autumn in the air, dampness, with a hint of smoke from some nearby garden fire.

Without any sense of direction they wandered through and out on the other side, from where they could look down on what once had been a farm but was now being cleared for building. After sitting for a while watching the confused activity below, they turned right and found themselves in a narrow lane between two large gardens.

Darkness was about to fall and with it came rain. So not being sure how far they were from the guest house, when they saw a narrow path leading to some large trees they ran up to shelter. The hedge beside where they ran was privet and still clothed in green, but as they pressed into it to avoid a soaking, Lowri looked through and saw an old house.

'Marion, look at that! Isn't it beautiful?'

Attracted by the air of peace it offered, they stared through at the neatly set out garden until the rain had ceased. Then they pushed through a weakened part of the privet hedge and stared some more.

'Can I help you?' a voice asked, and they turned guiltily.

'Sorry, we were just sheltering from the rain, we didn't mean to pry, but it's a lovely house and—'

The man laughed. 'It's all right, don't worry. I agree with you. I own the place but I don't live here. In fact, no one does after this month. The tenant is moving away.'

'I feel sad to think of it being empty. It should be a much-loved home, filled with happy people,' Lowri said, then apologized again. 'Sorry, I think we'd better go.'

'Are you just visiting, or have you moved in around here? I know most people, as I run the local ironmongers and paint store.' He offered his hand. 'Geoff Tanner. You've probably seen my shop on Steeple Street. Call and say hello if you're staying a while. My wife Connie loves having visitors. Oh, and by the way, the house is called Badgers Brook.'

After introductions were completed, Geoff left them to go into the house. Marion giggled as he moved away.

'I felt like a child being caught scrumping apples from his orchard, didn't you?'

'A bit,' Lowri admitted. 'He seemed pleasant, although he might not have been so kind if I'd introduced myself as the daughter of Jimmy Vaughan, suspected murderer!'

'Stop being dramatic, the world isn't full of people like your ex-boss, remember.'

'Filled with people who believe him guilty, though! Except you and me.'

'We'll probably find his shop as we explore,' Marion said.

'But I don't think we'll call in, do you?'

'Come on, we'd better find our way back to the guest house or we'll miss dinner.'

Over the next few days they ignored the constant rain and walked around the lanes, caught buses into Cardiff and to nearby villages, and began to learn their way around. Lowri went into the post office to buy postcards and in that familiar setting relived the shock of being told by Mrs Potter she must leave, that no one wanted to be served by the daughter of a criminal.

She had worked in the post office since she'd left school and presumed she would stay there until she married. Hope of a wedding had been ruined when her fiancé had died on the Normandy beaches in 1944 when she had been eighteen and he only a year older. Now she had been forced to leave the job she enjoyed, because customers refused to be served by the daughter of a suspected murderer. Marion was the only one to remain her friend.

The arrest and conviction of her father, followed by being told she was no longer required to work at the post office had been serious blows to her security. She felt lost, belonging nowhere and with nothing to hope for in the future but friendless, empty days. Marion would lose interest soon like all the rest, giving in to the pressure from others. Then with no job and her mother far away and her father unreachable, she would be alone. At the age of twenty-four the future was an empty place. Now their holiday was over, Marion would leave like all the rest.

While staying with Mrs Potter, she had used the time putting furniture, carefully labelled, into store and discarding all the surplus; memories of childhood burned in the ash bin, she thought sadly. Unable to get a job, she wandered around, searching for a place where she could settle. She cycled or went on buses, passing through towns and small villages as though expecting a place to attract her and persuade her to stay.

She had refused to go with her mother; that seemed like giving in. Staying around here had been a defiance, and half hid the hope that one day her father would return here, head high, to face those who hadn't believed in his innocence. She had felt that if she went too far away she would be losing faith in him, admitting he was guilty. Now she realized she had no choice. She would have to leave the place her father knew as home. She needed to find somewhere she could earn a decent living. But where?

Something took her back to Cwm Derw and she found herself walking along the lane with the wood on her left and the houses set back from the lane on her right. When she reached the house called Badgers Brook she walked up the path a little way and stopped to stare. It appeared to be empty; the windows lacked curtains, there was no smoke issuing from the chimneys, but it was more than those things: the place had an empty, abandoned look that she couldn't quite explain. It was as though the house was sad. She laughed at her fey imaginings. The man they had met in the garden told them the tenants were about to move out, so of course it would have an abandoned look.

She walked on up the lane but after a few paces she stopped, walked back and went right up the path to what appeared to be the back of the house. Peering through a window she saw a kitchen with a large oak table, a gas cooker and empty shelves. The walls were painted a cheerful yellow and with the door open into the hall, she could just see a part of what must be a living room, but now the flagstone floor was dusty and without a shadow to suggest any furnishings.

She heard the slam of car doors and turned to see Geoff Tanner, the man she and Marion had met on their earlier visit. A smiling woman followed him carrying a basket covered with a white cloth.

'Hello again – Lowri, isn't it? This is my wife, Connie. We've brought a picnic, won't you join us?'

'A picnic? At this time of the year?'

'Oh, Connie is a great one for picnics. We sometimes go to the beach and sit and look out at the sea. It's beautiful whatever the season.'

They went inside and beckoned for her to join them. She hesitated but encouraged by the smiling woman, she stepped inside.

Although the air was chilly, the house was warm even though no fire burned in the grate. As she and Connie walked through the empty rooms, Geoff lit the fire and fed it with wood from a log box in the hearth. Connie unpacked her basket and they sat in garden chairs that had been brought in for the winter and ate sandwiches and cakes and drank coffee from the flask Connie had brought. The place seemed to wrap her in comfort and peace.

'It's silly, I know that, but I can see myself living here,' Lowri told them. 'It's far too big and with no job I couldn't possibly afford it, but I feel in some strange way that I belong.'

'If it's for you you'll find a way. We have no one moving in at present and it's never empty for long,' Connie said.

She gently asked questions and at first Lowri was cautious, not explaining why she was without work. Then, knowing she was at risk of discouraging these pleasant and friendly people, she said, 'Even if I do manage to find a job – which is unlikely – you wouldn't want me as a tenant.'

'Why do you say that?' Connie asked.

'Because my name is Vaughan.' Connie and Geoff looked vague and she went on, 'My father is Jimmy Vaughan, he's in prison serving a sentence for a theft he didn't commit.'

Defiantly, she continued, 'Many people believe he murdered Ellis Owen, the man who really stole the money. Now d'you see why I haven't a job or a chance of living here?' Under patient questioning, she told them all that had happened.

'Stella Jones at the post office is looking for someone to help her, she's broken her leg,' Geoff volunteered. 'Tripped over her little dog she did,' Connie added, as Lowri stared in disbelief.

'I worked in a post office for years; it's all I've ever done!' Her shoulders drooped then as she felt the slight hope drift away. 'But it's no use. Once I tell her who I am, she'd find an excuse to say no. Everyone does.'

'Give her a try. If you've had disappointments before you can risk another one, can't you?' Connie began packing the basket with the remains of her picnic and Geoff dampened down the fire.

They smiled encouragingly. 'Come on, Lowri,' Geoff said. 'We'll give you a lift, it's on our way.'

'If the house wants you here, you'll find a way,' Connie said mysteriously. The post office was on the main road opposite the cafe, and it was closed.

'Stupid of us, we forgot it's half-day closing and there's us with a business ourselves,' Connie said with a laugh. She got out and knocked loudly on the shop door then called through the letter box. 'Stella, we've brought someone to see you.'

A few minutes passed as, with a dog barking an accompaniment, Stella made her way to the door grumbling about her crutches, her leg and the inconvenience of people calling when the shop was shut and Colin not there to help.

'Oh, it's you two, come on in. The kettle's on the boil.' She turned apparently without noticing Lowri, who hesitated at the door. 'You an' all, girl, shut the door mind, or there'll be a queue, Wednesday half-day closing or not.' Lowri did as she was told.

Stella's living room was overfilled with furniture and on one chair was a large railwayman's coat. Near it was a bed now occupied by a little terrier.

'This is Lowri,' Connie began as she pulled the kettle closer to the fire on the hob. 'Experienced in the post office and looking for a position in Cwm Derw.'

'A bit of luck finding her, wasn't it?' Geoff added. 'Sneaking a look into Badgers Brook when we saw her first.'

Between complaining about her leg and how difficult it was to find someone experienced and available, she began asking Lowri questions. 'Why did you leave your last job, then?'

'I didn't leave, I was sacked because people refused to let me serve them.' Lowri stared defiantly at Stella as she went on. 'My father is in prison for—'

'Have *you* ever been guilty of theft? Embezzlement?' Stella interrupted.

'No, but—'

'That's all right then.'

'It isn't! His name is Jimmy Vaughan and he's—'

'Wait a minute, that's the man who's suspected of murder, isn't it?'

'Yes.' Lowri didn't add her usual defence of him and declare him innocent of that too. This wasn't the time.

'You can't be accountable for what your father did – or didn't do,' Stella added quickly. 'Start tomorrow, could you?'

'Well, no, I have to find a place to live and—'

'Elsie Connors's guest house is empty.'

'And get furniture out of store, and…' she stopped as Connie shook her head.

'We have enough furniture gathered over the various tenancies to start you off and you can stay at the guest house for a couple of days while you get everything ready.'

Geoff smiled. 'See? If you really want something, it's easy.'

It was as though a great weight had been lifted and in her mind she saw her father's face smiling at her and knew this was the right thing to do. Badgers Brook had called to her, wanted her there, and as Connie had promised, every problem was being pushed aside to enable her to live there.

It was much later, when she was lying on her uncomfortable bed in Mrs Potters' house that she realized she hadn't even asked about the rent.

The next day she told Marion of her decision. 'I know you're right and I should accept that Dad will be in prison until he's an old man, but I've always felt I should stay here so Dad will be able to come back home. But Cwm Derw isn't far from where Ellis Owen lived when he embezzled that money from Dad's business. Marion, don't laugh at me, but that house, Badgers Brook, called to me, and everything has slotted into place once I decided to live there. Now I think that by living there, near where Ellis Owen lived when the embezzlement was discovered, I might learn something to prove my father is innocent.'

'You don't *know* that this... er – what's his name – Ellis Owen, is guilty, do you? It's only what your father believes, remember.'

'I do know it wasn't Dad and who else could it have been? If only the money would turn up, then the police would know it wasn't my father who stole it.'

'What d'you think of my moving into Badgers Brook with you?' Marion asked, changing the subject. 'I can always get cleaning work and we could share the expenses.'

Lowri stared at her. 'You'd come with me? But that would be marvellous. But your job and your family...?'

'My family won't mind. With a house full like Mam's got they'd be glad of the extra room. Yes, I liked the place and it would be an adventure, wouldn't it? Well? Yes or no?'

'Yes, oh yes! The rain shower that drove us to shelter near Badgers Brook has changed my life and perhaps yours too.'

'It's time I moved on. Like you, I've been in the wrong place for too long. Holding on to Mam's apron strings, and me twenty-four. Ashamed I should be. Now, who's the best cook? Housework is my forte as you know, but I'm prepared to try anything and everything.'

—

It was just a week before Lowri took over the tenancy of Badgers Brook. Geoff and Connie were quick to do as they promised and a couple of beds, a surprising number of chairs and some curtains were quickly delivered. She went to the post office on the following day and Stella Jones thankfully told an ex-school teacher she was no longer needed.

'Slow she was. No mistakes, mind, but so slow the little ones were driving their mams wild, standing so long and impatient to leave. Little ones aren't good at standing still.'

She was brief in her explanations, leaving Lowri to sort things out for herself and by arriving early and staying late for the first week, she soon grasped the few differences in the system from the way Mrs Potter had run her business.

The local people were curious about her, but from the back room, or the seat she had set up in the shop, Stella interrupted questions by reminding them that: 'The poor dear girl hasn't got time to gossip, I work her too hard, don't I, Lowri?' Smiling, Lowri agreed.

The furniture she and her mother had placed in store had been sorted and what she needed was on its way. She stood at the kitchen window on a bitterly cold Wednesday afternoon, looking out towards the lane, waiting for the arrival of the lorry. She was curious to examine the contents of her father's desk, which the police had returned after their investigations were completed. It was unlikely she would find something the police had missed, but she had to keep trying; her father depended on her. He had insisted he had kept diaries in which he had noted his suspicions and the changes in the account statements. Several of his diaries had turned up but there had been nothing to substantiate his accusations against the dead man, Ellis Owen. The important one was missing.

A stranger approached, opening the gate and waving as she walked up the path. Lowri stood at the door and waited for her to introduce herself.

'Kitty Jennings,' the lady announced. 'Me and my Bob live at the next house along the lane. Neighbours we are so I thought I'd come and say hello. Work at the post office, don't you? Lowri, is it?'

'Come in,' Lowri said opening the door wide. 'I'm waiting for some furniture to arrive.'

'Kettle on, is it?' Clearly knowing where everything should be, Kitty went in and filled the kettle and set a tray with four cups. 'Gasping they'll be, the driver and his mate.' She fished out a large pictorial tin from the bag she carried and set out some cakes.

An hour later, as the heavy van pulled up outside the gate, Kitty ran to fetch her husband, and after brief introductions, Bob Jennings helped the van driver to unload, placing the items where Lowri – and occasionally Kitty – instructed.

'You'd best come back with Bob and me for a bit of dinner tonight, tired you'll be. Too tired to cook a proper meal.' Bewildered by the way she had been taken over by the kind and willing Kitty, Lowri could only agree. When she went up the stairs that night, she had a comfortable feeling that by great good luck and against all expectations, she had fallen among friends.

Two

When Marion arrived, complete with a few treasures including a wind-up gramophone and some records, she went to the post office and placed an advertisement in Stella Jones's window offering her services as a cleaner. The response was immediate and over the first few days she went to several houses and chose ones where she agreed to deal with the regular cleaning. A few people took in summer visitors and at these she agreed to help on 'changeover day', usually a Friday. This involved changing beds and washing the linen as well as making sure everything was welcoming for the new arrivals.

From the first day she regularly visited her mother and although Lowri suggested going with her, she always made some excuse.

'It is a bit disappointing,' Lowri admitted to Stella one morning as she opened the shop door and let the first customers in. 'I was so pleased to think I'd have company but she spends a lot of time out of the house, either with her family or just walking. She's made it clear I'm not wanted. Don't you think it strange?'

'I love a bit of company, but I know there are those who need time on their own. My Colin is a very social man, loves people he does, but he often enjoys a quiet hour or two on his own at the allotment or our country cottage.' Accepting her friend's need for privacy, Lowri and Marion soon settled comfortably at Badgers Brook, the stout walls gave them a sense of security and once inside they relaxed and felt at home. Lowri was still a little disappointed that at a time when she needed friendship and support, Marion spent a lot of time out of the house. Lowri gave up inviting herself along and hoped one day that Marion would suggest they went together, but it never happened. When she suggested they went to see if they could find where the badgers lived, she was firmly reminded that although they shared the house, their lives were their own.

Although they shared the house and dealt with the running of it in equal partnership, the casual friendship they had enjoyed before her father's arrest hardly changed. They usually ate together, sharing the cooking and cleaning amicably, they discussed their day as they prepared for bed, but there was a barrier that Lowri knew she must not cross.

'I'm puzzled at never being invited to meet Marion's family,' she told Stella. 'It's probably because of my father,' she added sadly.

'Doesn't she talk about them?'

'Oh yes. She tells me about her sisters, brothers and the step family frequently, repeating some of the amusing events in the lively household, but evades any suggestion that I should visit or that they come to Badgers Brook so I can see for myself.'

'Give it time,' Stella advised. 'With a big family like her mother has, it must be difficult to cope with visitors – and taking them out must be like setting off on safari!'

There were no shortage of visitors to Badgers Brook. Very few days ended without at least a couple of callers at the house near the brook. Betty Connors from The

Ship and Compass often called during the afternoons, and she sometimes brought Gwennie Flint from the chip shop with her. Kitty and Bob often popped in and on Wednesdays, when she could get someone to bring her, Stella Jones came limping up the path asking if the tea was made. Between them Bob and Colin dealt with the garden.

Lowri loved the atmosphere of the old house and every knock at the door pleased her. Whoever was standing there was sure to have a smile, convinced of a welcome. What if Marion's parents didn't want to meet her; she wasn't exactly lonely. Her father's imprisonment must be the reason they were avoiding her but as long as Marion continued to share the house she could cope with the disapproval of her parents. One day, when he'd been pardoned, they would meet her father and realize how wrong they'd been to doubt him.

–

Lowri's father, Jimmy Vaughan, had had a fifty percent share in a small factory making underwear and specializing in night attire. When they'd been demobbed from the Navy, he and his friend Jack Morris had started their business when the factory had been stood down from making uniforms and other requirements for the forces, and, from nothing had built up their reputation.

They had taken on Ellis Owen to deal with the accounts as they had been unable to afford a qualified accountant and, with Jack Morris's son Dic sometimes coming in to help, they had struggled during those first few years. Dic Morris had his own business, designing and selling sculptures and jewellery, helped by his wife before her untimely death from influenza, but he found a few hours every week to check on their progress.

Helped by the end of clothes rationing in March 1949, the business had made steady progress and they were slowly and cautiously expanding. Then it suddenly began to show signs of trouble. Although the orders were still keeping their dozen employees busy, the profit was no longer there. Any savings they had were pumped into the place, but they began to realize that somehow someone was stealing. An investigation of the orders, both out and in, was quietly undertaken but nothing was found. It was Jack Morris's son, Dic, who found the evidence in the columns of the monthly totals. Close examination showed totals had been altered and figures were giving a false result. There was only one man for whom this deceit was possible, their accountant, Ellis Owen.

Ellis had been with them from the first day and when Jack and Jimmy's suspicions were aroused, they were foolishly hesitant to go at once to the police. Instead they gave him the chance to explain and he declared himself as puzzled as they were. He promised to work overtime in an effort to solve the mystery. Jimmy persisted in his demand to go to the police but Jack felt they owed the man the chance to prove himself innocent. So they did nothing, waiting for Ellis to come up with an answer. Although Dic and Jimmy tried their hardest to persuade Jack, he was reluctant. The three of them were friends. How could he accuse Ellis of stealing from them? Being in business himself Dic knew there was no doubt about the dishonest intent. The alterations were quite deliberate and all in one direction-reducing the money in the firm's profit and the balance in the bank. However hard Ellis Owen searched, he wouldn't find the missing money. It was gone.

When the truth that they had been systematically robbed was undeniable, Jimmy had officially accused Ellis. Before the police could act, he went to tell him to his face, hoping Ellis would admit it and save them a lot of trouble. The three of them had been friends and spent many hours together out of work, mostly fishing – either from the shore or out in a boat belonging to Ellis so Jimmy knew where to look.

He started at Ellis's home and Terri Owen, his wife, admitted she couldn't help. 'There's a storm brewing,' she said, looking up at the sky, 'so I don't expect he'll be fishing, although that was what he intended.'

'Did he take a rod and tackle?'

'Oh yes, my Ellis is daft enough to try, even in this weather. Nothing puts him off once he's made up his mind.'

Jimmy went to all the usual places where Ellis might be found, but there was no trace of him. On impulse, and finding himself only a few miles away, he went to Mumbles Pier, where he found the man calmly leaning over the side looking down at the water. The sea was wild that day and the signs were that it would get worse. Huge waves were lashing the shore and there was no one else attempting to catch fish, although there were several groups of people watching in wonder at the fury of the sea.

Ellis must have seen Jimmy approaching, although his angry shouts were lost in the tumult of the storm. He waved, then picked up his rod and box of equipment and began to walk towards him. As Jimmy drew closer he released his anger.

'Come here, you disgusting, thieving, unprincipled lout!'

Ellis began to back away from him, throwing his rod down he ran back on to the pier and Jimmy followed. Hesitantly a few people went forward but the wind was so strong they had to cling to the rails to make any progress and fear held them back. One called for someone to phone the police.

'What's the matter with you, Jimmy? What have I done?'

'Done? You've stolen our business, and don't deny it!' As Jimmy reached Ellis he began pushing him, shouts from both men almost unheard, ripped away by the raging storm. Accusations and counter accusations followed and soon blows were being struck and a serious fight ensued.

The police arrived and were on their way to separate the furious men but they were too late to prevent Ellis going over the side into the turbulent water. Jimmy went in after him, but although he stayed in the dangerous water until a couple of men tied themselves to a long line and hauled him to the shore, there was no sign of Ellis. Days passed and Ellis's body did not appear.

With so many witnesses, including the police, Jimmy was believed at first. But in the leeway the partners had foolishly allowed him, Ellis had cleverly rewritten the books, and added a few embellishments. Later, the court was told that evidence of theft pointed not at Ellis Owen, but at Jimmy Vaughan.

There had been many descriptions and counter descriptions of the events of that afternoon. Soon the rumour of attempted murder spread accusing Jimmy of pushing the man over into the sea to hide his guilt. It had only taken one man to say he had seen the flash of a knife blade for others to believe they might have seen the same. The foreshore was searched but no weapon was found and although their story was ignored, the rumours continued, fuelled by the confusion of that afternoon, the disappearance of Ellis Owen, and reinforced by Jimmy's arrest.

Back in 1945, both Jimmy Vaughan and Jack Morris had sold their houses to invest in their new business and they were both short of money as they had since had added further savings to keep the business afloat as things became difficult. The prosecution could find no evidence of Jimmy and Emily having more money than they declared, but suspicion was strong and the police believed that the money had been hidden and would one day be revealed, probably by careless over-spending. Jimmy had escaped the charge of attempted murder, but the shadow of it hung over him and his family.

For Jimmy, his greatest hurt was that his friend and partner Jack didn't believe him. His greatest fear was that with the only man who knew the truth being dead, there was no one able to prove any different and he would remain in prison for a crime he hadn't committed, and come out a broken man still under suspicion of murder.

Lowri had hidden her sadness and frustration at the unfairness of the sentence bravely, and smiled confidently at everyone, telling herself her father was innocent and therefore she had no cause to be otherwise, but she often cried herself to sleep thinking of her father in that awful place.

Part of her sadness was the loss of Jack Morris – Uncle Jack – and Auntie Cathy. Their son too had been lost to her. Dic Morris had been there all her life and was like an adored big brother. She felt the pain of losing them almost as badly as losing her parents. Seeing them pass her by without a word had been very painful, but now she had moved away and she must forget them and concentrate on her new life with new friends.

Living among strangers in Cwm Derw and settled in Badgers Brook, she had found peace. The house wrapped her in warm comfort and the atmosphere was calming, giving her a chance to accept what she couldn't change, and ease away the anger she had felt for so long. Cathy Morris had written to her three times and Dic twice, but she had thrown them all on the fire. Strangers had soon become friends and she no longer grieved for those she had lost, even loved ones like Uncle Jack, Auntie Cathy and Dic – him most of all. The past was forgotten, here was where she belonged.

She began to hope that with only her landlords Connie and Geoff Tanner, and Stella Jones at the post office, knowing her background, she might begin to settle down and cope with her despair. Then she saw someone who was capable of ruining her newly found peace.

Dic Morris, the son of her father's partner Jack, and her father's accuser, was standing outside the post office when she closed for lunch on the Friday of her first week. Her heart gave a lurch of shock. Then with some defence mechanism creating a childish response, she wondered how she could ever have thought him good looking. With his ancient coat, muddy boots and his untidy hair he looked like a tramp, she thought, the unkind, silent appraisal a spurious comfort. She refused to notice his dark, expressive brown eyes, so serious and concerned, and the way his hair curled around his face, swept by a turbulent wind.

'What are you doing here? What d'you want? Haven't you done enough?' she hissed, hoping to avoid anyone seeing her talking to him and remember him from the

28

time of the trial. She wished he would turn and go away. How did he find her? What did he want, to taunt her with more reminders of her father's dishonesty?

'Lowri, how are you?' he said calmly. 'I wonder if we can have a word. Perhaps at the café?'

'I've got nothing to say to you. Because of you my father's in prison, charged with theft and suspected of murder. Or have you forgotten?' She was still hissing, keeping her voice low, glancing around for fear of being overheard. She stared at him, eyes glaring, hiding her distress, then walked away. She had intended to go to the café for lunch but changed her mind at the sight of Dic. There was a bus due that would take her to the end of the lane and she would go home and make a sandwich, although at the sight of Dic Morris the thought of food made her choke. Aware of him following, she began to run.

As the bus swung around the corner past Geoff Tanner's shop, making its way towards her, she ran faster, waving her hand for it to stop. She was relieved to see no one at the bus stop, so she could jump on and with luck Dic would not find out where she lived. She sat and looked back to where he now stood, staring after the bus.

Dic went into the café and ordered tea and toast, then asked where the young lady from the post office lived. 'I feel such an idiot,' he said, smiling disarmingly. 'I'm a friend of Lowri's and I've lost her address.' Pleased to be of help to the handsome man, the young waitress gave him the name of the house and exactly where to find it.

Lowri had set the corner of the kitchen table and made herself some toast, and stood debating what to spread on it, when there was a knock at the door.

'Is that you, Kitty? Come on in, want a cup of tea?' She was taking the toast from under the grill when the door opened. She looked up, a smile ready to greet her friend, and saw Dic.

'Sorry, but I need to talk about the business and neither your mother nor my father is in a state to listen. Dad is still struggling to save the business and there are papers to sign, decisions to be made.'

'Why ask me? I'm the daughter of an embezzler and murderer, not to be trusted, or have you forgotten?'

'Lowri, I no longer believe your father stole from the business. All right, I admit that I shouted as loudly as anyone, I was so angry. I didn't think any further than the evidence in front of me. Ellis Owen left books and letters that showed your father's guilt. Ellis had set it out to imply that he was trying to catch your father, covering himself in case he were accused.'

'You know my father. You should have trusted him.'

'You're right, we should have been looking for evidence instead of venting our anger on your father. Now I want to find the truth. I've spoken to the police and to your father's solicitor but it's clear they aren't interested. So will you help me? Give me any papers you have? Jimmy spoke of diaries but some of these haven't been found. Is there anywhere we can look for them?'

Despite trying to be cynical, hope clawed at her throat and she felt like a child being shown something wonderful that she could never have. All she said, was, 'I don't believe you. This is an attempt to make me hand over what's left of the business to your father. While *my* father rots in prison! You think there's some money hidden away somewhere and *that's* what you want to find! Isn't that the truth?'

Dic shook his head. 'I will want to check your parent's finances again if I can persuade your mother to let me. I'm sorry, but I have to do that even though the police investigated thoroughly, then I can be sure.'

'So you do believe his guilt? That there's money somewhere? While my mother lives in a grotty little flat and... Get out! I don't know why you came, but it isn't with any intention of helping my father!'

She tried to push him towards the door, but he held firm and as she burst into tears, he put his arms around her and gently rested her head against his shoulder until the tears were spent. He handed her a handkerchief and she noisily blew her nose.

'Now see what you've done! Made my face all blotchy and I'm going to be late for work. Besides,' she added huffily, 'you don't smell very clean!'

'I've been walking along the beach and into the mud, collecting wood from an ancient fishing boat that's been immersed in the mud for years.'

She was curious enough to ask why.

'I make sculptures from the old sea-hardened wood. It's something I enjoy doing and the customers like them too. I make fish mostly, it seems relevant. You must come and see them some time.

'It's all right for you. Your business is still sound. While my father...'

'Yes, I know all about your father, you needn't glory in it all like an amateur actress!'

'How dare you!'

'I dare, because I'm trying to do something to help and you're just playing the gallery!'

'Trying to help? How? It's your evidence that put him in prison!'

'Bills were unpaid, accounts emptied, borrowing had been arranged without my father or your father knowing. Lowri, I keep looking at the facts and I can't put your father in the role of villain. There's nothing new to go on, except my instinct, yet I believe that somewhere there has to be evidence to show he was innocent of stealing from the business.'

'Too late, you were too convincing when he was in court. Remember?'

'He and my father were so proud of what they'd built. I don't believe he would have risked taking even a penny piece, let alone thousands of pounds. Without that charge of embezzlement, the rumour that he was guilty of murder doesn't make any sense. He'll have that hanging over him all his life if we don't get the truth.'

'Thank you.' She spoke softly, staring at the flagstone floor. When she looked up, she saw he was reaching for the door. A sudden need to ask him to stay, a longing to be held a while longer, was repressed when the door opened and Marion walked in.

He nodded politely and walked to the door. Sadly, Lowri watched him go. He was an echo of her life before the trial and a link with happier times. 'Will you come again?' she called. 'Bring the children. Please, Dic. They'd love it here.'

Walking back to her he said, 'Thanks, I will. Sarah-Jane and little Katie often ask about you. But first you and I have to talk – without interruption. I want you to search in your memory for anything that didn't come out at the trial. Anything, no matter how trivial, that might have some relevance.'

'There are some notebooks, with ideas and sketches for future designs and colour schemes which he intended to discuss with Uncle – your father.'

'Anything at all. And he's still your Uncle Jack and my mother's still Auntie Cathy.'

'No! They're not. They refused to speak to me.'

'No doubt they're ashamed of their gullibility, as I am. So when can we meet?'

'I work all the week. Saturday evening? Or Sunday?' she offered.

'Saturday, my parents have the girls all day.'

–

On Saturday the post office closed at one o'clock and she hurried home after a brief visit to the shops to buy food for a simple lunch for two. Marion wouldn't be there. She had gone home to see her parents, something she continued to do quite often. Saturday was her day off from the various cleaning jobs she had undertaken when she had joined Lowri in Badgers Brook. So whatever Dic had to say he could say it in confidence. She was aware of a candle-flame of hope, likely to be puffed out in moments, but she was comforted by the frail, temporary glimmer.

She set potatoes to boil and had water simmering ready for the vegetables, the sausages were already slowly cooking in a pan of onions. She knew this meal was one of Dic's favourites. Before his wife Rosemary had become ill, she had been a frequent visitor to their home and had learned many things about him.

He smiled as she placed the meal before him. 'How did you know this was my favourite?' he asked as they began to eat at a small table set near the glowing fire.

'Rosemary was a friend of mine, remember,' she said. 'You'd be surprised at how much I know about you.'

Dic had never been afraid of talking about his wife. He had told Lowri soon after Rosemary had died of influenza, that to avoid talking about her was like pretending she had never existed. And besides, he wanted the girls to have constant reminders about their mother as their memories of her were almost non-existent. They had been very small when they had lost her. Two years ago when their mother had passed away, Sarah-Jane had been three and little Katie, not quite one year old.

It wasn't until after they had cleared the dishes and were settled into armchairs either side of the fire that he began to explain his reason for coming. 'My father was shocked but convinced by the evidence presented by the police, and was furious that he had been let down by the man who had been his friend as well as his partner,' he began. 'Now he has calmed down and time has passed, he's thinking about things more clearly and he agrees with me that the whole thing is completely unbelievable. Ellis Owen was the weak link, not your father. It must have been Ellis Owen who robbed them.

'Our parents had given up their homes and most of their savings to start the business and had taken Ellis on as they needed an accountant. He was experienced but unqualified, and starting off, they just couldn't afford the wages of a professional man, so they employed Ellis. He drew a wage, and appeared to live quite comfortably with none of the worries that owning a business brought.'

'Talk! Nothing but talk!' Lowri interrupted sharply. 'We can all talk, tell ourselves it can't be true, that my father is an honest and non-violent man, but where does that get us? A surge of optimism, sleepless nights dreaming of a happy ending and little besides! Thanks Dic, but I can really do without this!' She stood up and stepped back, dismissing him.

He didn't move. 'I haven't finished. At least let me finish.'

'Go on.' She sighed, her words sounding bored. She wanted him to finish and then leave her to go back to her defeatist acceptance.

'Ellis's wife Terri is moving away. Is that because it will be easier for her to spend money she isn't supposed to have, in an area where no one knows her?'

'Why did you come,' she said despairingly. 'Telling me you believe Dad couldn't steal or harm someone isn't going to change anything. There must be quite a few out there who will tell me that, but what we need is evidence and with Ellis Owen dead that can't happen.'

'Unless his widow starts to spend large amounts of money. It must be hard to have so much and not spend it. She's bound to give in to the temptation some time. She could buy a nice little house and live comfortably. Easy to give up the small flat where she and Ellis lived. She works in a cafe, doesn't she? How long will she go on doing that with all that money in her possession? The police would be sure to investigate if she revealed owning such an amount.'

'Would they bother? With my father in prison the case must be closed.'

'Not if we can offer new evidence. Don't give up hope, Lowri. If he's innocent, and I believe he is, then we mustn't give up. Think. Think about everything that went on during the weeks leading up to Ellis Owen's death. Somewhere there has to be some tiny indication of Ellis's guilt.'

She showed him the box of papers belonging to her father that she had brought with her and he patiently went through every one several times. 'Can I take these with me?' he asked.

Lowri shrugged, then she said sharply, 'I want them back, mind. They belong to my father and he must have saved them for a reason.'

'I promise, and no one will look at them except Dad and me.'

She was calm after he left. She sat near the fire, frowning as she worried her memory into giving up its secrets and offering a spark of hope. Darkness fell and she still didn't move until she heard the door open and guessed that Marion was home. She stood and greeted her friend then went into the kitchen to start preparing their meal.

Later that evening, after hearing the stories about Marion's visit to her large lively family, she told her about Dic's comments. Marion's reaction was familiar.

'Rubbish, Lowri! Forget it. Your father hasn't the smallest chance of a reprieve. Best you accept that and stop exhausting yourself with false hope.'

'But what if he's right and there is evidence out there? I'm trying to re-live those last weeks, wondering whether I have a snippet of information that would lead us to proving his innocence.'

'Rubbish and nonsense. You know that as well as I do. Coming here, encouraging you to hope, saying your father's incapable of what he's accused of, he's being so cruel. We know that! Proving it in a court of law is something different. This Dic Morris is a false friend if he comes here and upsets you with nonsense like this. Tell him to stay away.'

'He's coming tomorrow and bringing his two little girls.'

'Then I'll make sure I'm here so he doesn't get you in a state again.'

Despite trying to accept Marion's advice about ignoring Dic's fragile hope, she dreamed that night of being reunited with her parents and woke happy, until the truth dawned and left her dejected.

Sunday was a quiet day, the weather was cold but crisp and clear and once Dic's daughters had explored the house and the garden, they went for a walk through the fields and woods, watching a flock of fieldfare feeding on one of the fields, and listening to the calming sound of the brook murmuring through the woodland near Badgers Brook.

They pointed out the track made by the badgers and where birds had nested and Lowri told them stories about the inhabitants of the wood and the fields around. They lifted Sarah-Jane and Katie over difficult places and Dic's hand was always there when she needed help. She found the touch of his hand comforting, and the way his shoulder was there when they sat to rest. A link with the happy past and something more. The children's enjoyment of each new discovery added to her own and the whole visit was an oasis of calm in troublesome times.

–

Monday morning was not usually a busy day at the post office but on that day there was already a queue formed when Lowri let herself in by the side door.

'What's happening? It's like Christmas already,' she said as she removed her coat and gloves.

'You might as well face it, Lowri, the rumours have started and they're here to see you and hopefully find out a bit about what happened to your father. Don't worry, I'll sit in the shop and shout them down if necessary. You just carry on serving and leave the gossips to me.'

'You don't want me to leave? What if they refuse to let me serve them?'

'Maes Hir is the next place where they can find a post office as well stocked as mine. They get most of their needs here with me, not just their stamps and pensions and stationery, but their sewing and knitting needs as well as dozens of small items I stock to oblige them. And they won't like travelling all that way for a postal order for their football pools, will they? No, ignore anything they say and leave them to me. Right?'

The hours passed slowly as she forced a smile and replied casually to the barrage of questions. Innuendo was slapped down swiftly by a fierce Stella. Lowri went to the cafe at one o'clock hoping there wouldn't be a continuation of the whispered comments she'd suffered all morning. To her relief she saw Marion there, smiling widely.

'Finished early I did, thought I'd join you in case the natives were unfriendly.'

'I hope today will be the last of it. By half past five I don't think there'll be a customer who hasn't been in. It's been non-stop since we opened at nine and I'm exhausted!'

'Hard, was it?'

'Stella was marvellous. And Kitty and Bob Jennings came, made a cup of tea for us and managed to hush some of the worst of them. Stella's threat of refusing their custom cured others, so I think it will die down by tomorrow.'

But there was worse to come. To her amazement, Terri Owen, the widow of Ellis came in and stared at her as though seeing a ghost. 'What are you doing here?' she demanded. Then she turned to Stella. 'Do you know who she is?'

Stella gripped her stick and rose out of her chair. 'Lowri her name is, best assistant I've had this ages. Why?'

'Her father killed my husband, even though the police can't prove it! In prison he is, for embezzlement.'

'Yes, I know all about him being in prison. Lowri isn't the sort to be deceitful. The rest is slanderous, so just you be careful!'

There were a few more exchanges during which Mrs Owen warned, 'Like father like daughter, mind.'

Stella calmly agreed. 'That's right, innocent, the pair of them.'

Unbelievably, by the time the woman left, Lowri was laughing. 'Stella, you are amazing.' She went home more relaxed than since before the trouble had begun.

There was a note from Marion telling her she was bringing home fish and chips for supper and to put the plates to warm. It was so ordinary that it put the alarms of the day aside. With only two weeks before Christmas, the post office was too busy to worry about who served who, their needs were more important than attitude and if a few more than usual ostentatiously checked their change, Lowri pretended not to notice.

—

Dic came to Badgers Brook again on Sunday 16th December with his daughters. Marion had tried to persuade Lowri to cancel his visit, warning her of the misery he could revive by building impossible dreams. Lowri ignored the advice and instead decorated the house with as much Christmas cheer as possible, buying a tree from Peter Bevan, the greengrocer, who delivered it and helped them to set it up in a corner of the living room, from where its lights would shine out towards the garden. His wife Hope, who had once been a tenant of Badgers Brook, had sent a few handmade angels to hang from its branches and a fairy to sit on the top. Knowing there were children visiting, two little girls who had lost their mother, Hope had opened her heart to them and willingly added to what Lowri and Marion were preparing.

Dic arrived with the excited girls and with arms filled with parcels, which he added to the growing pile under the tree. Kitty and Bob arrived with a few records for Marion's wind-up gramophone and the mood was set for a party.

They had eaten and cleared away and were starting to play traditional games, Lowri carrying Katie when the going was too fast and laughter filled the air. It wasn't until the third knock that they heard someone at the door. Marion went to answer it and saw two policemen standing there.

The mood immediately changed. Dic pulled his daughters on to his lap, leaving Lowri and Marion to take the officers into the kitchen.

'Miss Lowri Vaughan?' one of them asked. Lowri could only nod, her breath was tight as she feared more trouble. 'Daughter of Mr James Vaughan, presently serving a sentence for fraud?'

'For goodness' sake tell me what's happened!' she shouted.

'It's your father, I'm afraid he's...'

For a moment Lowri imagined they were about to tell her he was dead, their faces were so solemn. 'Your father has escaped from prison.'

The words went on, reminding her that she was bound by law to inform the police if she knew where he was, or where he was likely to be hiding, but the words didn't really reach her brain. Expecting worse, far worse, she felt only relief. Once she'd recovered, she mentioned a few places where he had been before, the holiday cottage owned by an aunt, where they had spent many summer days. Another place near Merthyr Mawr where they had spent a happy holiday, but these were unlikely guesses, or she wouldn't have mentioned them. No, there was only one place her father would make for and that this house. He had escaped just to see her as he refused to allow her to see him in prison.

There was one other place he might use as a hiding place, an ancient, half ruined building once used by shepherds and walkers high on the cliffs above a Gower bay. She knew he would be there but she dared not go and see him. The police were certain to be watching her. But just knowing he was free and not far away made her heart sing.

The following morning, Lowri and Marion were aware of an increase in police presence, but they didn't worry too much. Surely her father would avoid places where they might expect him to be?

'Will you be all right if I go home for a day later this week,' Marion asked that afternoon. 'Mam's so busy with Christmas to prepare and all the kids getting excited, I want to give a bit of a hand.'

'Of course I don't mind. I don't feel at all uneasy being on my own here. Stay the night if you need to.'

'Heaven help! I couldn't stand that! Why d'you think I came here with you? Like my own bed, I do, and they're three deep in some of them at the moment. With his kids and her kids and their kids, it's chaos.' She explained to the police where she was going and when she would return and Lowri settled down in the quiet house and listened fearfully for shouts and activity that would indicate the rearrest of her father.

–

Marion went into the noisy house where her mother lived with her second husband and their combined children. Eight children, whose ages ranged from two up to eighteen were hard to control and Harriet didn't try. She had become immune to crying and shut her mind when one or another began to wail. It was the job of the older ones to look after the younger ones. She concentrated on keeping them clean and feeding them. Apart from washing day when she spent the hours sweating over a wash tub and a gas boiler, her long black hair tangled as she pushed it aside, her face red and moist, most of Harriet's day was spent in the kitchen preparing food. A part of every day involved shopping.

Marion was welcomed with relief when she walked in on that Friday morning. Her mother was sitting in the middle of the living room floor surrounded with paper, string and a few sparkling tree ornaments. A fir tree leant against the wall in a corner beside a bucket of cinders.

'There's a treat to see you, Marion, love.' Harriet gave a huge sigh of relief. 'Desperate busy I am. Go and sort the dishes from the table, will you? I haven't managed to wash up after breakfast yet. I'm determined to get a tree decorated before the kids get in from school. They'll love the surprise.'

'Just as well I brought these then,' Marion said, unpacking a shopping bag filled with newspaper-wrapped tree ornaments. Tarnished but unbroken, they would fill the bare branches and delight the younger members of Harriet's brood. 'Mrs Jones from the post office said she won't need them all.'

Ignoring the table still spread with the remnants of a meal, they worked together to fill the tree with the glittering items.

By lunchtime, order had been restored and after sitting down to a small meal of fried potatoes left from the previous day, Marion said, 'Mind if I go for a walk, Mam?'

'Yes, you go, love, and thank you. Worked hard you have and I'm grateful.'

Marion smiled. Her mother never failed to thank her for the help she gave. 'It's no wonder I'm earning my keep by cleaning,' she said, 'I've had plenty of training from you. Fast and furious you are and I think you're amazing.' She left the now orderly house and set off up the hill from where she could glimpse the distant sea.

Approaching the summit she looked towards the small overhang of rock under which sheep often sheltered and saw a tall figure standing there. He stepped forward and waved and she began to run towards him. Their arrangements were difficult to make but she usually managed to meet him whenever he left a message for her. Secretly of course, with him being married, but guilt didn't affect her joy when they were together. It was only at night, when she was alone, that she thought of his wife and knew what she was doing was wrong. Doubly wrong if she were honest.

On Christmas Eve they were told Jimmy had been recaptured. He had been found on the cliffs above the place where he and Dic's father had often fished for sea bass. Lowri noted that he had not been far from that ancient hut the men had used to store their equipment. Was there something hidden there, that he had been hoping to find? She didn't mention this to Dic, in spite of a growing need of him, she was not quite sure where his loyalties lay. Was he really trying to help her father, or was the return of the money his prime motivation?

So, Christmas was a subdued affair, thinking of her father locked up after his attempt to be free and wondering what he had hoped to achieve. Dic came on Boxing Day with the girls as they had arranged, and Marion cancelled her plan to stay with her family until the following weekend and came back on Boxing Day morning so she would be there when he came.

'To ward off any more of his false imaginings,' she told Lowri, who thanked her, even though she didn't quite know why.

True to Marion's expectations, Dic swore his determination was even greater. 'Jimmy risked having his sentence extended by getting out like that. He must have had a good reason. He wouldn't do it just to see your mother, much as he loves her, or you. I believe he was searching for evidence, so somewhere it must exist. Perhaps Mrs Owen knows something and he was hoping to persuade her to talk?'

Lowri couldn't help being encouraged. Marion seemed less than pleased.

True to form, as news filtered through of Jimmy's rearrest, Badgers Brook filled up with well-wishers. Betty

Connors came and she brought Gwennie Flint from the chip shop. Stella came in laughing, having been pushed on Colin's bike to save her leg from the strain of walking, Kitty and Bob, Geoff and Connie, the room was filled with talk and laughter.

Gwennie's husband had dragged himself out of an armchair to ask when Gwennie was coming home to get his supper. Lowri noticed a look pass between Betty and Gwennie, who replied, 'When I'm ready, Maldwyn. There was food if you roused yourself to get it, so now you can wait.'

So much for the Christmas spirit in their house, Lowri thought with a smile.

'Gwennie's Maldwyn is a work-shy lazy man and today, Gwennie is starting her New Year's resolution a bit early,' Betty explained.

Small gifts were found for the children, who were delighted with their new aunties and uncles, and it was midnight before the last visitor had gone. Gwennie amusingly was one of the last to leave, but Maldwyn had eaten and drank so he was no longer complaining about his lack of attention.

Marion made their usual cocoa and despite all the treats they had consumed, made toast and ate as though she hadn't fed for a week.

'It's Christmas,' she excused. 'We've been so busy entertaining I don't think I've eaten since breakfast!'

Lowri didn't argue. Tomorrow she faced a day at the post office, so why not make the most of the last few hours of the holiday? With a deprecating grin, she sliced more bread and settled beside the fire to toast it. She was smiling as they put the dishes into the bowl of hot soapy water, aware of the contentment of being surrounded by good friends.

'This house is special, isn't it?' she mused.

Picking up her night dress from where it had been warming near the embers of the fire, Marion sleepily nodded and both carrying lighted candles, they went up the stairs.

Three

Lowri had started to wonder what she would do once Stella Jones was well enough to return to her duties at the post office. Although the leg was still painful and she was restricted in what she could do, Stella was spending more and more time in the shop, checking stock, cleaning, re-ordering and at the same time, coming to help Lowri when a queue formed.

The run up to Christmas had brought a rush of customers, when everyone in the area seemed to be either waiting in the never-ending queue, or standing chatting outside the shop; Lowri had been too busy to think about future plans. Even now, with Christmas Day behind them the customers were still there in droves. Sending belated parcels, writing thank you letters, arranging get-togethers for New Year.

'We never see daylight during the weeks around Christmas,' Stella had told her as she lit another overhead light to brighten the gloomy day. 'The windows don't let in even the little bit of sun we do have. We cram them full of extra things for sale, blocking the light, then there's the customers leaning against them to gossip. It's like being in a cave!'

Lowri looked at the women outside the shop in thick coats and hats and waving umbrellas to emphasize a point, leaning against the small amount of glass still clear of gifts on offer. They were noisy, they kept Lowri and Stella frantically busy and sometimes they were argumentative about whose turn was next, but Lowri loved it. The occasional disagreements were without aggression, quickly forgotten and were often amusing, adding to the enjoyment of every day.

'Thank goodness Christmas and New Year are more interesting than you and your father, eh?' Stella said when they were closing the shop on the Monday before New Year's Day. 'Giving you a bit of peace, eh?'

'With luck 1951 will start with something else to talk about. Like the January sales,' Lowri agreed.

'Now there's an idea. Why don't *we* have a sale?'

'But they're usually to get rid of the last season's leftovers and we can hardly sell stamps cheap, can we?' Lowri laughed at the enthusiasm on Stella's face.

'There's all these gifts, mind. Aprons, and handkerchiefs and scarves for a start. And a few calendars and cards. We'll reduce the prices and get rid of them. If we stick the cards in the storeroom for next year they come out looking a bit shabby, and who will want this year's calendar? Right then, when shall we start?'

'What about next Monday? It's usually a quiet day on the counter, and I'll come in on Sunday and mark up the new prices if you like.'

'Good on you, Lowri, you're a gem.' Then Stella frowned. 'We won't have to knock too much off the price, will we?'

'Get below the nearest shilling and it'll look like a bargain,' Lowri promised.

–

When Dic called at Badgers Brook the following Sunday, the house appeared to be empty. The door was open and he stepped inside and called, 'Lowri? Marion?' Receiving no reply, he put down the New Year greetings card and the flowers he had brought and began to leave. Then he heard sounds coming from upstairs and his skin prickled in alarm. He knew Marion usually went to see her family on Sundays, and if she had changed her plans and stayed home, she would have answered his call.

He quietly went up the stairs, his heart racing, looking around him, wondering what he would meet. The bathroom door moved, and he headed for it, convinced that someone had just stepped inside. He didn't call again; whoever it was, hadn't wanted to be seen. Hardly a burglar; what could a thief expect to find here? But whatever the reason, it was someone who ought not to be there.

The landing floor boards creaked loudly – no chance of creeping up on someone, so he ran across fast and pushed open the bathroom door.

Marion stood there, wearing a dressing gown, a toothbrush in her hand and an expression of alarm on her face.

'Dic? What's the matter?'

Relaxed, deflated, he began to make his apologies.

'I called, but no one answered and I heard someone, saw the bathroom door move and…' He shrugged. 'I'm sorry, but I thought you had an intruder.'

'How very brave of you,' Marion said with a laugh. 'And there's me armed with a dangerous weapon, too.' She waggled her toothbrush. 'I'm just having a lazy morning, so why don't you put the kettle on and we'll have tea and toast.'

'Where's Lowri?' he called as he ran back down the stairs.

'She's gone to help Stella Jones at the post office, sorting out unwanted stock. They're having a sale, would you believe!'

They sat companionably and ate what was for Dic, a second breakfast.

Upstairs, a man sat on a chair behind Marion's bedroom door and waited.

Being told of Lowri's intention to come back in time for lunch, Dic went for a walk through the winter woodland, enjoying the quiet and peaceful place and wishing he had brought the children to enjoy it with him. Today he had wanted to talk privately to Lowri, which was the reason he'd left them with his mother. A private talk was not possible now, with Marion there.

He sensed that Marion disliked him and knew it was partly because of her protective attitude towards Lowri, trying to prevent her from dreaming of her father's release instead of getting on with her life – but there was something more. In his more fanciful moments he thought Marion was afraid of him in some way. She certainly mistrusted him, but he had no explanation of why, or about what. Maybe, he mused, Marion was enjoying being away from her home and living in Badgers Brook so much she was afraid of Lowri leaving? Getting married? That might give Marion feelings of jealousy toward every prospective male.

She needn't worry about me, he thought. Lowri was young and quite lovely, and he was a man of thirty-two encumbered with two young daughters. The thought made him feel momentary sadness. Encumbered was the wrong word, he loved Katie and Sarah-Jane and couldn't imagine life without them, but knowing he was destined to live alone, with no prospect of finding someone who could love them as well as himself, made him foresee a lonely future. He'd be living on the outside of other families, touching them, becoming a part of them from time to time, but always going home to that emptiness.

Lowri had prepared a rabbit stew which was sending out appetizing smells and when she got home just before midday, Dic was easily persuaded to stay for lunch. Aware of Marion watching him suspiciously, he said nothing of what was on his mind. It was Lowri who brought the conversation around to her father.

'Dad is not well,' she told him. 'Mam thinks he caught a cold sleeping out in the fields during his few days of freedom,' she told him.

'That was such a foolish thing to do. It won't help and might prolong the time he spends inside,' Marion said.

'I wonder why he did it? He must have had a reason. D'you think he has an idea of where he can find some proof and tried to find it?' Dic wondered.

'Stop it,' Marion said sharply. 'Here you go again, building up hope instead of concentrating on his wife and daughter rebuilding their lives. It doesn't help, Dic, in fact it's cruel!'

Dic turned to face Lowri, touching her hand lightly. 'I'm sorry if it upsets you. I can't stop hoping. Having confidence of a reprieve for your father isn't instead of you making a good life for yourself, it's a small part of it, and hoping for that miracle will certainly help your father through it.'

'Dad wouldn't have risked the business, so it must have been Ellis Owen.' Lowri spoke quietly as though thinking aloud.

'Ellis Owen loved the freedom of being out of doors. He was a keen sportsman, he loved sailing that boat of his, and canoeing, swimming and climbing. He liked taking those kind of risks, but he wouldn't have risked imprisonment, even for a thousand pounds or more. You're refusing to face the obvious!' Marion exclaimed.

'The "obvious" being that my father is a thief and stole from his own business?' Lowri glared at Marion and at once Marion apologized.

'No, Lowri! I'm sorry. I was trying too hard to stop Dic upsetting you. I didn't think what I was saying. Of course he's innocent. I just don't think it helps to keep on going over and over without anything new to add. It just re-opens the wounds and stops them healing.'

'I don't want them to heal. I don't want to give up waiting for a miracle. Can't you see that?'

'I keep going over it because I feel responsible for Jimmy's arrest,' Dic said. 'When he's proved innocent, I'll have that burden to carry for always.'

'There you go again!' Marion shouted. 'You don't mind upsetting Lowri so long as you feel better!'

Lowri protested, Marion apologized again and Dic looked at her wondering why she was so adamant about them accepting Jimmy Vaughan's guilt. It seemed to be more than her concern for Lowri, there was real anger in her voice when she criticized him.

It wasn't until several days later, that Lowri wondered how Marion knew so much about Ellis Owen, a man she had never met. Nothing about his love of dangerous sports had been in the newspapers. Or his love of being outside. She would have learned that he was a fisherman, that had been in all the newspapers together with the irony of the sea claiming him, but fishing had been only one of his interests and even she hadn't known he enjoyed climbing.

Lowri had read all the accounts of the trial, discussed every small detail with her mother time and time over, searching for some chink in the devastating case against her father. She had no recollection of such things being mentioned, so how did Marion know? From her own experience she was well aware that gossip knew no boundaries. A casually spoken word seemed to fly through the air it travelled so fast and so far. But she still considered Marion's remarks odd.

–

Dic decided not to go to Badgers Brook for a while. He was making everything worse, believing that holding on to hope had been the best way of helping Lowri to cope. Hope could be a false friend. He also needed to concentrate on his business and he had been neglectful of the essential restocking since the arrest and the trial. He and his wife had started a small business when he had come out of the Air Force in 1945. Rosemary had been a talented silversmith and she had made beautiful jewellery and small works of art, specializing mainly in wildlife. Dolphins, otters, mice, frogs, unlikely choices as gifts but amazingly popular because of the fine detail she could impart, giving each a character and a name.

He had added carvings to their stock making many lovely pieces from wood rescued from the wrecks embedded in mud on the beaches around the local coastline, or from bomb-damaged buildings, from which he made religious crosses and statues. Some were small but several had been very large, commissioned pieces that had ended up displayed in local businesses in entrance halls and offices.

Thinking of Lowri made work difficult, but he sat and stared at one of the pieces he had gathered on the day he had met Lowri, seeing its possibilities, making a decision on what he would extract from its uncompromising appearance.

As he studied it, he saw a boat, an odd shaped boat, a cartoon of a boat, with high sides opening out almost into wings, with a superstructure lopsided and with a small figure leaning against it. He reached out for a note pad and began to draw.

—

The sale at the post office started slowly but as people shared the surprising news, the shop began to fill and it stayed full until five thirty, when an exhausted Stella closed the door. Her hair was falling out of its customary neat pins and her face was flushed, her bright eyes shining in delight.

'God 'elp, girl, that was a day to remember! Who'd have believed people would go through all that just to save a few pence, eh?'

'Better than going to the pictures it was, watching some of them fight over a bargain. Did you see Mrs Richard and old Harold Francis arguing over the possession of a pair of oven gloves?'

'Had them for years I have. Nobody wanted them, content with a folded tea towel, mingy lot. But with threepence off they went faster than postal orders on football pools day.'

There was a knock at the door and Stella shouted, 'Can't you see we're closed?'

'Lowri, it's me,' Kitty called back. 'I think you've had a break-in. Bob's gone for the police.'

'Go you, I'll finish up here,' Stella said. 'Colin and I will come down later to see if you want any help with locks and things.'

With Kitty puffing beside her, Lowri ran to the bus stop.

As they went up the path towards the kitchen door, everything seemed normal. It wasn't until they went inside that the evidence showed. In the kitchen and the living rooms, cupboards and drawers had been opened, their contents thrown around the floor. Upstairs there was a repeat, with wardrobes and chests of drawers treated in the same way. Clothes had been dropped to the floor and coat pockets were pulled inside out, and even the hems of coats had been cut open. Every piece of furniture and every item of clothing had been thoroughly searched. But for what? She had nothing of value, except the joy of living in this house and now that had been spoilt. How would she ever feel the same peace after this?

Like a child she wanted her mother and father to be there, help her through it, and she also imagined how relieved she would be to see Dic walking in and taking charge. She felt vulnerable and very afraid. 'This has to be something to do with my father,' she told Kitty. 'There must be something we've overlooked and someone is determined to get to it first.'

'What could they have been looking for?'

'I don't know, but it makes me feel hopeful if someone is going to all this trouble to find whatever it is.' Kitty looked puzzled and Lowri explained. 'My father escaped to find something that would help him. I remember talk of some diaries in the weeks after his arrest, Dad believed they'd show he was innocent. Perhaps someone else wants to find them. That's definitely hopeful, isn't it?' she added tearfully.

Marion went home to her family and Lowri stayed with Kitty and Bob for the night. The following day, after checking and finding nothing missing, the police suggested that with nothing stolen, it must have been an opportunist thief, seeing the house empty and secluded, he had gone in looking only for money. Apart from the rent in the book ready for Geoff and Connie, and the money put on the window sill for the milkman, and the baker, the thief had been unlucky. For herself there was the mess and the creepy sensation of knowing strangers had handled her personal possessions. She set to and began washing everything washable and sponging down things that were not.

When Dic heard about the attempted robbery he took the girls and went to see Lowri on Wednesday afternoon, when the shops were closed for the half-day. He drove down, intending to invite Lowri out for a drive and a meal, something Sarah-Jane and Katie considered a treat.

Aware of Marion's mistrustful presence when she came in from her morning cleaning job, he said nothing about the burglary until Lowri mentioned it. Then he was reassuring. 'It won't happen again, the police were right it was an opportunist thief who by now is far away. There are quite a number of tramps wandering around the countryside and not all of them are honest.'

Lowri talked about it: the shock, the feeling of unease, the way her confidence had been knocked. 'It's as though I've deserved it in some way, by carelessness in not checking every window when we're both out, or perhaps giving the impression that I have a lot of money here.' She stared at him in horror. 'You don't think someone believes I am hiding the money my father's accused of stealing, do you?'

'Come on, you need to get out. Sarah-Jane and Katie want to take you for a drive, and stop somewhere for high tea in a smart tea shop, which must include cream cakes.' He unwillingly invited Marion to join them and was relieved when she refused, explaining that she had to go to her Thursday job a day early.

He didn't intend to mention the robbery again, but as the girls were tucking into their cakes, something occurred to him and he asked, 'Lowri, have you checked the coat you were wearing when the robbery took place? And the handbag you carried?'

'Why would I do that? He couldn't have stolen from those things – I was at the post office when he broke into Badgers Brook!'

'I don't mean check for something missing, but to see if there's anything he might have been searching for and didn't find.'

'You mean he could be back?'

'No. From what I understand, the search was extensive, there's no need for him to come back. But if you look in your handbag and pockets, you might find something you'd forgotten or ignored.'

She frowned. 'My handbag is full of junk and if something disappeared I wouldn't miss it, but as for there being anything there of value... well, nail files, a few keys, money, make-up, nothing a thief would want.'

'Sorry. I just wondered if there was something important in a pocket or your handbag that you haven't given a thought to.'

'So you do think it was something to do with my father?'

'I don't know what I was thinking of, the police are probably right about a stranger passing through. But look anyway, will you? See if there's anything belonging to your father that you'd forgotten about. Just in case.'

She nodded and tried to remember if there was anything in her possession that could be of any use to someone else, and failed.

'There's one more thing,' Dic said as they pulled up outside her home. 'I don't know why I'm asking this, but will you promise to say nothing of what I've asked you to do to Marion? I can't explain, but indulge me, please.'

As they stood up to leave the car, she nodded, but curiosity showed on her face. 'Marion is a good friend,' she said. 'She stayed with me when no one else did, when all the people I'd considered reliable turned out to be false friends.'

'I know, but I want us to share any thoughts we have that might help your father without including anyone else, not a soul, not even your friend, Marion.'

–

The next day, Thursday, the empty shelves in the post office declared the sale over. The dark day emphasized the spaces left by the sale and Stella didn't like it at all. 'I'll have to start filling up again or the customers will think we're closing,' she said ruefully. 'Lovely to get shot of all that old stuff though.'

'Will you extend your stock now? There are plenty of things that people need. Children's clothes maybe? Or perhaps kitchenware?' Lowri suggested. 'There's room for a few more shelves and even a display cabinet now we've cleared out all those half-empty boxes.' There was no reply and she turned to see Stella staring out into the heavy rain, a glazed smile on her face.

'Children's clothes,' Stella breathed. 'I've always dreamed of stocking children's clothes. Pretty winter dresses and warm jumpers, and shorts and dippers for the summer when they go on holiday to the beach. Lovely that would be.'

'You already sell buckets and spades,' Lowri encouraged.

'And socks with turned down tops for the boys to wear to school, and black stockings for the girls. Oh, I can see how welcome that would be, save a trip into Maes Hir or Barry.'

Lowri shared the excitement but was reminded that as her employment was temporary and about to end, she wouldn't be there to enjoy it. 'Stella, can you tell me how much longer you'll need me here? I have to start looking for something else as soon as I know.'

'You aren't thinking of leaving, are you? I couldn't manage the extra business without you here.'

'I thought, as soon as you're fit again I wouldn't be needed.'

'Needed? Of course you're needed, girl. Lovely it's been having you with me. I'll be glad of a bit of leisure later on, when the weather's better. Me and my Colin aren't too old to enjoy a day on Barry Island sands. You can take over and I can go out for an afternoon now and then. No, I don't want you to leave.

'I thought now your leg is almost better...'

'Come with me to the warehouse next Wednesday afternoon and we'll start looking at what's available.' She stopped and stared at Lowri with her bright knowing eyes. 'Unless you're fed up and want a change?'

'Why would I need a change from this place? There's never two days the same! I'd love to stay on if you need me.'

'Right then. Next Wednesday I'll fix for us to start looking for our new stock.'

It was as she walked to the bus stop that rainy day, that she remembered what Dic had asked her. Going back to Badgers Brook after the pleasant afternoon with him and his children, thoughts of her father had been temporarily soothed away. The coat she had worn to work on the day of the robbery was hanging in her wardrobe and as she put away the mac she was wearing, she remembered. A search of the pockets revealed nothing except a handkerchief and several used bus tickets.

Emptying her handbag on the bed, she was embarrassed at the amount of useless rubbish she had collected. More bus tickets and shop receipts, small change that had escaped from her purse, her house keys, make-up and a mirror. There were other oddments too, like pencils and some stale sweets. As she searched through, discarding the unwanted items, she noticed a key of which she had no recollection. It wasn't from their previous home, and looked more like a padlock key than that of a door.

She went to call Marion to tell her about her mystery, but remembering Dic's request, she held back. She slipped the key into a pocket of her summer jacket hanging in the furthest reaches of the wardrobe and refilled her capacious bag. It could hardly be important if she couldn't remember its use.

–

The young man who met Lowri and Stella on the following Wednesday at the warehouse was charming and obviously attracted to Lowri. Showing them as many of their lines as they wanted to see and showing no sign of being bored, he waved away a woman assistant who stepped forward to help. He was very fair, his hair straight and worn longer than was usual. His eyes were blue and longing for an excuse to laugh. He introduced himself as Ken Hardy and although he talked to both of them, his admiring eyes rarely left Lowri.

The clothes were fairly expensive but the quality was good and Lowri knew that people would pay if they considered the money well spent. There were party dresses for little girls, each with its own stiffened muslin under-skirt, and simple woollen skirts with matching jumpers – clothes for every occasion.

As Ken spread out one outfit after another, Lowri imagined Sarah-Jane and Katie wearing them and wished Dic were there to see them. It was half an hour before Ken Hardy reminded them with an amused smile, that they might like to look at clothes for boys too.

It was as they were leaving, having spent more than Stella had intended, and had arranged to borrow a rail and a glass fronted chest of drawers, that Ken Hardy invited Lowri out.

'Cinema, or a dance? Or a walk and a place for lunch?' he suggested. 'You choose.'

'I don't know.' She hesitated, wondering why as she did so. He was good looking and she knew she would enjoy his company, so what was holding her back?

Stella had overheard, as she had been making arrange-ments regarding opening an account, and she whispered, hoarsely, 'Go on, girl, have a bit of fun.' Turning to Ken,

she added, 'Wednesday's her half-day, give her time to
"doll" herself up, won't it, us closing the shop at one.'

'Stella!'

'Wednesday it is,' Ken said, shaking her hand and
seeming reluctant to let it go. 'I'll call for you at six and
you can decide what we do.'

'You don't even know where I live!'

'Oh but I do. Stella told me while you were drooling
over party dresses for little girls.'

Her cheeks were warm with pleasure and self-
consciousness and Lowri was relieved to get out, aware of
the other members of staff watching her curiously. As they
were closing the door Ken called to them, 'Your order will
be packed in fifteen minutes. If you'd like to wait I can
deliver them and give you ladies a lift home at the same
time,' he offered.

The van was large and the three of them sat in front,
Lowri in the middle unavoidably close to Ken. She
couldn't join in the conversation easily. She hadn't been
out on a date since Henry Roberts had been killed. She
felt gauche and child-like and was glad when the journey
was over and they climbed down outside the post office.

'Shall I take you the rest of the way?' he offered and
Lowri at once shook her head. 'Thanks, but I want to
help Stella unpack and get the clothes on to hangers.'

Something in her voice warned Stella not to disagree.

'Good on you girl,' Stella said, as they went into the
shop. 'Pleasant young man, so go out and enjoy yourself.
We don't know him mind, so make it a café, so you can
be sure before being on your own with him.'

'Don't you trust him, Stella?'

'Of course, I wouldn't have told him all about you if
I hadn't. Never does no harm to be sure, though. And I

found out a bit about him too. Not married nor engaged, he's twenty-six and lives with his parents, likes dancing and plays darts in the pub team. How's that for a start?'

'Shall I take him to The Ship and Compass and challenge him to a game of darts, so your Colin can sit at the bar and keep an eye on him?' Lowri teased.

'Never harms to be sure,' Stella repeated. 'Special you are, young Lowri and don't forget it.'

Lowri frowned. 'D'you know, I am rather special. I've just realized, it's the sixteenth. Today is my twenty-fifth birthday!' She was laughing as she walked back into Badgers Brook clutching a cake Stella had given her. 'Marion,' she called. 'Come and have a piece of birthday cake!'

–

The grand opening of the new collection at the post office shop the following Monday was greeted at first with suspicion. People came and looked at the window display, handled the garments when they called for their pensions and postage stamps and shook their heads over the prices. 'I'll wait for your next sale,' a few called, and Stella smiled at their joke and muttered insults under her breath.

Gradually the clothes began to earn approval. Stella kept the prices as low as she could and knew they compared favourably with other places. Mrs Nerys Bowen, who owned the ladies dress shop on the corner opposite Geoff Tanner's ironmongers called and admired her selection and bought two outfits for a friend's children. Respected as a woman of taste, her delight in her purchases encouraged others and on the day Lowri had arranged to go out with Ken Hardy, they knew they would soon need to restock.

'Are you looking forward to your date with Ken?' Stella asked on that Wednesday morning and was concerned to see Lowri frown. 'Don't worry, you don't have to go if you aren't sure. Ring him from here and tell him you've got a galloping infectious plague, or are needed for something important.'

'I don't want to go, not that I don't like him, but because I can't get involved.' Stella guessed the reason. 'You think he'll drop you when he finds out who your father is? Why would he?'

'Why wouldn't he?'

Stella put on her coat and went around to The Ship and Compass, where she knew Marion was working that morning. 'Come and talk to her, will you?' she said after explaining the problem. Marion did so willingly. Anything that would discourage Dic Morris, with his constant talk about rescuing Lowri's father from prison, was welcome.

So Lowri went and, ignoring Stella's half serious advice, she chose the pictures, where she could learn something about Ken's sense of humour, followed by supper, during which they could talk. The conversation was easy and time went fast. She was disappointed when they stood to leave the restaurant and go to his parked car. Still talking and laughing, exchanging stories of their recent past, he drove her to Badgers Brook, where a light shone from the kitchen, lighting their path, but she didn't invite him inside. She thanked him for an enjoyable evening and just smiled her non-commitment when he started to talk about 'next time'. She wasn't sure. Liking him too much, or not enough, each had its problems. There was the spectre of her father's situation to contend with, and if she began to warm to him, that threat was likely to end it all. Best to take it slowly.

'Vain you are, that's your trouble,' Marion said when she told her about the evening and its hesitant ending. 'What makes you think he's so smitten he's already thinking of a serious courtship? He might be the kind who takes a girl out a few times then looks for something new. And why shouldn't he?' She smiled then and added, 'Nice he is, mind. I wouldn't say no to a date.'

'Then you think I should go again, if he asked me?'

'Of course. Unless he's got B.O. or halitosis, of course.' Then they were both laughing as they discussed their attitudes to the advantages and disadvantages of the various men they had known.

Marion was relieved that Lowri had found someone to take her mind away from her father's plight and hoped the friendship would continue. Better than Dic and his constant reminders of the insoluble fact of Jimmy Vaughan's imprisonment.

Lowri had heard of Stella and Colin's shed on the allotment where they grew most of their vegetables for the year. She had never been to see it, as winter and the cold frosts and snows of January were not the ideal time. She had also heard Stella refer to her country cottage. She hadn't realized they were one and the same.

It was as they were closing the shop for lunch a few days after her first date with Ken Hardy, with overnight snow covering the ground 'waiting for more', according to Stella, that she was invited to walk around and see the place.

Colin was on the late shift at the local railway station and he gathered up a few bags of stale food to feed the birds – something Lowri learned that he did every day – and they set off, Stella carrying a small canvas bag containing flasks of soup and some fresh bread.

'I've never known such a place for picnics,' Lowri said with a laugh as she was handed a second bag with milk and a few biscuits. 'Haven't either of you noticed the snow?'

'Beautiful it is. Just beautiful.'

They trudged along the narrow lane leading to the field that had been divided into equal sized plots, each with its home-made shed to hold gardening tools. The whole area was covered in snow, a perfect carpet on which the only patterns were the tiny footprints of birds where they had gathered to devour the scattering of crumbs left by others.

The birdsong was surprising for so late in the day and added its magic to the scene. Stella opened the shed door and Lowri was surprised to see the interior was more like a kitchen, with gingham curtains and neatly arranged shelves. Two chairs were unfolded and set out near the table to which Stella added a carefully ironed tablecloth and, to Lowri's amusement, a vase of dried flowers. Tins were opened to reveal cups and saucers, salt and pepper, and soup bowls, each one wrapped in tissue paper.

With limited heat from a primus stove, they ate the hot soup with neatly sliced bread and Lowri declared she had never enjoyed a meal more. Later, when even the small primus stove couldn't keep them warm any longer, she walked along paths made invisible by the covering of snow, as Colin pointed out areas in the white blanket where his various crops would be. Sticking through the icy covering, the tall stalks of Brussels sprouts leaned drunkenly and, ignoring the cold, Colin picked some and filled a small bowl.

'I'll go and wrap some for you and Marion,' he promised and thanking him, she walked on to where a hawthorn hedge made a barrier to the field beyond.

'This plot belongs to Gwennie Flint's husband, Maldwyn,' Stella said, waving an arm to encompass more of the pristine snow. 'Lazy man he is, and does very little to grow his crops. My Colin and a few of the others do a bit now and then, feel sorry for Gwennie they do. She runs that fish and chip shop almost single handed, out these cold mornings dealing with the potatoes when the assistant fails to turn up, and him in bed waiting impatiently for his cup of tea. Lazy man he is, and he can be unpleasant too.'

She wandered back discussing future plans with Colin while Lowri stood looking back and smiling at the pleasure Stella found in her country cottage. Then, for no reason at all, she stood up on an abandoned pile of bricks, grasping a branch for security, and looked over the hedge.

A man was walking in the field beyond, striding across her view, his legs rising and falling in a caricature of the goose step as he navigated his way through the deep snow. There was something familiar about the figure and she almost waved as she tried to place him. She stared curiously, running names and possibilities through her mind: Peter Bevan? Ed Conners? Geoff Tanner?

It was none of these, but something tormented her memory, the way he walked through the difficult terrain was obviously distorting his usual gait, but there was something about the angle of the head; he walked tall and with his shoulders held determinedly back, a small man trying to compensate for his lack of height?

A bucket upturned over rhubarb was close by and she climbed up for a better view, stretched on tiptoe, prepared to wave if the man was someone she knew. The man looked towards her, then hesitated in a sort of crouch, and quickly changed direction to walk away from her. Despite the difficult terrain, he began to move faster.

She felt a coldness that was nothing to do with the temperature. The man she was watching, was without doubt, Ellis Owen, the man her father was suspected of murdering.

'Colin, come quick, who's that man?' she called. But by the time Colin had climbed up beside her, the man had disappeared into the next field and was lost to sight. The hedge was thick and there was no visible exit, no way she could run after him. Who would believe her? Yet she was certain it was Ellis Owen she had seen. He had filled her nightmares for so long, she could see his face just by thinking of him. Clear too was the way he walked. She often recognized people by the way they walked, and he had a way of holding his head that no one else could copy. In her heart and her mind, there was no doubt. No one would believe her, in fact she was already beginning to doubt her own eyes, so what should she – could she – do?

Four

The man was gone from sight but still Lowri stared. She must have been wrong. Yet there was something about the walk, the angle of the head, stretched up and slightly back. Her father had often teased him about it.

'You all right, Lowri?' Stella called anxiously, as she ran to where Lowri stood looking over the hedge.

Lowri turned towards her and asked, 'How can I get into the next field?'

Stella and Colin pointed to a gate, hidden in the tangles of hawthorn and ivy and Lowri ran and struggled to pull it open. When she could not, she climbed over and, ignoring the scratches from the sharp branches and the chill as she landed in deep snow that rose over her boots and soaked her skirt, she ran to where she had last seen the man. Following close behind, were Stella and Colin, calling, asking her who she had seen.

She reached the place where the man had suddenly changed direction when he had seen her and looked along the line of snow prints which were at right angles from his initial direction. The trail led to a narrow road and when she reached it, the passing of traffic had obliterated all trace of him. As Stella and Colin reached her, panting and concerned, Lowri told them what she had seen.

'You have the man on your mind so much, it isn't surprising you think you've seen him,' Stella comforted.

69

'I remember when my grandad died,' Colin added, putting an arm around her shoulders and leading her back. 'I couldn't believe that he was gone. Several times I ran after a man who looked like him, called his name, "Grampy!", only to see a stranger when he turned his head. I was only about seven,' he added. 'Missed him dreadful I did.'

'I'm twenty-five,' Lowri replied. 'And I'm certain that man was Ellis Owen.'

'Stranger things have happened, mind,' Stella said, with a warning glance at her husband. 'Oh yes, it could happen, no doubt about that. Truth stranger than fiction, indeed.'

Lowri walked home in a daze. The buses were running now the main roads had been cleared but she needed to walk and clear her head. Of course it wasn't Ellis Owen. How could it have been? He had died in that wild sea. Yet hope, dormant within her, had reawakened. She had always dreamed that, as the body was never recovered, Ellis Owen might still be alive.

Her face revealed her shock, and when she walked into Badgers Brook, Marion looked at her in concern.

'Lowri? What is it? You look frozen, and as though you've had a shock. Is everything all right?'

'Cold, that's all,' she murmured, forcing a smile before going up to her room to remove her outdoor clothes. She stared, unseeing, at the clothes in her wardrobe and frowned. Was she going mad? Allowing imagination to make a distant view of a stranger into someone who could solve all her worries? It was impossible. Ellis Owen fell into the sea when the storm was it its height and was never found. The last few words echoed in her brain. Was never found. Hope – never far from the surface of her mind – leapt anew. Couldn't that mean it wasn't impossible? That there was a chance, however slight, that Ellis Owen had survived?

She lifted out the summer jacket and felt in the pocket. The key lay dully in her palm and she stared, urging it to give up its secret. But then reality flowed painfully back and she knew that it was most likely to mean nothing. If it belonged to her father she would know its purpose. There had been no secrets in their family. It was probably one her father found and dropped into his pocket as he would have picked up a coin.

She tried to make a connection between a mysterious key and the man who was presumed to be dead and at the bottom of the sea, but she knew too little about him. She visualized him walking across the field and told herself the uneven surface and fear of slipping on the snow could have accounted for his stiff, upright gait, but maybe not. Despite trying to ignore the foolish hope, she still felt certain it had been Ellis Owen and the thought made her heart race.

She wished she hadn't told Stella and Colin. She couldn't tell anyone else: it was too fantastic. She half smiled as she imagined Marion's cynical response and she certainly wouldn't upset her mother with such a story. There was no one – except Dic; he would at least listen to her. She would ring him, make light of it, pretend to be embarrassed at her own stupidity, and perhaps, just perhaps, he might believe it possible. Hope never dies, she thought sadly. Not even when the only hope is for a miracle.

She hadn't seen Ken Hardy since their evening at the pictures followed by supper. She had avoided going to the warehouse when Stella went for fresh stock and had been vague when he had telephoned and invited her out. It was early in February when he called at the post office just before one o'clock and invited her to lunch in the café. Instead, making the excuse it was her turn to bring in the coal and logs for the fire, she invited him back to Badgers Brook and made Welsh rarebit – scrambled eggs on toast with the addition of the dry end of their cheese ration.

He was very formal as though afraid of offending her, and went to look at the garden, decorated with a fresh fall of snow, unmarked and shining in the sun.

'This is a beautiful place, Lowri. You were lucky to find it vacant and waiting for a tenant.'

Offering him some Wellingtons belonging to Bob Jennings who, together with Colin Jones tended the long garden, they walked around and she explained where the various crops would grow, similar to the tour she had been given by Colin in his allotment the day she had seen – thought she had seen – Ellis Owen, a dead man.

He surprised her by recognizing many of the trees, and the birds that fluttered around searching for food and together they filled the various feeding areas she and Kitty regularly tended. She began to relax and enjoy his company; perhaps he wouldn't be another false friend, and would accept the truth about her father if she should one day explain.

She walked ahead of him, wondering about the time, afraid of being late to re-open, then she suddenly felt a sudden blow on her back. She turned and ducked in time to avoid a second hit. Ken was pelting her with snowballs! She was amazed. Then, as a third whizzed past her head, she bent and gathered a handful and threatened him, arm held back. A fourth reached its mark and she threw hers and joined in with great enthusiasm. An icy shock when

72

one hit her neck was quickly followed by another on her shoulder. Gritting her teeth she pelted him, snow flying through the air leaving a powdery trail from her carelessly made missiles.

It was then that Marion came around the house and stared at them in disbelief. Laughing she scooped up the soft feathering snow and lobbed overarm to each of them in turn. They were so intent on each other they hardly seemed to notice, then as one, they turned and chased her back indoors.

Lowri's face was rosy with the exercise and laughter and her eyes shone. Ken didn't remark on how lovely she looked; he had the feeling that compliments wouldn't sit easily on her, that she would take them as casually meant when he wanted to be believed. Instead, he touched her wet hair and said, 'I think you'd better change before going back to the shop. You look as though you've been swimming!' Still laughing and puffing from their game, they returned to the house, stamping the snow from their boots.

'I'll be late and Stella will worry,' she said as she looked at him after rubbing her hair dry, and said happily, 'Fun though, wasn't it?'

'The best,' he agreed, touching her cold cheeks with his hands. Then he looked out at the less than pristine garden and added, 'This place grabs you and makes you happy, doesn't it?'

'You feel that too?'

'This house and you. Everything you do makes me happy, Lowri.' He held her close, stared into her eyes for a moment then kissed her. She responded at first but then began to pull away when they were disturbed by a movement at the door. He looked at her and saw an expression in her eyes that concerned him. It hadn't been disappointment at the interruption, but a relief it had happened and ended their closeness. Had he moved too fast and ruined his chance of something more than friendship?

'Don't worry, I'll bring the coal and sticks in, even though it isn't my turn,' Marion said with pretend annoyance, as she came in shrugging off her coat. 'You go off and leave it all to me.'

Lowri was uneasy and was aware of a feeling of guilt. An image of Dic Morris came into her mind and for some inexplicable reason she felt the fun of the brief interlude draining away. It was as though the fun in the garden would have disappointed him, but why that should be she couldn't decide. Ken took her back to the post office and when Stella asked if she had been swimming, she burst into tears.

She couldn't explain. Amid the confusion in her mind were several fears. One being the inevitability of Ken finding out about her father and walking away. Another was mixed up with Dic and the strange feeling that he should have been the one playing and laughing with her in the garden. Why should that be? She gave up trying to work it out and sipped the tea a concerned Stella had made, washed her face, then went to the counter and smiled at the customers.

Ken was waiting to give her a lift home when she left and they went back to Badgers Brook, but he didn't stay. He guessed that with Marion likely to be there, the evening would lack the magic of that snowy afternoon. He also sensed that Lowri's mood was more sombre and wondered whether she had regretted the brief show of affection between them. Lowri saw him to the door with an ill-disguised indication of haste, and he kissed her lightly as he left.

The day had unsettled her and without explaining to Marion, Lowri put on her coat and heavy shoes and walked up the dark and slippery lane to the phone box.

'Dic,' she said when he answered, 'I know you'll think me crazy, but last week I thought I saw Ellis Owen.' She went on under his questioning to tell him exactly what had happened.

'I don't think it's unusual for people to imagine they've seen someone who has died,' he said unknowingly repeating Colin's opinion. 'But it's usually when they've lost someone they love.'

'So that could be true of me. Through this man, I lost someone I love, my father. And all my friends too. So you're probably right and I allowed my imagination to run away with me.'

'That's the most likely, but what if I come down and we talk about it? What about Sunday?'

'Sunday will be fine. Bring Sarah-Jane and Katie,' she added quickly, and wondered why. She liked the little girls and enjoyed their company, but she knew their presence would make serious talk impossible. Talking about her belief that Ellis was alive would reduce her conviction and she needed something to cling to. Was she avoiding facing the truth, that she had so obviously been wrong? Was she just a foolish dreamer, unwilling to face facts? Or worried by spending time alone with Dic, the brotherly man who was stopping her from falling in love with Ken?

Sunday dawned into one of the rare days of sun and mild calm that February sometimes throws up as a welcome interlude in the darkness of winter. The girls were well wrapped and when they arrived soon after eleven o'clock Dic at once suggested a walk, reminding her that the girls loved the woodland.

'Coffee first,' Lowri said.

Dic made a few comments about his week, adding quietly, 'Mum sends her love. She asked me to remind you that whatever has happened, she's still your Auntie Cathy.'

'I wish we could all go back to how we were,' Lowri said with a sigh. 'But that will never happen. Your mother and father believe my father's guilty. How can I forget that and call them Auntie Cathy and Uncle Jack?'

Dic wanted her to believe his father had changed his mind and was still her Uncle Jack, but he knew she was right to stay away. His father was still angry and if he met Lowri she would sense that in moments. He wanted so badly for them all to be reconciled, but unless his father could be convinced that Jimmy Vaughan wasn't the thief, it would never happen.

Jack had been working every hour he could to put the ailing business back on its feet and, exhausted and constantly on the edge of disaster, he refused to listen to arguments in Jimmy's favour. If anything changed, it would only be when Jimmy proved his innocence and there didn't seem to be the slightest chance of that.

He looked at Lowri, smiling as she listened to the children talking about the story book she'd bought for them as she prepared coffee. Leaving them for a moment, she warned, 'I haven't told Marion about seeing Ellis Owen, mind. I can't face her reminding me that it's nothing more than wishful thinking. Even if it is.'

'We'll talk as we walk through the wood, where we can discuss it freely,' he assured her.

It wasn't to be. The sunny promise quickly died away. The day became dark and overcast, the clouds lowered threateningly and soon precipitated into heavy rain.

Lowri stood looking down the garden as the milder temperature and the rain ruined the beauty of the once white garden. She smiled as she remembered the snowball fight, the unexpected companionship and fun of that brief interlude.

Then Marion called from upstairs, 'You'll have to cancel your walk, mind. It's pelting with rain. And a good thing too, it'll get rid of this messy snow.'

For Lowri the memory was suddenly destroyed, just as the rain was ruining the once beautiful white world beyond the window.

They played games with Sarah-Jane and Katie and only in whispered snatches discussed the figure Lowri had seen walking across the field that day.

'If you'd told me at once, I might have followed his footprints in the snow and found out where he had gone.'

'How could I? It was too fanciful to be believed. Besides, I climbed into the field and followed as far as the road, from where the snow had been cleared by traffic. I was mistaken. How could I have seen Ellis Owen? He's dead. Drowned in a storm.'

'Stranger things have happened,' he said, squeezing her hand reassuringly. 'If it happens again, ring me at once.'

'Unlikely. The man I saw was probably hurrying because he was a poacher, walking stiffly because he had parts of his gun down his trousers!'

'Something else our Ellis Owen used to do,' he told her. 'A real outdoor man he was.'

-

Betty re-read the letter with growing dismay. A group of ramblers was coming through Cwm Derw the following day and would like her to provide a snack lunch for eight people. This was something she often did and something she enjoyed. She put on her coat and went to find 'Willing-But-Won't'. He wasn't too reliable and she would need him there if she were to cope with the extra eight people wanting food.

He was still casually dressed and looked as though he wasn't long out of bed. His mother fussed and promised he wouldn't be late and assured her he would be there early on the following day. As Betty walked away, she laughed as she heard the mother's voice raised as she warned her son what would happen if he lost his job. 'As soon as I can find someone better that's exactly what will happen!' she muttered aloud.

'Talking to yourself?' Gwennie Flint came out of a shop and stood in front of her friend.

'Walkers coming tomorrow expecting lunch. I've been trying to persuade "Willing-But-Won't" that it's a good idea to get there on time.'

'Food isn't a problem, is it?'

'No, but I need a barman who knows what he's doing and at least pretends to enjoy it.'

'You wouldn't give my Maldwyn a try I suppose?'

'Gwennie, you're my friend but your Maldwyn isn't, well...'

'Isn't fond of work?' Gwennie finished with a sigh.

'I'll keep him in mind if I'm stuck, I promise,' Betty said hurrying back to The Ship.

Lowri called in to The Ship the following evening with vegetables from Kitty and Bob and was surprised to see the bar full of strangers.

'Came for lunch they did but they didn't leave,' Betty explained. 'They've booked in to my brother's bed and breakfast for the night. They walked through the wood and as far as the cliffs and now they're back and challenging the locals to a game of darts. See who's struggling to finish on a double?'

'Ken?' Lowri called. She watched as he threw the dart into double seven then went to congratulate him.

All plans to return to Badgers Brook were forgotten and she joined the group and tried her hand at darts, joined in a singsong as the mood became more maudlin and the evening ended with the ramblers shaking hands with everyone and promising to come back soon.

Ken drove her home and she felt happiness like fizzy bubbles inside her. Ken always created fun out of ordinary things. It wasn't until much later, as she described the evening to Marion, that she wished Dic had been there to enjoy it too.

—

Dic, encouraged by Lowri's vision of Ellis, went to Swansea and around the bay to Mumbles a few days later and spoke to several local fishermen, gathering information about the tides. He was told that a body going into the water at high tide at the place where Ellis Owen had disappeared, could have been taken almost anywhere along the coast. It could have drifted around the headland as far as Bracelet Bay or even further, to where the sandbanks known as the Mixen sands were situated. One coast guard told him a body could have been taken across the channel to the coast of Devon!

He walked along the beach as far as he could, then along the road where it cut through the rocks and down to the pier. He continued past Bracelet Bay with its view of Mumbles Rocks and the lighthouse, past the smaller bay of Limeslade to the beginning of the coastal path to Langland. He looked out to sea where, now the tide was low, he could make out the slight disturbance that revealed the Mixens.

On rare occasions, when a very low tide and calm seas allowed, the Mixen sands were revealed, and Dic had been shown photographs of a group of people sitting in deckchairs apparently picnicking in the middle of the sea on the temporary dry bank. A boat had been standing by, but out of shot, so not to spoil the amusing picture.

There was no chance of Ellis being saved by the Mixens on the day he had purportedly drowned. The sea had been wild and conditions had offered no escape.

His only chance would have been if he had been carried out by the tide and currents and miraculously found himself against the rocks without being hurt and had been able to clamber to safety. Or had been washed against an anchored boat. But there were few boats in the bay on that day; the owners had taken them in for safety having been warned of the storm to come. Only crafts belonging to foolhardy owners, who lived a long way off and had decided to take their chances, were left bobbing on the angry waves, two of them wrecked against the sea wall. If he had miraculously survived, where was he? Surely he'd have returned to his wife?

He had to be dead and Lowri mistaken in her sighting of him. Common sense told him that, but Lowri was not yet ready to face that irrevocable fact, and he would carry on nurturing that seed of desperate hope until she was.

–

Since the snowball fight and the evening at The Ship, Lowri and Ken gradually began to see more of each other and he became a regular visitor to Badgers Brook. During the dark weeks of the year they walked in the wood or called to see Kitty and Bob, where he would ask interested questions about the garden, and was eventually invited to visit Stella and Colin's 'country cottage'.

The snow was gone and the fields and allotments looked drab with dead foliage and moist debris, yet the day had a beauty of its own. Seen closer, the trees were already showing promise of spring. There were small catkins on the hazel and birch trees, and the deep green of the evergreens and the startlingly lovely gold of the willows had come into their own.

Ken and Colin even spotted a few bright primroses in sheltered places, and below the hedges there were the unfolding leaves of wild garlic which was gradually forcing out the once widely spread bluebells. Seeing it with Ken taught her to look more closely and to listen to the sound as well as the sight of the birds flying around, anxiously searching for food in the few hours of daylight.

The afternoon, looking at familiar things Ken's observant eyes pointed out, was enjoyable and the almost constant thoughts of Dic's disapproval faded. Sharing the tea Stella provided in her country cottage made her feel like part of a couple and the hour passed pleasantly.

Before they left, she couldn't resist walking down and looking over the wet, leafless hawthorn hedge into the field beyond. The snow was gone and the field was empty. She foolishly willed the man to reappear so she could accept he was a stranger and put aside her foolish dream.

One day soon she would have to tell Ken about her father. She was looking forward to their meetings more

81

and more and was afraid that by saying one brief sentence: 'my father's in prison' they would end. No explanation would be given, just the fading away of their friendship, the lack of invitations and plans. Despite the wonderful afternoon, and the way he looked at her as he tucked her arm in his, she was saddened, aware of the inevitable end of it all.

'Tell him, and the sooner the better,' was Marion's advice.

'Perhaps a couple more weeks,' Lowri said. 'It's been such fun, having Ken to go out with after all the years I've been alone.'

'He's fond of you and he'll realize that you aren't tainted by your father being convicted. Tell him everything, then he'll understand.'

To Lowri the words sounded like a mother pacifying a child with false words.

'The missing money is the stumbling block to accepting that,' she said. 'The prosecution convinced a jury that Dad had been embezzling money from the business and that was why he had to kill Owen. How can I expect him to understand that? Even saying it aloud it's hard to convince myself sometimes.'

'Anyway, he has to be told. It will be harder to convince him if he learns from someone else.'

'I suppose it's a miracle he hasn't found out already.'

'There you are, a small miracle! Now all we want is a big one!'

Smiling at Marion's attempt to cheer her, Lowri decided that she would tell Ken the next time they met. But the small miracle was not to be, she had waited too long.

They met at five thirty when the post office closed and Ken handed her a bag of sweets, coconut macaroons, her favourite. His sweet ration was usually spent giving her little treats on their dates. He had the car and they drove towards the cinema, but he pulled into a lay-by and turned off the engine. Turning in his seat, he stared at her, his expression almost invisible in the pale light from a nearby street lamp.

'What is it?' she asked. 'Is something wrong with the car?'

'You've been evasive when I've asked where your parents live,' he said, his voice catching in his throat. 'Is it because your father is in prison?'

'Who told you?' she asked in a low voice.

'It doesn't matter who, what does matter is it should have been you.'

'I couldn't. I'm sorry, Ken. I've lost so many friends since this happened and I didn't want the same to happen to you.'

'Perhaps I'd have walked away, if you'd told me straight away, I don't know. But finding out after all these weeks is an insult.'

'You'd better take me to the bus stop. I'll find my own way home.'

'You believe I'd do that? Your opinion of me must be even lower than I thought.'

'Sorry.'

'I think we should abandon the pictures, but shouldn't we go somewhere and talk about what happened? I'd like to hear your version rather than the newspaper reports which is where I have my information from, after someone put it on my desk this afternoon.'

'What did you do?'

'I read enough to learn about the trial, waited until the shock had subsided, then threw it into the waste-paper bin. Loudly, so everyone could hear, I then announced that the gossip was not necessary as I already knew.'

'I'm so sorry,' she whispered. As Ken started the car and drove off, Lowri shrank back in her seat struggling to hold back tears. She would never be free of this. Never.

They drove back to Badgers Brook and with Marion visiting her family they were able to talk. Ken listened in silence as she told him the story of her father's arrest and sentence. 'So, with this Ellis Owen, whom your father believed was responsible for stealing from the business, now dead, there's no one to prove otherwise,' he summed up.

Hesitantly, she told him of her foolish belief that she had seen Ellis. 'I know it was only wishful thinking,' she said before he could comment. 'But his survival is the only chance my father has of being reprieved. So I believed it – for a while at least.'

'D'you think every person guilty of a serious crime is able to convince his loved ones he is innocent?'

'Dad *is* innocent!'

'I can't imagine my father harming a soul, and even faced with the most damning evidence, I would still not believe it.'

'So I should accept his guilt and forget miracles?'

He turned to look at her, with such compassion in his eyes that she felt a lessening of her anxiety, a sensation that she was no longer alone. 'I wouldn't,' he said softly.

Although he kissed her as he left, there was a lack of warmth. She was saddened by the realization that news of her father's predicament had created a space between them, an awareness that he had metaphorically taken a few steps away from her. They continued to meet but there was a tension that hadn't been there before. She was afraid their feelings for each other were on a slow slide into oblivion and there was no one to blame but herself. She should have told him, trusted him.

-

Since Lowri and Marion had become tenants of Badgers Brook their friendship had grown, yet there were still parts of Marion's life into which Lowri was not allowed to enter. Besides visits to her family, and the odd hours she worked, Marion often went for walks, always on her own. On these occasions, she insisted that she needed to relieve herself of excess energy, and although Lowri was offered a casual invitation to go with her, she was left with the strong impression that her presence was not really required. Lowri would watch her friend set off at a gentle run, down the path and across the road, where she would jump the ditch before disappearing among the trees.

It took her a while, but at the end of February, when she and Ken were walking the few steps home from a visit to Kitty and Bob Jennings, she suddenly laughed and said, 'It's a boyfriend!'

'What is?' Ken asked, sharing her smile, aware that a joke was about to be explained.

'Marion's secrecy! I think she has a boyfriend and for some reason doesn't want to tell me about him. D'you think he's much younger than her? Or covered in spots? Or so dull she'd be too embarrassed to introduce him? Perhaps her parents don't know and when she says she's going home, she's really meeting this secret friend.'

They exchanged ideas about the unseen young man as they unlocked the door and went inside. The gas light was low and Lowri pulled the thin chain to bring it to its full strength, then whispered, 'Shall I face her with it? Demand the truth?'

'The truth about what?' a voice asked and Lowri jumped, and found herself in Ken's arms. 'Marion! What are you doing in the dark?'

'I've been sleeping and you noisy pair woke me rather suddenly. What time is it?'

'Eight o'clock. Are you ill?' Concerned, Lowri went towards Marion and saw to her horror that one side of her face was badly scraped. Blood had seeped through where the skin had been pulled away and her eyebrow was cut and still bleeding. 'Marion! What happened? What have you done?'

Ken went to the kitchen where he knew they kept their minimal supply of medication and brought out cotton wool and some salve. He scrubbed his hands then, while Marion sat trembling with shock and explained what had happened to Lowri, he bathed her injuries and applied the ointment.

'I went through the wood following the tracks of the badgers,' Marion told them. 'Then I went further and climbed the hill. Evening mist was creeping across the fields and I realized I'd gone too far and it would soon be dark so I hurried back. I came along the track to the right at the top of the lane, creepy place it is after dark. I picked up speed, tripped over the rough grass and fell down the side of the track. I did this as I rolled through bushes into the field below. Stupid, eh?'

'But what were you doing on that side of the wood?' Lowri asked, offering her friend a cup of hot sweet tea.

'I had a lift for part of the way then I walked around the outside of the wood instead of cutting through. It was getting dark and I thought I was less likely to trip. I forgot how terribly overgrown that track has become, idiot that I am. It was so overgrown and dark I imagined someone watching me and I ran. Mam told me someone once tried to kill himself by running his wheelchair off the track. Someone who lived in Badgers Brook. Thinking of this I was really spooked, I certainly wasn't concentrating.'

Lowri glanced at Ken and they shared a frown of disbelief. Whatever happened to Marion, she was not telling them the true story. Ken left soon after and Lowri asked no more questions. Marion was secretive and obviously not telling her the truth but she didn't want to pester her after the shock she had suffered. Tomorrow she would persuade her to talk, and hopefully find out what had really happened.

For a fleeting moment she wondered whether the mysterious boyfriend had hurt her, but realized that the injuries did not appear to be the result of a fight. Neither did they represent a fall through bushes and on to a soft, soggy, wet field. Besides, on the clothes Marion had discarded and which Lowri brought down for washing, there wasn't even the smallest patch of mud.

When Lowri woke the following morning there was no sign of Marion. A note on the table told her that her friend had an early start at the house of Mr Morgan, a man for whom she occasionally cleaned, but whom she had never met. This wasn't surprising, several of Marion's clients, as she called them, were out all day and left money and instructions for her.

At lunch-time, after eating a snack at the cafe, Lowri went to the telephone box and spoke to Dic. She described Marion's accident, exaggerating the mystery to amuse him.

'Whatever she did, it wasn't falling in to a muddy field. It looked as though she'd scraped her poor face on a brick wall! Perhaps it was a rock face and she's a climber, a modest and anonymous member of a rescue team?'

'Or perhaps her secret lover is a hermit, living in a cave far from human contact apart from her visits? Or she steals birds eggs? Or photographs rare creatures, wearing camouflage and hanging from dangerous ledges like a bat?'

Whether it was the fear of laughing aloud, remembering Dic's comments, Lowri hesitated to ask Marion any questions that evening and as days went by and the skin on Marion's face, legs and arms slowly healed, the moment passed and it was no longer easy to bring up the subject. Her friend was a perfect housemate, apart from her determination to keep part of her life a secret and Lowri knew that if she offended Marion by demanding answers, she would have difficulty finding someone else who would share Badgers Brook with her so amicably.

–

Dic was restless. Work needed his concentration and the figures he designed just wouldn't grow under his ministrations. He had almost finished the humorously crooked boat, which he intended giving to Lowri, and he put it aside. A moment's carelessness and it would be ruined. He closed the shop thankfully at five thirty and went to collect the children from his parents' home.

His mother was out with Sarah-Jane and Katie. They had gone to the pantomime and wouldn't be home for another hour. Dic took the opportunity to talk to his father.

'Dad, how d'you feel about Jimmy Vaughan after these past months? Do you still believe he's guilty?'

'I swell with anger every time I think of him. We'd started from nothing and built up a good business and he ruined it by stealing the money we should have been putting back into the business. It would have trebled the size in another year and he ruined it by impatience and greed.'

'Don't you ever wonder if he was set up by someone else?'

'Ellis Owen, you mean? No, I don't. Ellis didn't have the intelligence. He might have had more opportunity for fraud, being responsible for the accounts, but Jimmy had always overseen what Ellis did, and looking back, his interest was unnecessarily thorough. No, Dic, I have no doubts that he was guilty of fraud.'

'And the murder? You knew Jimmy for years, can you believe him guilty of killing someone for money? The amount was substantial, but as you say, it was less than he stood to make over the next few years.'

'I couldn't believe it at first, but when the case was made in court there seemed no doubt. I try not to think of him these days.'

'Why? Do you have doubts?'

Angrily, Jack stood up and glared at him. 'I know what's going through your mind! You've been seeing Lowri and feel sorry for her. It's clouding your judgement. It was you who first pointed the finger at Jimmy, remember. And your evidence that convicted him. So wishing won't change anything. The facts were clear. Jimmy lost his temper when Ellis threatened him with the police, then the fear of being discovered turned him into a murderer.'

'But this is so out of character, you and he built the business and it was on the way to a real success story. I just can't believe he would change so much that—'

'Forget him!' Jack shouted. 'And forget Lowri, she's your uneasy conscience. Getting a man imprisoned for fraud, and suspected of the death of Ellis is on your conscience and something you'll never forget while you keep seeing Lowri and feel sorry for her!'

In the silence that followed his father's tirade, Dic heard the sound of a car outside and he took a deep breath and turned to greet his daughters. They ran in, rosy-faced, both trying to tell him about the performance they had enjoyed. He knelt down and hugged them and asked questions until their need for food overcame their excitement. Then Katie, aged three, reached into her pocket and brought out some warm, soft toffees. 'I saved these for Lowri,' she told him proudly. 'I wanted to eat them but I saved them for when we go to Badgers Brook.'

'Can we go tomorrow?' her sister pleaded. 'We want to tell her about the panto and sing her the song we learnt.'

Dic glared defiantly at his father and said, 'Of course we can. We'll go at the weekend. Now, sing your new song to me.' Dic was aware of his father's anger at the mention of Lowri, but smiled at Sarah-Jane and Katie and encouraged them to perform.

Together they sang the silly song that 'Buttons' had taught them and he hugged them and told them he was proud of them. But the moment, so precious, was spoilt by the stiff-backed anger of his father, that seemed to fill the air around him. As they sang it a second time, Dic smiled and imagined the scene at Badgers Brook as they performed their new song for Lowri. Relaxed and happy in that warm and wonderful place, away from doubts and anger, just the joy of watching his daughters in the peaceful companionship of Lowri.

He explained his father's anger to his mother and Cathy sympathized. 'I've been unable to talk about it but I've never believed Jimmy was guilty,' she whispered. 'A man died and Jimmy must be partly responsible because of the fight they had, but none of it is Lowri's fault. Give her my love when you see her, try to explain, tell her I miss her, will you?'

Without saying anything further to his father, afraid of causing another argument, Dic took the girls to Badgers Brook on Sunday afternoon and found the house full. Kitty and Bob Jennings from the lane, and Stella and Bob from the post office, plus Betty Connors, glad of a break from her full-time job at The Ship and Compass, Gwennie Flint and Geoff and Connie, the owners of Badgers Brook. As he ushered the children in, he wondered whether the gathering was to celebrate a birthday.

'No birthday,' Lowri said in reply to his question. 'There's never an excuse needed. This house gathers people in and instantly there's a party.'

'My mother must have guessed,' he said. 'She sent you a few sandwiches and a cake.' He handed her a couple of carefully wrapped packages. Knowing they were from Cathy Morris, who had never spoken to her since her father was arrested, made her want to throw them into the bin, but she thanked him and added them to the pile of overladen plates in the kitchen, and filled the kettle. 'Tea now and food in an hour. All right?'

Solemnly, Katie pulled out the now misshapen toffees and handed them to Lowri. Lowri knelt down and hugged both girls and thanked Katie for her present, sharing an amused glance with Dic. They then announced they had a new song and proceeded to sing it three times.

As the food was being set out on the long Welsh oak table in the kitchen, Dic managed to have a few private words with Lowri.

'I know your father's situation seems hopeless,' he began, 'but there must be something somewhere that will break the chain of evidence. Someone searched your belongings. It wasn't a normal opportunist thief, nothing was stolen, so he must have been searching for some specific thing.'

'Don't build up my hopes any more, Dic,' she said sadly. 'I've been foolish, dreaming of a miracle and imagining I've seen Ellis Owen. I have to stop, accept what can't be changed and get on with my life.'

'Of course. You *must* do those things, but while I have this niggle in the back of my mind, like you, I will never really give up hope of that miracle.'

She hugged him and whispered a tearful, 'Thank you.' She stepped towards him and his arms came around her, he lowered his head until his cheek rested on her hair. She was reluctant to move.

'Anything you find, or remember, I want you to tell me and no one else. Right?'

'Right,' she promised.

'Can I borrow that key?'

'Of course.'

'It might fit the hut your father and mine used when they were fishing early morning or late at night.'

'That's very unlikely. The police have searched it several times, most recently when my father escaped. There'll be nothing to find.'

'I still want to look.'

She found the key and he held her hand as they went to the kitchen where the impromptu party was underway.

Scars were still visible on Marion's face and arms, but everyone had accepted her story about falling on the track beside the wood.

'That's where poor Ralph Murton fell from his wheel-chair,' Stella said.

'Talking about falling, did you hear about a young woman who almost fell from the cliff a week or so back?' Connie asked. 'Apparently she was hanging on to a rope but was having difficulty getting back up and a man passing in a small rowing boat called for someone to help. A man appeared and she was hauled up. When the police arrived there was no sign of them.'

'How stupid, fooling about at the edge of a cliff,' Marion said quickly. 'You wouldn't catch me doing anything that dangerous.'

Lowri said nothing, but she was thinking of the evening Marion was sitting in the dark, covered with unexplained scraped and bleeding skin.

Leaving the children at Badgers Brook that afternoon, Dic went to see Tommy and Rachel Treweather, the farmers on the other side of the wood. They owned the hut on the cliffs and he wanted permission to go there.

'I have the key,' he said, holding it out, although he wasn't certain it was the correct one.

Tommy looked at it and shook his head. 'That might have been the padlock key, but it's been changed. The place was repaired a while ago, some birdwatchers wanted to use it and they tidied it up. There's a proper lock now but I don't have a key yet.'

Dic looked outside the hut but there was no way of getting inside. A new lock had been fitted and the door strengthened. He found the discarded padlock in some debris but the key didn't fit.

Ken had arrived when he got back to Badgers Brook. Lowri was taking his coat and Katie and Sarah-Jane were tucking into some sweets he'd brought. Dic greeted the man, hiding his disappointment behind a smile. Ken would ruin the atmosphere built up by the others. He didn't belong there.

It wasn't until he was on his way home that he admitted the feeling engendered by Ken's arrival and Lowri's warm welcome, was jealousy.

Five

Ken stayed after Dic had taken the tired little girls home and Betty had gone with them, glad of a lift back to The Ship. Colin went into the garden with a torch to find some onions Bob had offered him from those hanging in the shed. While the women sorted out which dishes belonged to whom, Ken said to Bob, 'I find it strange that Lowri accepts Dic Morris as a friend, when he was the one who put her father in prison.'

'Lowri isn't the sort to bear malice, even over something as important as this. She knows that the investigation he undertook was expected to find Ellis Owen guilty of fraud. After all, it was Lowri's father who asked him to look for evidence. He had no control over where the investigation later led, especially once the police took over.'

'It was Jimmy Vaughan who asked for an investigation of the accounting? But doesn't that suggest he was innocent?'

'Sadly not. What was found was well hidden, and it was only Dic's thoroughness that unearthed it.'

'Double bluff, you mean?'

'That's what the police based their case on.'

'And the money?'

Bob shrugged. 'From what I've learned, the police believe Jimmy has it and will serve his sentence happily, knowing it'll be there when he comes out.'

'You believe he's guilty?'

'I don't know the man, so how can I tell? From what I read in the newspapers and what Lowri has told me, Ellis Owen seems the most likely, and if he stole the money it might never be found now the man's dead. There's no sign of the money, which means either Jimmy is guilty and has hidden it somewhere, or Ellis's wife is being very careful not to spend any of it. But again, Ellis could be the thief and Terri Owen know nothing about it. Ellis could have hidden it so well that no one will ever find it.'

'And Emily, Lowri's mother?'

Bob shrugged again. 'I imagine the police will still be watching her, perhaps Lowri as well. The appearance of unexplained money would confirm that their case against Jimmy Vaughan was sound.'

'Or not? Depending where it turned up?'

'I don't think it's kind to give Lowri and her mother hope. Too many experts are convinced that Jimmy stole from his own company.'

Standing in the hall, hidden by the half-open door, Lowri listened and felt the weight of unhappiness increase with every word. She stepped back into the kitchen and said brightly, 'All the dishes washed? Pity, because I think we'll dirty them again. I feel the need for another cup of tea.'

Colin, discarding his boots on newspaper spread just inside the door, enthusiastically agreed. Like many people, he found the atmosphere of Badgers Brook a happy one and was always willing to stay a while longer.

Dic was in his shop a few days later, serving customers and in between working on a model of a leaping fish which he intended to enhance by tipping some of the scales with silver. He missed his wife, whose skills as a silversmith had been far greater than his own, even though they had both attended the same course. Working with wood was his greatest joy but he occasionally used silver to add sparkle to some of his better pieces.

The comical cartoon boat with its captain, was in the centre of the window and the interest and amusement it gave to passers-by, was satisfaction enough for the time spent. One day, when the moment was right, he would give it to Lowri. Perhaps when she saw him as more than a doting brother? He shook his head, dismissing the thought. Now *he* was hoping for miracles!

He wondered whether a talk with Ellis's wife Terri, might unearth some glimmer of hope which he could offer to Lowri. He hadn't known Ellis well, having met him only a few times when he had called at the office to see his father. Thinking about the man now, months after his tragic death, he tried to bring back to mind something of the man's character, but all he could remember was his enthusiasm and energy, his quick movements, his sharp wit and the ease with which he conversed.

Not a man to hide anything, he mused. Ellis had been open with everyone, always a ready smile, quick to make friends, no pretence or guile. He couldn't see him in the role of fraudster and cheat, but unless the jury were correct and Jimmy was guilty, his charming smile had hidden his true character remarkably well.

On Wednesday afternoon after the shop had closed, he ate a sandwich and went to see Terri Owen. She stared for a moment as though trying to place him, then opened the door wide and invited him in.

'Dic, what a pleasant surprise.'

'No reason for the call,' he admitted. 'I've been wondering if you are all right, coping, you know.'

'I'm managing well enough,' she replied, as they sat beside the roaring fire. 'But an event as horrifying as this doesn't end when the court case finishes and the jury go home. Everything that happens leads to something else and an event as horrific as this, well, I don't think I'll ever recover.'

Dic offered soothing words and waited for her to go on.

'There are so many threads to unravel, things that need an explanation but with Ellis dead there's no one to give them. It goes on and on.'

'It's worse than a natural death, I can see that,' he said, following her as she went into the kitchen to make tea.

'I'm having to sell the house and move to a small flat, and even then I'll have to find a job to help me to manage,' she said.

'You mean there's no money?'

'Of course there's no money!' She stared at him in horror. 'You think that…'

'No, Mrs Owen! I'm sorry. I didn't mean the stolen money – that didn't enter my head. I was thinking of insurances and savings,' he said quickly. 'Most men provide for their family.'

'I'm sorry. I'm so touchy these days. You'd be surprised at the number of people who expect me to move to a grand house and live a comfortable life, imagining there's a stash of money hidden in my mattress!'

He took the kettle from her shaking hands and filled it. 'I'm sorry,' he said again.

'If there had been any money the police would have found it,' she added sadly. 'Searched the house, they did. Every inch. It doesn't feel like my home any more. In fact I won't be sorry to leave.'

'But you've lived here all your life, isn't it possible for you to wait a while, see if things will settle?'

She stared at him, her eyes bright with unshed tears as she set out cups and saucers. 'I might as well tell you the truth – we were going to sell it anyway. Just before he drowned, Ellis had asked me for a divorce.'

Dic's first thought was regret for the sad woman facing him, but it was immediately followed by disappointment. There wasn't the slightest chance of Jimmy Vaughan being freed. Terri's grief and humiliation seemed so genuine, she couldn't be holding on to the stolen money.

'Do you know his reason?' he dared to ask, sensing in her a need to talk.

'Usual sordid reason, there was another woman, but I have no idea who she is.'

'He didn't give you all the facts?'

'Oh, he intended to. He'd promised to tell me about a girl who was going to have his child, and said he hoped that when I'd thought about it I'd understand. Understand? How could he do that to me?'

'I'm so sorry, Mrs Owen. I had no idea. You were remarkably brave, through the investigation and court hearing.'

'My mind was all over the place, thinking about his death and of how I'd have lost him anyway. I won't be at peace until I find out who this girl is. And there's another thing. With the continuing murmurings about my having the money, I won't be free of this until the money is recovered. I only know that I don't have it, and, you know, I don't believe Jimmy Vaughan has it either; the fight that ended with Ellis's death was for nothing. So where does that leave us?'

He asked why she hadn't told the police that Ellis had been planning to leave her.

'How could I? They'd have said it was more likely to have been Ellis, stealing money to support this girl and her child. I couldn't face that, people whispering, laughing at me.'

'What if that had been the case? Jimmy Vaughan might not be in prison now.'

'Of course he would! There was a judge and jury who said he did it. He stole the money, Ellis wouldn't have done that! Even if he were besotted with the girl.'

'You should have told them though,' Dic admonished softly.

—

Lowri invited Ken to lunch on Sunday, but he refused, eventually agreeing to call during the afternoon and perhaps stay for tea. He seemed friendly enough when she saw him at the warehouse where she had gone to pay the monthly account for Stella, his smile as full of pleasure at the sight of her as always, but there was reservation in the way he avoided touching her, keeping his hands well away from hers. He didn't invite her into his office to attend to the business either, but brought the ledgers out into the customer's area and stood behind the wide wooden counter where the assistants checked measurements and counted out tea towels and dusters and the rest of the varied stock.

The edge of excitement was gone and she felt the lack of it. Was this because of Jimmy's gaol sentence, or because she hadn't trusted him enough to tell him? Sunday saw the end of the previous day's rain and the sun shone brightly, adding sparkle to the dripping trees, strengthening the green of the grass to a spring-like richness and emphasizing the brightness of the berries that had survived the winter, on a few holly trees and firethorn hedges. She awaited Ken's arrival with some anxiety. She liked him and didn't want to hear him say goodbye. He had opened up her life in a way she had once thought had gone for ever; the thrill of dating, the warmth in his brown eyes that had promised better joys to come.

Time passed and he didn't appear and she began to believe this was the end. He had said nothing because, after such a brief friendship, there was nothing to say. He would just fade from her life. The thought took the colour out of the day and she knew she had hoped for so much more. So when a knock at the door announced a visitor, she ran to open the door and was unable to hide her disappointment on seeing Dic and the girls. It was only momentary but she knew Dic had seen her reaction and had been hurt.

Making a fuss of Sarah-Jane and Katie filled the first minutes as she took their coats, admired their dresses and exchanged boots for slippers. Only then did she look at Dic and smile a greeting. 'I'm so glad to see you,' she said – and meant it. There was something so reassuring about him. He gave all the comfort and friendship she wanted and asked nothing in return.

Dic didn't talk to her but watched as she set the big oak table for tea. A cake made with the usual lack of proper ingredients was the centrepiece, and there were plates of sandwiches decorated with a few quarters of pale tomatoes. A couple of small vases containing some leafy branches and bluebells were placed at either end to make it look festive. Sadly, Dic suspected the effort had not been for him.

This was confirmed a few moments later as the door opened after a knock, and Ken walked in. 'Goodness, is this another party? There always seems to be a reason for celebration in this house.'

He greeted them all, took a small box of Dairy Box chocolates from his pocket and sat down. 'The chocolates are from my parents' ration,' he explained. 'It's a small offering but there should be a couple for each of us.' He placed the unopened box near Sarah-Jane and Katie, for them to examine the cover and decide on their choices, promising them first pick.

Lowri was uneasy as the two men eyed each other and they began the meal. She soon become aware that the unease was within herself and did not emanate from the men. She concentrated on the girls' chatter and by the time they had eaten, the mood lightened. However, she was relieved when Kitty and Bob came, bringing some firewood and stayed a while.

Perhaps, she thought later, when Marion was home after a visit to her parents and they were heading for bed, I've been so hurt by the way people treated me after the arrest of Dad, that I've lost the ability to relax and enjoy the company of friends.

Dic had left early, having to get the children home and to bed. Ken hadn't stayed much longer and it was Kitty and Bob who had waited until Marion returned, aware of Lowri's need for company.

As they washed the cups after their usual cocoa and biscuits, Lowri asked, 'Where did you go today, to see your Mam and Dad?'

Marion nodded. 'They're glad of some help on Sundays. With the kids to get bathed and settled into bed, and their clothes ready for school.' She laughed. 'D'you know, I spend a couple of hours ironing sometimes twice a week. I don't mind though. My mum is marvellous and I'm so grateful to her.'

'Grateful?' the choice of word seemed an odd one to use.

'Yes, grateful, for the wonderful childhood I had and for the way she's always willing to help, even though her life is so full and chaotic.'

Lowri couldn't see how Marion's mother helped her, it was clearly the other way round, but she smiled and agreed. 'I'm going to ask for a Monday off and go to see my mother next week. We write, and talk on the phone, but I want to see how she is, talk about her visits and find out how Dad's coping. She assures me he's fine, but talking to her, I might learn more. Will you be all right on your own?'

'Good idea. Of course I'll be all right! I feel safe and secure in this house.'

'Even after the break-in?'

'A chance, hoping to find some money, that's all that was. No, you go and don't worry about me. If I do feel nervous, I'll call on Kitty and Bob.'

The following Saturday, Lowri went to the post office with her case already packed and left at twelve o'clock. She had seen the flat before her mother had moved in but not since the few pieces of furniture from her home had been installed. The door opened as soon as she touched the gate of the converted semi, and her mother ran out. They hugged each other tearfully, Lowri hiding her alarm at how her mother had aged in the weeks since they had last met.

Lowri's first questions were about her father as they walked up the path to the door. She was apprehensive about going inside, wondering if her mother had settled, or had refused to unpack and make herself comfortable, still believing the move was a temporary one, just until Jimmy was released. She sighed with relief when she stepped into the living room. It was comfortable and cosy, filled with familiar things. It was crazily overcrowded, as her mother had tried to fit in all her valued pieces, but it was set out attractively and shining with loving care.

During the visit, she took out the small key which she had brought after Dic had given it back to her, partly out of curiosity and partly from fear of it disappearing while she was away. 'Mam, do you recognize this?' she asked.

Her mother picked it up, then shrugged. 'No, dear. What's it for?' It was Lowri's turn to shrug. 'I don't know. I found it among my things. Could it be Dad's?'

'Unlikely. I'd recognize it if it were. We didn't have secrets, did we? No, it's probably for a box long gone. Or your old desk, perhaps?'

'That went for firewood years ago. But you're probably right, it's about the correct size.' She put it back in her handbag, safe in the compartment that had an extra zip.

Tearfully they exchanged their news and talked about Jimmy. Lowri had the impression that her father was suffering but was making light of his ordeal to help Emily – as her mother had been doing for her. She looked around the crowded room and remembered the beautiful home they had been forced to leave.

'Mam, can't you find somewhere a little better than this flat? Somewhere with a garden? I'm sure you miss it. I manage well enough and could help a little with extra rent.'

'There is still some money in the bank.' Emily told her. 'After the sale of the house with its heavy mortgage there wasn't much, but your father put some aside for emergencies – and the police know about it,' she added defensively. 'I could take a larger place, but I want the money kept for when your father is released. He'll need some help to get started on rebuilding his life.'

'The best way you can help Dad is to make your own life comfortable. You being happy has always been his main concern.'

'But what if he comes out soon and—'

'Mam, if that happens it will be wonderful, but it might not, and you can't stay here for years, can you?'

Emily lowered her head and stared at the floor with its faded carpet. 'I have to believe he'll come home soon,' she whispered.

'Then what better way to wait for him than in a house of your own? He has to believe in a future too.'

'Houses are quite cheap in some areas,' Emily said thoughtfully. ''Specially those near the prison.'

'You could take a few boarders, you'd manage quite well.' Lowri knew that having someone to look after was what her mother needed.

'You're right, darling. I must have a proper home for when your father comes back. He'd hate a small cramped place like this. I can tell him all about it, and explain what I've done, describe the wallpaper, ask him about the choice of paint, he'll be involved from the very first moment.' She smiled at Lowri as though the idea was already in progress.

Lowri smiled. 'You're so wise, Mam. Knowing there's a home waiting for him will help him through the time. Imagine, we could soon all be together again.'

'It won't be long now,' Emily said. 'The money is bound to come to light and he'll be freed.'

Aware of the importance for her mother of believing that, Lowri agreed and offered to go with her on the following day to see what properties were for sale.

As they looked at a neat cottage on the edge of the town, she told her mother that Dic was a regular visitor to Badgers Brook, and saw a wince of pain on her face. 'He wasn't responsible, even though we thought so at the time,' she went on. 'Dad asked him to search for evidence and, well, Ellis Owen was too clever for him – not that it did him much good.'

'I can never forgive Dic, or Cathy and Jack,' Emily replied. 'Jack was your father's partner. They had worked side by side as they built the business, yet he and Dic didn't doubt that your father was guilty. Not for a moment.'

–

While Lowri and Emily were looking at the few properties for sale, back in Badgers Brook, Marion awoke and turned to the man lying beside her. 'You'd better stay here and I'll bring breakfast up. In fact,' she added with a smile, 'what about lighting the bedroom fire and making a day of it? If anyone calls I can go down and pretend to have a cold.'

He laughingly agreed and together they set the coals alight and, after eating toast and drinking tea, they settled back under the blankets. They spent the morning lazily and, hoping no one would disturb them, they went down to eat, and listen to the wireless for a while, then went back up to the warm, cosy bedroom. Drowsy and comfortable, they closed their eyes. Lowri wouldn't be back till late.

When Lowri returned home, the house was empty. The fire was low but was soon revived, and there was a tray set, a loaf ready to slice, and a pot of something tasty simmering on the hob. She was hungry and cold after her journey and ate two bowls of the hambone flavoured lentil soup before wondering where Marion might be. Probably visiting her family, or even working. Her hours were irregular, cleaning to suit herself as well as her clients, sometimes during the evenings, and she could be anywhere. Lowri settled near the fire to think about her visit to her mother. Silence wrapped around her like a comfortable blanket.

She had been in an hour when she heard a noise from upstairs and called. There was no reply and with memories of the thief breaking in so recently, she picked up a poker and began to climb the stairs. She pushed open the door of her bedroom, which was just as she'd left it. In Marion's room, the bed was unmade and both pillows were dented as though two people had recently used it. She backed out on to the landing, shock making her clumsy and she knocked against the banisters putting out the torch she carried. She scrabbled around the dark landing until her fingers found it and continued her search, more nervous after the temporary darkness. She pushed open the other doors but fear and the feeling of vulnerability between her shoulder blades made her eyes refuse to take in anything. She looked but saw nothing, her nerves were so taut.

The house was empty, but as she stood irresolutely at the top of the stairs, she felt a draught and realized that her window was wide open. Why hadn't she noticed before? A draught must have caused the noise she'd heard. Irritable with herself, she slammed the window and fastened the latch and went back downstairs. The back door stood open and she gripped the poker more firmly. Then Marion came in, and tension fell from her like a warm shower. She felt a bit foolish having chased an imaginary burglar around the house, so she said nothing.

'You're back!' Marion said in surprise.

Jokingly, Lowri looked down at herself and said, 'Well, so I am!'

They hugged and began to question each other about their weekend apart. 'Ken called, having forgotten you were away,' Marion said. 'I came back from a walk on Saturday and he was sitting in the armchair, reading your copy of *Three Men in a Boat*, and laughing loudly. Quite at home here, isn't he?'

'Strange, I did tell him I'd be away. And tell me,' she asked with a suspicious grin, 'who else came calling? D'you have a secret lover?'

To her surprise, Marion nodded. 'Yes. I do and you might as well know that the reason he's secret is because he's married. There, so now you know.'

Shocked, vividly remembering the visual evidence on Marion's bed, but determined not to show it, Lowri hugged her and said, 'It's none of my business, and I can only wish you luck. I hope it works out for you.'

'Oh it will. We have to be patient a while longer, that's all.'

Lowri lay awake for a long time but she wasn't thinking about the complications of Marion's life, or even her parents, but about Ken. Why had he called when he must have remembered she'd be away? Surely it hadn't been him who had left the telltale indentation on Marion's pillow? For no particular reason she could have explained, she relit her candle and looked around her neat room for signs of something being moved. There was a piece of red material caught in the wardrobe door and, puzzled and a little afraid, she opened the door. The clothes on the rail were neat enough, but some of the sleeves, which she always tucked in folded against the garment, were hanging loose. A red jacket was marked with a slight indentation having been shut in the door.

The key? she wondered anxiously. Was someone looking for that key? Could that someone be Ken Hardy? She took it from her handbag and stared at it, pleading with it to give up its secret.

–

On the following Wednesday afternoon, she took an order for a few items from Stella and went to the warehouse to see Ken. When she suggested they went to a cafe he agreed, and they sat in a tea room and he ordered scones and tea. She tried to talk about her visit to her mother and what she had learned about her father, but he was clearly uninterested.

'Sorry,' she said finally. 'I know how boring this must be for you. Tell me about your weekend. You called at Badgers Brook. Did you forget I wouldn't be there?'

'I did remember you'd be away, but I called anyway. There's usually someone around. I had a chat with Bob, who was tidying the greenhouse. Did you know he's an ex-policeman? I waited a while, had a cup of tea with Marion, then came home.'

'Mam is leaving the flat. She's hoping to move into a small house and take lodgers; so she has a place ready for when Dad's released. She still believes that evidence will come to light and—'

'Lowri, I don't want to talk about your father. He's in prison for...' He avoided saying the word. 'And well, that fact keeps coming between us.'

'You mean you're like the rest? That his presumed guilt has brushed off on me? I'm no longer Lowri Vaughan, I'm the daughter of a thief and maybe a murderer too? Is that how it is, Ken?'

He hushed her with a flapping hand. 'Quiet, you'll have the cafe in uproar.'

She jumped up, throwing Stella's list of requirements in front of him and walked out. A bus was just leaving the stop and she waved frantically and the driver stopped for her to get on. She hurriedly paid her fare then, without really considering it, changed her mind, jumped off at the next stop and made her way to Barry.

Although it was Wednesday and Dic might not be at the shop, she knocked on the shop window and saw the inner door open. He recognized her and opened up and saw at once that she was upset as he ushered her inside.

'Ken's just another false friend. He doesn't see *me* any more,' she said, 'he sees a woman who has the blood of a murderer running through her veins.'

'I think you have to give him some time,' Dic said, taking her coat and pushing the armchair closer to the fire. 'He feels it more because you didn't tell him.'

'I hadn't known him long enough for such confidences.'

'It must have been a terrible shock, however he learned of it.'

'But I'm still *me*!'

'Remember that you and I have lived through it step by painful step.'

'Yes, we lived through it but on opposite sides!' She stood up and pushed him away. He caught hold of her shoulders and pulled her towards him. 'I don't know what I'm doing here.' she shouted. 'Let me go!'

'Just calm down, Lowri, you've been hurt time and again, and even though I was involved with your father's arrest, I'm your friend and always will be.'

After a while she stopped resisting and stood quietly as he held her in his arms. 'You smell of mud again,' she muttered into his shoulder, which shook with his laughter.

'It's this jacket. I'm just off to the boatyard to see if Jake has any pieces of wood I can use.'

As they drove the few miles to where Jake Llewellyn had his boat repair yard, he told her that Ellis Owen had asked his wife for a divorce just before he died. 'I don't think the police were told, at least, it didn't come out at the trial. But it might have been the reason for him stealing money, to give him a fresh start. I don't believe his wife has knowledge of the missing money. What d'you think?'

'When did you find out?'

'A few days ago.'

'And you said nothing.'

'I wanted to, but not with other people around. Ken, Marion and half of Cwm Derw always seem to be at your house, there's never a chance of a private conversation.'

'You won't have to worry any more. Ken won't be coming again.'

'More fool him,' he said softly.

She pressed a little closer to him. Somehow it made the disappointment easier to bear.

Jake greeted Dic by calling, 'Oh, here he is, Dic Morris on the scrounge again!' He smiled and offered his hand. 'Lowri Vaughan if I'm not mistaken. How's your dad coping?'

It was a relief to talk about her father without facing disapproval. Jake had known her father and Dic's father since they were children at school. On the rare occasions Lowri had gone to the boatyard, she had been treated like a little princess. She spoke to him about her mother's plans while Dic walked around searching for old wood from which he could sculpt figures, boats and animals.

'Where's the big fellow?' Dic asked.

'He's taken the trailer to pick up a boat from Swansea,' Jake explained. 'Good chap he is, I wish he'd stay, but I don't think he will. He's just licking his wounds after some business venture failed. He doesn't want to talk about it so I don't ask questions.'

The afternoon ended by Lowri walking to the school to meet Sarah-Jane but Dic couldn't take her to his parents' home where he would collect Katie; he didn't want her upset by his father's attitude. Instead, she caught the bus for the first stage of her journey back to Cwm Derw. The day had been enjoyable and she was feeling contented as she walked into Badgers Brook. Ken was sitting there, continuing to read *Three Men in a Boat* and he looked up and smiled as she discarded her coat.

'Why don't you borrow it and save having to come here to read it?' she said.

'I've brought a picnic, Connie's the expert, she advised me and lent me her vacuum flasks so we can take hot coffee.' The non-sequitur threw her momentarily.

'What's a picnic to do with that book?'

'What are you taking your coat off for, we're going out!'

'It'll be dark soon!'

Carrying a woven basket that she recognized as Connie's, he led her towards the wood. Anemones and bluebells covered the floor under the trees and although it was early spring, the trees were already showing their greenery. He threw a Welsh tapestry rug over a mound where they could rest their backs against the trunk of a tree and they sat, and ate and talked about everything except her father.

'See how easy it is?' he said as they wandered back to the house slowly, his arm around her, kissing her hair and then her cheek before discarding the baggage and taking her into his arms. 'You and me, together, no one else intruding, that's just perfect.'

That night she woke anxiously from a dream in which she was walking away from her father who was locked in a cage for which she had the key. Towards dawn, she dreamed she was kissing Ken, and she was wonderfully happy, until she saw Dic watching them. She awoke restless and with painful feelings of guilt.

–

'When am I going to meet your mysterious friend?' Lowri asked the next morning as Marion was setting off to work.

'Not for a while. We can't be seen together, not until the divorce comes through,' Marion explained. 'He doesn't want me to be cited as co-respondent. Shaming that would be.'

'Then where do you meet?'

'We don't see each other very often, but we sometimes manage an hour, in some isolated place, a cafe or a park, somewhere far away from his wife. It's quite exciting really.'

Lowri gave a sideways grin. 'So you wouldn't mind if I went away again for the weekend?'

Marion blushed slightly. 'Thanks,' she said. 'Now I have to go, this Mr Morgan leaves a long list of jobs for me and I have to make an early start. Fussy beyond he is, but he pays me well.'

Lowri was thinking of Marion and the tangle she had become involved in and wondered if she would ever find a love of her own. For a while she had believed Ken might be the one, but as with so many other friendships, what had happened to her father had intruded and although the Connie-style picnic in the wood had been wonderful, there was still a doubt that she and Ken would stay together.

She called out, 'Good morning,' to Stella and unlocked the shop door, flicking the sign from 'closed' to 'open' as three impatient customers walked in. She began serving, her mind efficiently dealing with the variety of services but still wondering about Marion.

Customers came and went, packing the small shop, then drifting off to allow her a breather, before another rush of people crowded in, arguing about who was next, filling the place with their chatter and laughter. When Stella came in with her first cup of tea, Lowri was tidying a shelf on which they displayed socks and stockings.

'You manage this place well, young Lowri,' Stella said, opening a tin of biscuits.

'Thanks. I love it. When I worked for Mrs Potter, we only sold things like envelopes and wrapping paper. It's more interesting with the added stock you carry.'

'Think you could manage on your own?'

'On my own?' She stared at her employer, afraid she was ill. Thinking quickly to avoid suggesting it, she asked, 'Planning a holiday are you? Lovely that'll be. Of course I could manage.'

'A holiday? Can you imagine my Colin leaving his allotment for more than a day? No, dear, I just want an occasional day out. Me and Gwennie Flint, we'd like to go off early one Monday and go and look at Barry Island beach, or perhaps take a trip into Cardiff.'

'You aren't thinking of retiring, are you?'

'No, I'd miss it too much to think of giving up. I thought paying you a bigger wage to take on more of the routine and me doing just a bit less than at present. I'll be helping out at busy times and I'll be handy if you need a holiday, or a honeymoon,' she added with a tilt of her head, a twinkle in her beady eyes.

'No chance of that,' she said, but her mind wasn't on what she was saying. She was imagining running the place, being a permanent part of Cwm Derw. It felt good and she smiled at Stella, who still stood with her head on one side, waiting for her response.

'I'd love to do more…' she said slowly.

'But…?' Stella encouraged.

'But I was going to ask if I might have a few days off, and that isn't a very good start, is it? It's my mother. She's moving out of the flat she took when my father began his sentence. We had so little time to get out and we threw a lot of stuff unexamined into boxes. We need to go through it all, take our time, and discard the things we don't need.'

'What about if you take a week, then come back and start learning about keeping the books?'

Lowri looked at Stella with real affection. 'You're so kind,' she murmured. 'I just hope I don't let you down.'

'Never no chance of that, girl. Now, isn't it time for a cup of tea? This one's gone cold.'

Lowri wrote to her mother that evening and told her about Stella's suggestion. She arranged to go to the flat and search through the piles of papers and mementoes that had been crammed willy-nilly into an assortment of boxes when they had left their home. As soon as her mother had found a suitable place, she would take the week Stella had promised and help her move in. Much of their furniture was in store and sorting that out as well as buying the extra beds she would need, would be quite a task. A week was a long time to be away from Badgers Brook, although she didn't think Marion would complain.

When the house was chosen it was only a matter of a few weeks before Emily was given the key to fourteen Hanley Place. At the end of April, Lowri went to join her mother carrying an extra, empty suitcase, knowing there would be her own memories to bring back. The feeling of being a resident of Cwm Derw, building her own home, was comforting. She gave the address to Marion and to Stella but she was surprised to receive a letter just a day after she had arrived. It was from Dic, just a short note offering to drive up and bring her home as she would probably have quite a lot to carry. Flattered by his thoughtfulness, she pushed it into her pocket and said nothing to her mother. Emily had made her feelings about Dic, Jack and Cathy Morris very clear.

When she went out later to post some letters and arrange for her mother's food rations to be registered in a nearby grocery store, she telephoned Dic. Aware of the pile of treasures she had already chosen to keep, and knowing that among her father's books there would be many she would want, she accepted his offer gladly. Just before he arrived, that would be soon enough for her mother to know he was coming. The furniture had been placed in the rooms, the cleaning completed and a list of what they needed to buy had been made, ready for their foray into town. There remained only the boxes of papers and her father's favourite books. These had been pushed into the smallest bedroom and were something neither woman wanted to tackle.

On the day before Lowri was to return to Badgers Brook, they went into the cluttered room and began. Several piles threatened to topple over as they made decisions on what needed to be kept and what could be discarded. The discard pile seemed reluctant to grow. Everything seemed to have either relevance to the future or to be a part of Jimmy's past life he might want to revive. Lowri found a book of poems her father had loved, copied out in his own hand. Afraid of it upsetting her mother to see it, she tucked it away to read later.

'What time are you leaving tomorrow?' Emily asked, as they put the last of the boxes into the loft-space. 'Mam, don't be angry, but Dic Morris is coming to take me back. He offered, guessing there's be a lot for me to carry.'

'Nonsense. You can take some of it and leave the rest till your next visit. I don't want that man here. His father ruined our lives with his accusations.'

'His father, Mam, not Dic. That's the same as when people blame me because my father's in prison.'

'It was Dic found the evidence of theft.'

'Yes, but Dad asked him to look for it.' She hugged her mother. 'I do understand, Mam. It helps to have someone to blame, I do it myself. Although Ellis Owen is dead, I blamed his wife for making him steal, I thought she must have been demanding and greedy. Now I know she wasn't any of those things. Ellis wanted a divorce. He'd found someone else.'

'Ellis was leaving Terri? But that didn't come out at the trial! It might have changed everything. Lowri, we must inform the police and they'll make her explain why she kept crucial information from them. This might be the break we've been looking for.'

'Don't build your hopes, Mam, please. And don't tell Dad and give him hope of an early reprieve. It might be nothing, she could be inventing it. Until we know more we have to stay calm.'

'Who was she? Perhaps she's the one who will help us find the truth.'

'Terri doesn't know, and I doubt whether the woman will come forward, would you?'

'But that could be where the money is. Lowri, we have to find her.'

Lowri told her mother the little she knew and it was with less resentment that she welcomed Dic when he arrived the following morning at midday.

Aware of Emily's attitude towards him, Dic walked around the house, admired the rooms and discussed the garden, careful not to mention anything that could be misconstrued. Emily was clearly convinced that it was only a matter of a couple of months more before Jimmy rejoined her now they knew about Ellis Owen's affair with a young woman.

Dic joined in the pretence and wished it had a basis in reality and not fantasy. Where would they find the woman, and would she talk if they did? It was all very unlikely and he wished he hadn't told Lowri what he had learned by talking to Terri Owen. It had just made everything worse.

Piling all her chosen treasures on the back seat, Lowri turned and waved until her mother was no longer to be seen.

'I hate leaving her there,' Lowri said as they settled into the journey. She told him about Stella's plan to leave more of the running of the post office and shop to her. 'So I seem to be putting down roots. Rightly or wrongly, my life seems to be in Cwm Derw.'

'I'm glad,' was all Dic said in reply. She seemed unaware of the disappointment in his voice.

Six

For Lowri it had been a long emotional day, starting early to sort out as much as possible before she left, and with the tension of her mother's attitude towards Dic making things worse. Then the long journey home. Dic didn't suggest coming in when they reached the front gate of Badgers Brook, aware of how tired she was. Before they unloaded the car of its assorted boxes, Lowri walked up the path to open the door. She stopped, her hand on the handle as the sound of an argument met her. She waved an arm to stop Dic from bringing the first of the boxes and walked back to meet him.

'I think Marion and her mysterious boyfriend are having an argument,' she whispered with a smile. 'Shall I make a lot of noise, so he can sneak off without being seen? Or go around the house and in through the garden door and hope not to interrupt them?'

Without another word, grinning like conspirators, they crept around the side of the house into the garden and through the lit window they saw Marion walking towards the hall with the shadowy figure of a man in front of her. They couldn't hear the words but from the pitch of her voice and the gestures, they knew she was still in the throes of a row.

'It looks like he's going out towards the lane; he'll see the car,' Lowri whispered.

'Then lets get back and make a lot of noise.' Dic put an arm around her and guided her back around the side of the house. The kitchen door opened and they heard the low tone of the man and the higher, angry voice of Marion as the argument continued.

'Hi, Marion, it's me. I'm back,' Lowri called. The kitchen door immediately closed, and the key turned noisily in the lock, shutting the two antagonists inside.

'Oh dear, now what do we do?' Lowri groaned.

'We stop hiding as though we were the ones with a secret to keep. Come on, round the back and through the garden door. It's bound to be open.'

As they neared the corner with a view of the big garden, they heard a door open and saw a man jump out and run down to where there was a weak part of the hedge. Before she could call Dic's attention to the man, he had slipped through and his footsteps could be heard running down the narrow lane.

Lowi was shaking. 'Dic, did you see him?'

'No, I only heard him pushing through the hedge and running off. I was too late to see him. Why, did you recognize him?' He laughed. 'So Marion's mysterious man is a secret no longer. Who was he, anyone I know?' He was standing close to her and was aware of her body shaking. 'Lowri? What is it? Who was he?'

'No one! I didn't see him properly. I was too late.'

Knowing from the sharpness of her tone and her obvious discomfort that was untrue, Dic guessed it was someone they knew. Names raced through his mind, people who would cause her distress to be revealed as Marion's lover. His strongest suspicion was that it had been Ken Hardy she had seen. Ken visited sometimes and on the most recent occasion he called when he had known Lowri wouldn't be there. How innocent it would seem for him to be there. But the man had run away, and besides, Ken wasn't married. Although, he thought, that might be a lie to protect his secret. As they walked back to the kitchen door, where Marion waited for them, he wondered why such secrecy was necessary? Did Ken Hardy hurry away because he'd be unable to explain why he and Marion were having such an intense disagreement?

Still pondering the possible explanations, he left the two girls to talk and carried the boxes in and put them on the kitchen table. Then he left, refusing an invitation to stay for supper. He put down the last box, kissed Lowri lightly, and promised to call again soon. 'Remember, I'm only a short drive away if you need me.'

She thanked him and wished he would stay. The vision of the man she had seen running down the garden and through the hedge was as clear as a photograph. Ellis Owen, and this time there was no doubt. But who would believe her? Oh why hadn't Dic been close enough to see him too? He knew the man well and a glance would have been enough for him to recognize Ellis.

Logic forced her to question herself. How could Ellis be alive? If he were, then why hadn't he been in touch with his wife? Perhaps he had and Terri was lying to them all, playing the part of grieving widow while she hid the money and protected him?

What was Marion's role in this? Was he her secret lover? Or was she a friend who was helping him to stay free? Whatever the explanation, how could she face Marion and pretend nothing untoward had happened? Surely her face would make it apparent? Taking a deep breath she went back into the living room.

Marion was clearly embarrassed. She fussed around arranging Lowri's boxes in the living room, between dashing in and out of the kitchen preparing a light supper. She chatted cheerfully throughout their meal, her nervousness adding vivacity to her conversation as she asked about Lowri's visit to her mother's new home.

She made no reference to the hasty departure of her boyfriend or the argument Lowri and Dic had interrupted. If she noticed how subdued Lowri appeared, she said nothing, presuming it was tiredness and her being upset at parting from her mother after a week together. Lowri said very little, answering her questions in a dull monotone.

'All right, are you?' Marion finally asked. 'Tired for sure, all that humping furniture and the long journey.'

Lowri raised her head and stared at her friend. 'Marion. Who is he?'

'Who's who?' Marion tried to sound flippant.

'Your boyfriend. I saw him leave, and thought I recognized him.'

Marion was startled but recovered swiftly and shook her head. 'He's not from round here and there's no way you two could have met. No, you don't know him and I can't tell you who he is, not yet. Not until his wife has agreed to the terms of a divorce. Demanding ever so much, she is. Bitter and angry, even though they haven't lived as man and wife for almost five years.'

Lowri said nothing more. If he was discussing divorce with his wife, then how could it be Ellis? Confusion and disbelief vied with the picture she still held in her memory of the man pushing his way through the hedge. Was she going mad?

Unless she were a very fine actress, Terri Owen was convinced she was a widow. She was having to sell the house and find a job to support herself. She couldn't be so convincing if it was all a pretence. Lowri fiddled with the piles of boxes for a while, then went to bed, bidding her friend a cursory 'Good night'.

Marion sat for a while, anxiety clouding her eyes, and it was after midnight before she filled a hot-water bottle and went to her bedroom, but still sleep wouldn't come. The temptation of an empty house in which to meet had been irresistible. In fact, that was one of the reasons she had agreed to share the tenancy with Lowri; the luxury of a comfortable, albeit an occasional, place to meet. The other reason had been a need to keep an eye on Lowri, stop her becoming too obsessed with wasting her life trying to find proof of her father's innocence. She longed to be able to discuss her situation with someone, hated keeping it all from her friend, but there was no alternative. This was how it had to be.

Before going to the post office the following morning, Lowri carried all the boxes up to her bedroom. Some, containing papers and files which had been returned by the police, she locked in the wardrobe. She didn't know why, there was nothing other than the mundane day-to-day minutiae of running the business. Any papers that were important would have been held by the police or taken by Dic's father, Jack Morris, who still ran the factory. She wished she had listened to her mother and burned it on the garden fire they had built to discard so much that was of no use. Trawling through it only added to her unhappiness.

She browsed briefly through the books and personal notebooks she had brought back. More poems and observations on birds and wild flowers he had written out for her when she had been young. Words of a few songs and nonsense verses. She was tearful remembering how happy they had all been before Ellis Owen had ruined it all.

She shook off the shock of seeing Ellis Owen and the sadness of her father's memories, and later cheerfully told Stella and Colin all that she and her mother had achieved. 'Three rooms furnished and ready for lodgers. A smart bathroom and the lovely kitchen – we bought a table that's big enough for six people to eat in comfort.'

'What about a sitting room, they won't want to stay in their rooms, will they?' Colin asked.

'There are two rooms downstairs and Mam will have one and the other will be for the lodgers, or paying guests as she will call them.'

'She'll make them comfortable, for sure. She's the motherly type,' Stella said nodding wisely, even though she had never met Emily.

On that first day back the customers all wanted to talk, wanting to know where she'd been and asking questions about the house her mother had bought.

'It's got a big mortgage, mind,' Lowri told them, even though it was untrue. 'Mam didn't have much money – she and Dad had sunk it all into the business.'

'Pity 'elp her. She's so brave, making a new life for herself,' several commented. 'And a place for Dad for when he's released,' she would add.

Needing to wallow further in nostalgia, she planned to look through the rest of the books and notes that evening. With Marion out, supposedly visiting her parents, she looked forward to a quiet evening in which to do it. She bought a corned beef pasty and some bits of salad for her meal and she had just opened the first of the notebooks when there was a knock at the door. Kitty and Bob came in and they were quickly followed by Connie and Geoff, who arrived at the same time as Ken Hardy. Accepting the inevitable, Lowri put aside the first box of papers she had begun to examine, and put the kettle on for tea. She brought out a cake her mother had given her, and Connie, true to type, unpacked a few small cakes and everyone made themselves comfortable.

They were all interested in Emily's plan to keep lodgers to help pay her way and praised her resourcefulness. Pushing aside her own concerns Lowri made light of the problems her mother had overcome and made it sound like a great deal of fun.

She was aware of Ken watching her as the chatter gathered pace around them and when their eyes met, his crinkled with amusement. He stayed after the others had gone and helped stack the dishes in the kitchen. He leaned against the sink and stared at her before asking, 'What's wrong, Lowri? Your laughter lacks the true ring of happiness tonight. Is everything really all right with your mother?'

'My mother's fine. She has chosen those who she'll have as paying guests, and everything will be fine.'

'And you? Are you "fine"?' he asked.

'Of course.'

'Tell me, Lowri. I might be able to help. I'll certainly try.'

He was still wearing that smile and laughter showed in his eyes, almost black now, in the distorting light from the gas lamp. She saw beyond the smile and knew he was serious. Taking a chance, prepared for ridicule, she said sharply, 'All right, call me stupid, but I believe I've seen the man who my father's suspected of murdering. There, now you'd better hurry off before I embarrass you by coming out with even more nonsense!'

'Where did you see him?'

She stared in surprise. 'You believe me?'

'Of course I don't believe you! I'd need more than your say-so to convince me a dead man is walking around Cwm Derw! Tell me where, and when.'

'It was in the field beyond Colin Jones's allotment. He saw me and quickly changed direction and ran off. I know it was him; he had a distinctive way of walking and besides he was startled when he saw me watching him and reacted so fast, he was obviously as shocked as me. I tried to follow, it was when the snow was on the ground, but his footprints were lost when he reached the road.'

'Have you seen him since?'

'Well, I'm almost convinced he was here, having a furious argument with Marion. How stupid is that?'

'You asked her of course?'

'I asked her to tell me the name of her boyfriend, but she refused.' She began filling the kettle to wash the dishes, turning away from him to hide her tears. 'How could it have been him. I must have been mistaken. It's too fantastic. If Ellis Owen is Marion's secret lover, then this would be the last place she'd bring him. Besides, Marion says he's asked his wife for a divorce, so that doesn't add up, does it? I can talk myself out of believing he's alive, but the hope sneaks back and catches me unawares sometimes.'

'So you know it's nothing more than a dream?'

'Most of the time,' she admitted.

He stepped closer and put his arms around her. 'When you feel unable to cope without the dream, talk to me. I'll listen for as long as you need to talk.'

She relaxed against him, not wondering what had changed his mind from unwillingness to discuss her father's situation, just thankful for it.

–

Dic was concerned about Lowri, afraid that the person she had seen running away from Badgers Brook was Ken Hardy. If Ken was Marion's secret boyfriend, then Lowri must be feeling dreadfully alone, Dic thought to himself. Yet he didn't want to put his suspicions into words. When she was ready, Lowri would tell him and until then he had to be patient. He phoned her at the post office and called a few times but although he tried to persuade her to talk about Ken, she avoided discussing him, and she also refused to talk about the man she had seen running away from Badgers Brook, so both suffered their doubts in silence.

Dic called at Jake Llewellyn's boatyard a few miles inland from Barry's pleasure beach from time to time. He went to look at boats and sometimes sketch them for the models he made. He also begged pieces of old wood from the repairs Jake carried out, using the odd shaped pieces for his work. On a Wednesday at the end of May, he took little Katie and went to see if there was anything of interest.

Jake saw them parking the car and filled the battered kettle and placed it on the primus stove. As they entered the office, he took out a bottle of Tizer and with a cursory wipe of a mug, poured a drink for the little girl. 'Hello, beautiful girl,' he said handing her the mug, 'and who's this ugly old man you've brought along?'

Katie giggled, her eyes sparkling, her face half hidden by her first sip of the fizzy drink. 'It's my dad, silly,' she said.

'So it is! Kind of you to bring him along.' Still joking and teasing, Jake waved a hand towards the corner, where he had thrown a few pieces of wood he thought Dic might use.

While the kettle boiled and the tea was made, Dic picked up several pieces of wood. He picked up a few unusual shapes and stared at them, visualizing what they might make.

'Can you make a model of my old boat, *Olwen*?' Jake asked him. 'I've tried but I don't have your skill and it never looks right. It was named for my mother and she's seventy next month and a model of it would be a nice birthday present for her.'

'Have you got a photograph? I can't remember her well enough to make an accurate model.'

'I can do better than that.' He pulled a couple of curled and faded snapshots from the wall and without turning around called, 'Alun?' at the top of his voice. A scruffy, bearded man appeared carrying a bucket and mop. Katie, who had been exploring the samples of woods and varnishes, saw him and ran to her father's side in alarm. He was a strange sight. The man was untidily dressed in an overcoat and Wellingtons, which were covered in mud and paint stains. 'He does the cleaning,' Jake explained in a low voice. 'And good he is, too. I don't know much about him. Some sort of cook he was by all accounts. He might have been once but he doesn't look the part now! Something happened to ruin his life and he's never been able to do a proper job since.' He found some paper and a few pencils for Katie and started drawing a boat which he coaxed her to complete, to distract her from the man who had frightened her.

The man didn't come any closer, he just stood and waited for Jake to tell him what he wanted. 'Can you shift the junk from around *Olwen*, so Dic can sketch her?' he asked. 'Tea in a few minutes, we'll come and help when we've had it.'

'No. No need,' the man replied gruffly, and walked away to the furthest part of the yard, where he began to throw things aside.

'Miserable old devil, but he keeps this place tidier than it's ever been,' Jake whispered. They watched as the man opened up a view of the old boat. 'We had a few good times in that boat, your dad and Jimmy Vaughan, and me. Sometimes Ellis Owen too. Expert swimmer he was, and he could handle a boat better than most.'

'Not even the strongest swimmer could have survived that storm, though, could they?'

Jake shook his head. 'No one. Sad mind, him losing his life like that.'

'Sad for a few others too. It's affecting Jimmy Vaughan's wife and daughter badly.'

'I can't believe Jimmy Vaughan's locked up. Working in that clothing factory was bad enough, but being locked up, it must be hard for him. Always one for the out doors, old Jimmy. Fishing, sailing, camping and climbing cliffs for a dare. Almost as foolhardy as Ellis. I can't imagine how he's coping.' He looked quizzically at Dic and asked, 'D'you think he did it?'

'Robbed his own firm?' Dic asked. 'No, I don't. At first the facts seemed to point to him being the thief. But not now. Unless the money turns up, most will continue to believe it, mainly because of the suspicion of murder that went with it. I think the case for murderous attack was weak without the theft and there's no sign of the money.

If Jimmy didn't steal the money, then surely Ellis's death was an accident?'

'Too many witnesses insisted he held the man under.'

'A form of mass hysteria, maybe? Like the knife: one saw it and others convinced themselves they had too. It must have been impossible to see anything in those conditions.'

'You think he could be alive?'

'Lowri has that hope in her heart and it won't go away.'

'His missus would know, wouldn't she?'

'Not if he had a girlfriend helping him.'

'Fantasizing you are now, Dic, my boy. Fond of young Lowri are we?' he teased.

'She has me wishing for a miracle now,' Dic admitted.

The three of them went to where the remains of the once proud *Olwen* lay. The large untidily dressed man walked away after moving much of the pile that had blocked their view of her. Dic and Katie drew sketches and Katie proudly showed hers to Jake, who gave her sixpence for it and fixed it on his wall. There was a discussion on the type of sails and a few other details long gone, and Dic and Katie left to go to the school to collect Sarah-Jane.

That evening, after the girls were in bed, Dic spread out the drawings of the boat but he couldn't concentrate. He was restless, frustration making it impossible to settle. He wondered where and how he could find some small, overlooked piece of information that would lead him on to find proof of Jimmy Vaughan's innocence. If he were innocent, surely there must be some way of proving it? Better still if it was revealed that Ken was a part of the deceit. He badly wanted to be the one to find that proof and he went to sleep imagining the look on Lowri's face when he told her.

–

Lowri watched as Marion dressed ready to visit her parents. Several times she had suggested she went with her but still Marion made excuses. 'Mam's so busy and the house is so chaotic,' she always explained. 'Our Mam would spend all day clearing up if she thought she might have a visitor. So I never take friends home.'

Marion's family didn't live very far away and, working in the post office, Lowri wondered if she had actually met her mother Harriet without knowing. She didn't even have any idea what the woman looked like, she'd never even seen a photograph, yet she and Marion had shared a house, and confidences, for months. She thought of the people who used the post office and although there were several Lewis's, none fitted the little she knew about Marion's mother.

Marion set off for the bus stop at the end of the lane but before she reached it, she glanced around then slipped into the trees. A man was leaning against a beech tree and came forward and took her in his arms.

–

Dic still suspected that Ken Hardy could be Marion's secret lover, mainly because of Lowri's shocked reaction. Marion visited her parents often and could use the visits to hide the fact that she and Ken were meeting. The mention of the man having a wife was easily explained as a pretence, a way of covering his identity. It would also explain her reticence to invite Lowri to visit her family, which in itself was strange.

He called at the post office the next day, buying stamps as an excuse to see her and he smiled politely at a woman in her late forties, carrying a little girl about two years old. As the woman and her child left, Dic asked, 'Isn't that Marion Lewis's mother?'

Lowri looked surprised, but shook her head. 'No, she's Mrs Davies, not Lewis.'

'Doesn't Marion have a stepfather?' Dic said teasingly, his head on one side, a smile on his lips. 'And wouldn't she have changed her name?'

'Oh, how stupid of me! I've been trying to think of a Mrs Lewis who fits with what I know.'

'What d'you mean, don't tell me you've never met her?'

'Marion is unwilling for me to meet her family.'

'Then come with me on Wednesday. I'm delivering a rocking horse, which I restored for her. It isn't what I normally do, but this time, I agreed.'

'That little girl, is she Marion's baby sister?'

He nodded. 'I think her name is Sandra.'

'Then she is Marion's mother. How strange that she avoids us meeting. The mother seems very friendly.'

'Come with me and we can lie and plead innocence.' And perhaps find out whether the secret boyfriend is Ken, he thought.

Curiosity overcame any qualms Lowri had about going where she was clearly not wanted. Marion can't have any reason apart from embarrassment over her mother's untidy home. If she went once, and made friends with her brothers and sisters and her mother, then those worries would be soon forgotten. On Wednesday she went home

133

and prepared a light meal for herself and Dic and at two thirty they set off.

She thought the garden gave a good inclination of what was to come, with broken bicycles and two ancient prams thrown carelessly on the front lawn – although lawn was a euphemism for a patch of weeds and bare earth. The door was open and two children were just outside, playing with buckets and spades, making mud pies in what might once have been a flower border. The woman who had been pointed out to her as Marion's mother came to the door, recognized Dic, and invited them both inside.

After a smiling welcome, they were led through a kitchen that was overcrowded with clutter but surprisingly clean, into an orderly living room. Armchairs and a couple of small couches were set around a cheerful fire protected by a fire-guard, and on a coffee table were a few children's books, one open, as though Harriet had been in the middle of reading to the two children who sat on the hearth staring at the newcomers.

Lowri at once picked up the book and began talking to the eight and nine year olds who, she and Dic were told, were home from school with head-colds. At their request, she continued with the story, leaving Dic and Harriet to carry in the rocking horse.

There was great excitement when the splendid toy was brought inside and Harriet had to stop the two mud-modellers from bringing half the garden in with them. 'Stay put!' she warned them. 'I'll fetch your slippers and get a bowl of water ready for hand-washing.' Accompanied by loud protests, the mud was cleared and the two children ran in to join the rest, taking turns at riding what would soon be a favourite toy.

They were offered tea which was served in good quality china. 'Apologies for not having any biscuits,' Harriet said. 'They never last in this house.'

'I'm not surprised. I only have two girls and they take some filling!'

'We have eight between us,' Harriet said proudly. 'Some are mine, some my husband's and some ours. It's hard work, but it's a wonderful life. Marion is a great help. My husband's a teacher and has short days and long holidays, so he's here more than most men. Although,' she added, 'he does have a lot of work to do at home, marking and preparing lessons, but at least he's on hand.'

They were told the repaired rocking horse had been bought as a birthday present for Sandra who would be two the following weekend. 'Can you believe it, she wants a party!' Harriet said with a laugh. 'As if there isn't a party here every day of the week! But she'll invite a few friends, no doubt.'

As Lowri and Dic walked back to the car, Sandra was in Harriet's arms waving goodbye, with four others hugging their mother's skirts. Lowri said, 'I find it even more curious that Marion didn't want me to meet them. It's a wonderful family and she should be proud of them. Her mother and stepfather cope amazingly well and they're all so happy.'

'The evenings are the worse, according to Mrs Davies. Getting them all fed, washed and up to bed she describes as a whirlwind, chased by a thunderstorm, battered by an avalanche, with clothes everywhere and food dropped and drinks spilt, and arguments about pillows and towels and pyjamas.' He laughed. 'Yet every morning, her husband and the children probably march out of the house as neat and tidy as any family you've ever seen. They are a remarkable couple.'

At Badgers Brook Ken was waiting. He didn't look pleased to see Dic. 'Where have you been?' he asked. 'You knew I'd be here.'

'Sorry,' Lowri said. 'I didn't think we'd be so long. Dic had a delivery to make and I went with him.'

'Something interesting?' He wanted to add 'more interesting than me', but he held back.

'Dic has restored an old rocking horse which we delivered to Marion's mother. It's a birthday present for Marion's little sister.'

'I thought Marion didn't want you to meet her mother?'

'As it happens I already knew her. Like most people in the vicinity of Cwm Derw, she comes to the post office. I just didn't know who she was until today.'

Dic stood with his hands in his pockets, unsure whether or not to leave. Lowri decided for him. 'Shall we have a cup of tea? The weather's warm enough for us to sit in the garden. Get the chairs out, will you, Dic? And can you knock on Kitty's door, please, Ken? She might like to join us.'

She touched Ken's cheek with her lips as she passed him to go to the kitchen.

'Safety in numbers?' he whispered. 'We never get a moment alone.' He didn't stay long. He made vague excuses of having office work to do and left with a kiss for Lowri and Kitty and the briefest of nods for Dic.

He didn't drive straight home but stopped at The Ship. 'No barman again,' Betty complained as she began serving a group of strangers who had just arrived. Ken helped her hand out the plates of food and collected the glasses.

'"Willing-But-Won't" isn't coming in, would you believe. He has a touch of flu and has to rest. I'm sure he's telling the truth, but it always seems to coincide with a particularly busy time. Twelve cyclists have booked supper and unless I can get my brother to help I'm on my own. As half the cyclists are staying with him it's unlikely.'

Ken promised to stay until the meal had been served and Betty thanked him, grateful for his kindness. 'But I really have to find someone I can rely on before the busy summer months,' she said.

–

Lowri and Dic were alone when Marion came in. 'I met your family today,' Lowri said in greeting.

'I had to deliver a rocking horse I'd repaired,' Dic explained.

'What a wonderful family. You're so lucky. Little Sandra is sweet,' Lowri said.

'All of them, not just Sandra,' Marion said sharply. 'She's a favourite because she's the youngest, but they're all lovely.'

'I agree,' Lowri replied quickly. 'I mentioned Sandra because I can't remember the names of the others.'

'Mam's Thomas, eighteen. Mam's twins, Dave and Ray, seventeen. His Jennifer fifteen. Bobby, ten. Margaret, nine, Sandra, two – theirs!' Marion chanted angrily.

They ate the meal Marion prepared, but there was little conversation. Marion was curt almost to the point of rudeness, and anger sparked in her eyes. When Dic had gone to collect his daughters, Lowri didn't know what to say to ease the situation.

'I'm not ashamed of my family, if that's what you're thinking,' Marion said, noisily piling the dishes and throwing the cutlery into the bowl.

'Ashamed? Of course not. That never crossed my mind! Proud you should be. You're very lucky to belong to such a happy group.'

'Well I'd prefer it if you don't go there again. Right?'

'Right,' Lowri echoed quietly. Puzzled by Marion's attitude, she asked none of the questions that buzzed around her mind. Perhaps one day Marion would explain and until then it was safer to say nothing.

A few days later, Lowri bought a soft, cuddly doll for Sandra's second birthday. She labelled it and left it near Marion's handbag, but when she returned that evening, the gaily wrapped package was still there.

–

The gossip that filled the post office was usually only half remembered by Lowri. For Stella, with years of experience of serving and at the same time listening, much of what was said remained in her mind. But whether it was because Lowri's thoughts were never far from her father's predicament and those involved in it, she remembered little, yet the half whispered comments about Gaynor Dallow caught her attention.

She had never met the woman as far as she could remember, but the name had a familiar ring. She gathered from the comments overheard as she served a shop filled with chattering customers that Gaynor was in her early twenties and had just given birth to a child. She had no husband and there had been no sign of a boyfriend. So could she be the girlfriend, for whom Ellis Owen had been about to leave his wife?

'Who is this Gaynor Dallow?' she asked Stella, as she was closing up that evening.

'Very glamorous she is, dark hair all shining curls, and blue eyes, gorgeous figure which she dresses to show off. Nothing "tarty" about her, mind, even though she did get herself in a spot of bother and ended up with an illegitimate baby. "Irish looks" many said. Lovely girl. Clever too, mind. She used to live in Barry. In fact, didn't she work for your father and Jack Morris for a while? I think she helped with the accounts.'

Startled, Lowri said, 'That must be from where I remember the name.'

She handed the money and books to Stella, refused an invitation to stay for a cup of tea and hurried home. The facts fitted, and Gaynor was certain to have known Ellis if she worked at the clothing factory. She could easily be the woman Ellis was hoping to marry. So did she have plenty of money that couldn't easily be accounted for? There must be a way of finding out. Her father didn't have it and it had to be somewhere.

She couldn't talk to Stella about her suspicions and Ken would be sceptical, but she had to talk to someone or she'd burst. After a meal, during which Marion hardly spoke, obviously still angry about Lowri's visit to her mother, she went out. It was a long way and required two bus journeys but she would go and see Dic.

To her disappointment the rooms behind his shop were in darkness. He must be with his parents. Dejected, knowing she couldn't call at the Morris's home, a place once as familiar as her own; she would no longer be welcome. She returned to Badgers Brook.

Marion was cleaning the kitchen cupboards. Lowri apologized. 'I'm sorry, Marion, it was my turn for cupboards. I meant to do them at the weekend but I forgot.'

Marion shrugged. 'I don't mind. Cleaning is something I find soothing. It frees my thoughts and takes away irritations.'

'You're still angry with me for visiting your mother?'

Marion threw the cloth she was using into the hot water and stared at her friend. 'I like to keep certain parts of my life separate, that's all. I don't mean to be secretive, but although we're friends and share this house, my work and my home are my business.'

'But I tell you everything – or practically everything,' she amended.

'That's your choice, I just don't want to do the same.'

'Then I won't go there again. Although, if she comes into the post office, I won't be rude and pretend we haven't met, mind,' she warned.

'Mam doesn't come to Cwm Derw very often.'

'Will you take the gift I bought for Sandra? You needn't tell her it was from me.'

Marion nodded. Wringing out the cloth again, she continued with her cleaning and Lowri went into the living room feeling like a schoolgirl who had been dismissed from the headmistress's office in disgrace. As she added coals to the fire for the last hour of the evening, she suddenly saw how ridiculous they must have sounded. The stilted conversation, and her being reprimanded like a child; she began to giggle. She heard Marion close a cupboard door and turned, expecting her to be angry. The laughter grew and she knew that if Marion began another complaint the laughter would be impossible to control. She looked up, her face red with the heat of the fire and the efforts to be serious and saw that Marion too was failing to hold back her mirth.

Neither could talk for a long time and when they did, apologies were pushed aside. The two friends sat together, both relieved at the end of the silly disagreement.

'I was pompous beyond,' Marion said. 'A stupid idiot is what I am, with no more brain than a scrubbing brush.'

'And I'm a busybody with a long nose.'

'I was ashamed of Mam with her eight children.'

'And I listen to too much gossip at the post office and it's addled my brain.'

'Where did you go tonight?' Marion asked. Lowri was on the point of explaining about Gaynor Dallow but something stopped her.

'It's all right, you're entitled to your secrets.' Marion said as Lowri hesitated. She smiled to take the criticism out of the words. 'I thought you might have gone to the pictures that's all.'

'I went to see Dic, but he was out.'

'All the way to Barry? Any reason?'

'Not really. I was fed up with us not talking and I wanted some company.'

'After serving half the village with stamps and postal orders and the like, you must have been desperate for company,' Marion said with a giggle.

In spite of Marion's efforts the laughter wouldn't return. Lowri was left with the feeling that behind the casual questions was a real curiosity. For someone who liked her secrets, Marion asked an awful lot of questions, she thought rebelliously.

'I wanted a cup of cocoa, but it seems I'll have to make my own,' she said, brightly. She went into the kitchen and rattling the cups and saucers, wondered what it was that always stopped her confiding in Marion. She'd been hesitant even before Dic had warned her. Friends gradually get to know each other and exchange confidences. Since they had shared Badgers Brook, she had become quickly aware of how secretive her friend could be. It had made her wary of telling her too much because there had been nothing in return.

First there had been the boyfriend who only visited when she was away from home. Then the revelation he was married. It had been clear from the moment they had become closer friends, after the arrest of her father, that she would not be a welcome visitor at Marion's mother's home. What else was Marion keeping from her?

She had the vision of the man running down the garden and disappearing through the hedge. Would Marion's next revelation be that Ellis was alive and was her lover? She smiled grimly. That was too fantastic, even for her wildest imaginings, but there certainly were other secrets to learn. The thought frightened her as she remembered her room being searched. After Marion was in bed, she went down and checked that the doors were firmly locked. Then she checked the key again before settling to sleep.

–

It wasn't until the following Sunday that she saw Dic. He arrived early in the afternoon with Sarah-Jane and Katie and invited her to go with them for a walk.

'I'll come,' Marion said, surprising them both. Lowri hid her disappointment having hoped there might be a chance to tell Dic about Gaynor Dallow.

Because of the words buzzing around in her head longing to be spoken, she was tense as they walked through the beautiful woodland, with birds flying anxiously around busily searching for food to feed their young. Lowri pointed out to Sarah-Jane and Katie the few remaining wild daffodils which she had found on her wanderings. Bluebells spread a hazy carpet of blue under the trees and on the field beyond they found their first cowslips. She picked ribwort and showed them how to make popguns out of them. Leaving Dic and Marion to talk, Lowri walked with the little girls and marvelled with them at every new discovery.

Dic caught up with them as they walked along the top of the field, from where they looked down on a building site which once had been the Treweather's farm.

'Is there anything wrong?' he asked Lowri.

She shook her head and smiled. 'No, it's a perfect day for a walk, with signs of spring everywhere. I think Sarah-Jane and Katie might like to take back a few branches and watch the leaves opening. I always enjoyed that.'

They walked back and from the garden Dic took a few branches from a large horse chestnut tree, where the sticky buds were already starting to unfurl. As Dic took them to the car, Lowri followed and, aware of Marion's persistent curiosity, she called after him, 'Will the girls eat beans on toast? There isn't much here to put in sandwiches.' She deliberately spoke quietly so he didn't hear and she ran out and said, 'Dic, I need to talk to you, but without Marion being aware.' Louder she said, 'Beans on toast? Not a traditional Sunday tea, but will it do?'

He walked back with her, an arm on her shoulder and replied easily regarding the food, but said nothing about the rest. They stayed later than usual, the girls playing hide-and-seek and dancing around to music played on the gramophone. Then they admitted to being tired and Dic gathered them up and prepared to leave.

'I'll be in Cwm Derw tomorrow, perhaps we can meet for lunch? It's about time I returned some of your hospitality.' He turned to Marion. 'You too?'

'Yes, why don't you come?' Lowri added.

Marion shook her head. 'I have Mrs Griffiths and Mr Morgan tomorrow, I won't be able to. But thanks anyway.'

Hiding her relief, hoping the invitation discouraged Marion from guessing she had something urgent to talk about to Dic, Lowri stood beside Marion and waved as the car drove away. As she waited for sleep to end the day, Lowri wondered if she were becoming a bit neurotic about Marion and Ellis Owen and her father and would be better to do as many suggested, and allow things to drift away in sorrowful acceptance.

The chances of the woman called Gaynor Dallow being Ellis's secret lover and mother of his child *and* the possessor of the stolen money, was more like an Enid Blyton story for children than possible proof of her father's innocence. Yet hope wouldn't die. If Gaynor Dallow did have the missing money, surely that would be the first step towards her father being pardoned? She breathed a sigh of relief. Once they found her, Dic would know what to do next.

After once more checking that the doors and windows were locked, she slept peacefully and dreamed of seeing her father walk out of the prison gates where she and her mother, and Dic Morris waited for him. As she awoke, with the dream still tormentingly real, she wondered vaguely why Ken had not been there.

Seven

When Ken was told by one of his assistants that a young woman wanted to see him, he presumed it was someone looking for work. As he went out to the customers' area the usual response was running through his mind; he would take her name and details and would contact her if a vacancy occurred. So he was surprised to see Marion.

'Marion? Is something wrong?' When she hesitated, glancing at the two women putting together an order, he gestured for her to follow him and led her into his office.

'It's Lowri,' she began. 'I'm worried about her.'

'She isn't ill, is she?'

'Not really, but I think she's becoming too obsessed with the dream of her father being freed. He's guilty. He has to be. No one is sentenced for something as serious as fraud without convincing evidence, he must be guilty. And there's also the strong suspicion of murder too, but Lowri won't accept it.'

He smiled wryly. 'I don't think I would either. How can we expect her to believe her father killed someone? Could you?'

'I can't imagine my gentle father or my stepfather wanting to hurt someone. But at the time, her father was filled with hatred. Couldn't that explain it? If we believe the evidence, he'd been stealing money and had been found out by this man, Ellis Owen. His anger towards the man must have been terrifying. He must have been robbing the firm for a while and believed he'd got away with it, then Ellis found out. Difficult to contain his anger then, wouldn't you say?'

'I didn't know Jimmy Vaughan, but I've met his daughter and nothing she's told me has convinced me that the man could hate that much, even if he were guilty of fraud.'

'If?' she asked doubtfully. 'Of course he did it. Lowri is incapable of facing facts. Jimmy Vaughan was seen fighting the man, in the water, at the top of a high, storm-driven tide. He survived but Ellis Owen didn't.'

'I have to agree with that, there were plenty of witnesses, but you can't expect Lowri to accept it. By doing so she'd be admitting that her father's guilty.'

'Will you talk to her, try and persuade her to stop hoping? I think it's ruining her life.'

Ken stared at her. 'A term in prison doesn't only affect the criminal. The sentence hurts the accused man's family and friends too and the pain must be immense.'

'But you'll talk to her? Think of a way to take her mind off the vain hope of a reprieve?'

'I'll try,' he said.

'Something happened recently, something she won't talk to me about. I think she's convinced that it will lead to her father's release. Try to make her talk about it, better to dash her hopes now, rather than let her build it up and watch her fall into another disappointment. I don't know how much more she can stand.'

'I'll try,' he repeated. 'But how can I expect her to tell me what's on her mind? I've never given her any encouragement to hope for miracles, in fact I've always tried to make her face facts, so what can I say to make her change her thinking?'

'You could hint that you're beginning to fall in love with her – she badly needs a friend, and a loving friend would also keep her away from Dic, who keeps her futile hope burning.'

'I couldn't do that! That would be cruel, unless I meant it.'

'Couldn't you convince her, for a little while?'

'I do like her, but her father being in prison is just too much of a stumbling block to our relationship. I'm too fond of her to pretend otherwise and then have to let her down.'

'Just to give her something else to dream about. Please, Ken. It would be kindest in the long run. She'll waste so many years of her life if she isn't helped.'

'There has to be a better way of helping.'

'You think of something. I can't!'

'I could invite her to meet my family.'

'Brilliant. That isn't a commitment but it will be an encouraging step. Yes, Ken, do that.' Ken still looked doubtful as she pleaded, 'Please, Ken, find out what this latest thing is, what information she has that she thinks will help her father. Then tell me, and together we can help her dismiss it and face the future without dragging the tragedy with her like a loose anchor.'

When Marion had gone, he sat for a while thinking about his feelings for Lowri. There was no doubt that her father's situation had been in the way of a growing attraction. He liked her and knew he could so easily fall in love, but it could never be. Every time he allowed his thoughts to wander that way, a reminder of Jimmy Vaughan, a picture of him in a prison cell, burst in and ruined it. How could he encourage her to think beyond her father's plight, without leading her on to disappointment? He could never allow himself to fall in love with the daughter of a man capable of murder.

Marion's suggestion that he could pretend his feelings were stronger than they were, and there was a future for them, would be justified if it helped her. Then he could encourage her to talk. That wouldn't be difficult. The difficulty would be walking away. If only she could forget her father and concentrate on the future, then he might be able to cope, allow his feelings to grow. Not while she was so determined to prove the man's innocence. Remembering Marion's words he smiled at her analogy – 'dragging tragedy like a loose anchor'. Living close to the sea, even those who had no connection with it used sailor's expressions, he mused.

–

Lowri still hadn't spoken to Dic about the woman with the young baby, who had once known Ellis Owen. Each time they met, there was someone else present and Lowri believed the possibility of a lead was too precious to share until they had made enquiries. She was mentally prepared for disappointment but hope refused to be dashed. Until she had discussed it with Dic she did nothing, except find out where the young woman, Gaynor Dallow was living.

Adding to her suspicious that the woman might be holding the missing money, she learned that Gaynor lived in a small house and earned a little money working at home, finishing garments for Hope Bevan, the dressmaker, the wife of the greengrocer, Peter Bevan. Did she appear to have more money then she earned? She tried not to become excited, knowing she had to hold back until they could learn more about the woman, but it was hard to contain her optimism.

She and Dic had arranged to meet for lunch, but once again the opportunity to talk about the young unmarried woman with a child was thwarted. Ken called at the post office the day she and Dic were to meet and to their further dismay he joined them, chatting amiably to them both, successfully preventing a private talk.

On Sunday morning Lowri and Marion were preparing their lunch. A small joint of meat comprising three week's ration – saved as a special treat – and potatoes roasted in carefully hoarded dripping, plus vegetables. They planned for it to be just the two of them but as usual, the morning was busy with visitors.

Betty Connors from The Ship and Compass called and was invited to stay and eat with them. Kitty and Bob brought a few vegetables but left soon after, Stella and Colin came, and stayed for coffee as Colin wanted to go into the greenhouse to check on his seedlings. At one o'clock, as they began to serve the meal, there was yet another knock at the door and Ken arrived.

Laughing, Lowri invited him in, saying, 'Thank goodness we did extra veg. Marion, here's another lost and hungry soul!'

Ken didn't explain that he was expected home for a late lunch but accepted the invitation with alacrity. His mother knew he might be delayed. 'Thanks,' he said, taking off his coat and sitting at the table. 'Only four of us?'

'Oh, they've had their usual busy morning,' Betty told him, helping herself to swede and carrots and the smallest sliver of beef. 'No one suffers loneliness living in Badgers Brook!'

While Betty and Marion dealt with the dishes, Ken asked Lowri if there was anything worrying her. When she assured him that she was perfectly content, he said, 'Tell me about your father, what sort of a person he was – I mean is. Talk about him so I can get to know him.'

'Why?' she asked curiously. 'You give the impression you'd rather forget he exists.'

'I confess that finding out about him was a shock. It changed the way I felt about you, for a while at least. Like most people, I've never been involved with anything like this before.'

'Neither have I,' she said dryly. 'So why the sudden interest?'

'Because of how I feel about you,' he replied. 'I'm fond of you – very fond – but this got in the way. I know I shouldn't have let it, but it was such a shock and, I didn't deal with it very well and I'm sorry.'

'You weren't unusual in that. All my so-called friends cut me off and became strangers. Even distant relatives now ignore Mam and me. So don't feel guilty.'

'But I do.'

The gramophone was playing softly, being wound up regularly by one or the other of them, dance tunes that had Marion jigging as she passed to and fro putting dishes away and clearing the table. Betty made coffee then announced she was leaving.

'Come on, Lowri, let's walk Betty back to The Ship and wander through the fields for an hour.' Ken invited. 'Just you and I,' he added softly, his eyes telling her things she was happy to know.

Puzzled by his change of attitude and excited by it, she gathered her coat and gloves and they set off. Once they had parted from Betty, he slipped an arm around her waist and pressed her against him. Laughing at nothing in particular Lowri knew there was a significant change in their relationship and it was one she welcomed.

For Ken his emotions were in disarray. What he felt for Lowri was no pretence and only the problem with her father prevented him declaring how he had felt from the first moment he had seen her. To be connected with such serious crimes was something he could never have imagined, and despite his words, his subconscious insisted that by being Jimmy's daughter, Lowri was implicated in those crimes. He tried to put the fears aside. Logic told him he was being stupid but still the doubts held him back like steel bands around his heart.

The fields were muddy in places but keeping to the unploughed edges they managed to stay clear of the worst of it. When they reached a small woodland he put his arms around her and kissed her. She closed her eyes and relaxed into the warmth of knowing she had found someone who cared. He stared down at her and she looked at him longingly until he kissed her again. They stood for a long time, hearts beating close to each other, the temptations of love in her eyes, reciprocating the desire shining in his.

'I want you to come and meet my parents and brothers,' he said. 'I think it's time we got this on a firmer foundation, don't you?'

Lowri didn't think she could be happier as they returned to the house, arms around each other, her head resting on his shoulder.

'From now on, you tell me everything – your hopes and worries. We share it all. Right?' She reached up and touched his cold cheek with her lips. 'Every little thing.'

'In fact,' he added as they opened the door, 'you can begin by telling me what's been on your mind these past few days. Marion is worried about you. She's afraid you're thinking too much about your father's reprieve and not enough about your own needs.'

It was as though a shutter had descended, shutting off the wonderful afternoon and its promise of a happy times ahead, leaving her alone in a cold, dark place. 'There's nothing that worries me,' she said, trying to speak calmly. 'The only worry I have is whether I ordered too many winter socks for the shop, with summer around the corner.'

'Good,' he said, kissing her as he helped her off with her coat.

The kiss felt different: casual, lacking the excitement of the earlier moments and she was overwhelmed by sadness. His increased affection had been a ploy. He wanted her confidence, so she would tell him when she had discovered something new to help her father's case. Then he could discard it, laugh at it, and make her see how impossible her dream of a miracle really was. Love was on his terms and to accept it, she had to forget her father, or at least forget her hope of his reprieve. She couldn't pretend he no longer existed, not even for Ken. Was Marion right? Was she becoming dangerously obsessive to the detriment of friendships? Would she grow old alone and friendless because of her determination to prove her father was innocent?

When Ken left she walked with him to the gate and was partially reassured by the strength of his arms and the tenderness of his kiss. Should she refuse a chance of happiness? Ken had made it clear that he wanted to forget Jimmy Vaughan, but could she do the same? Avoid mentioning him when Ken was near? She watched as the car disappeared along the lane and knew she could not.

Betty Connors was angry. The delivery was due and 'Willing-But-Won't' had worked his notice and the new bar assistant had changed his mind and wasn't coming in. She had asked her brother Ed to help sort out the heavy boxes and set up a new barrel for the beer to settle, but he had just sent a note with a local boy to say his wife was ill and he couldn't come.

No one was able to help her and she foresaw several such incidents in the future. She really had to get a reliable assistant. She looked up and down the road, thinking of the many families that lived close enough to use the place as their local and thought there had to be someone who would do the job, but house by house as she went through the various families, she couldn't think of a solitary soul.

The draymen did what they could and took the stock into the cellar through the double doors set in the ground outside, but the cellar needed rearranging and she set to with a regular glance at the clock. She would never finish by opening time. In her haste she was careless as she carried a box up the stairs into the bar and the edge of it caught on a stair and she fell. Walking upwards, she should have been all right but her foot slipped on the stair and she fell down and down until she landed at the bottom, with her leg across the lowest step taking the weight of her body. The box was on top of her and she managed to move it, but was aware of a pain in her arm as well an excruciating pain in her leg.

She lay there for a moment, recovering, then tried to get up. It was no use, she would need help. The old clock on the cellar wall told her it was ten thirty. No one was likely to look for her for an hour and a half. She called a few times, accepted the futility of it and rested. She tried to take her weight off her leg but each time the pain stopped her moving.

Alun Harris was delivering a boat for a customer and at Cwm Derw he stopped and got out to walk around and perhaps find a café. He parked near The Ship and walked over, knowing it was too early, but seeing the door open wondered if the landlord could tell him of a café nearby.

The bar was empty and he went to where the doors to the cellar were wide open and called, 'Anyone home?'

'Down here, come quick, I need some help,' Betty called back. A few more words and Alun went down to find Betty sweating and obviously in pain.

'Telephone first,' he said, and following her directions, used the phone in her sitting room to call an ambulance. Then he went back to see how he could help.

On first seeing the huge man leaning over her, white teeth exposed in a smile within the thick beard, Betty had wanted to scream, but the man's eyes, remarkably blue, and his voice was so calming that she quickly changed her mind.

'I don't think I should move anything until the experts come,' he said, covering her with his coat. 'I'm afraid of doing damage if your leg is broken.'

'Oh, don't say that,' she wailed. 'I'm opening up in less than an hour.'

Alun didn't think so but he declined to reply. He bathed her face with cool water and talked to her while they waited for the ambulance men, who, when they arrived, lifted her carefully on to a stretcher and took her to hospital.

She handed the keys to Alun and said, 'Lock up, will you? And tell Ed what's happened. We'll need a new barrel, so will you ask him to do that, too?' She told him where to find the guest house. 'Thanks,' she said, 'whoever you are.'

'I'm Alun, glad I could help,' he told her with a smile. 'Don't worry, I'll see everything is secure before I leave.'

He found the guest house behind the post office, but Betty's brother Ed was unable to help. 'I'll open up this evening, but I have guests to see to and my wife is ill,' he explained.

'What d'you want me to do?' Alun asked.

'Just lock the pub and put a notice on the door,' Ed advised.

When Alun returned to the place there were several people waiting. After a moment's hesitation, Alun went inside, phoned Jake to explain the delay on the delivery of the boat and opened the bar. In a brief lull, he opened the new barrel. He found the brass tap and the bung-starter easily. He tapped the bung through into the barrel and fixed the tap in place. Then he drilled the spile in the top of the barrel, the place through which it had been filled, and it was ready to go.

Everyone wanted to know, 'Where's Betty?' and 'Who are you?' and he amiably answered their questions and promised that her brother Ed would know more when he came in later.

He phoned the hospital before he left and was assured that the leg wasn't broken as he had feared.

Betty came home the following day to find her brother there. He showed her the takings from the previous day's lunchtime session carefully written out, the money in a bank bag in the till.

She had to rest for a few days but fortunately there was no serious damage. No one knew who Alun was so she couldn't even thank him.

–

Dic hadn't seen Lowri for a while and knew he should, but he was busy building up his stock of sculptures and gifts ready for the busier months ahead. The work was meticulous and slow and he had to put everything else out of his mind and concentrate wholly on what he was creating.

There were few tourists who found Cwm Derw and most of those were walkers and cyclists, who were notoriously unwilling to spend on unnecessary purchases, but Dic's shop, near the popular seaside resort of Barry, attracted them in large numbers. He needed to offer a variety of attractive gifts of all prices and appeal if he wanted to earn enough to keep him through the winter months. He'd been busy with commissions too, mostly plaques for various sports organizations, ready for their prize-giving. Between all this work, there was little time to drive to Cwm Derw.

There were a few pieces that had been on his shelves for too long and he decided to take a stall at the Maes Hir market and sell them cheaply. He wondered whether Lowri would like to go with him and help. He decided against taking three-year-old Katie, knowing she would soon become bored, and arranged with his ever willing parents to look after her. He telephoned the post office in Cwm Derw just before lunch and invited Lowri, who enthusiastically agreed.

Although Wednesday was half-day closing for both of them, Dic decided to close the shop in the morning, and on hearing this, Stella told Lowri she would give her the morning off too. So it was soon after eight when Dic set off for Cwm Derw, leaving the girls with his mother who would take Sarah-Jane to school and look after Katie.

The prospect of a day out was a good one. He rarely went far and hadn't had a holiday since the birth of Sarah-Jane. As he passed the warehouse, he saw Ken parking his car and waved, but didn't stop.

Ken watched as the car headed on its way towards Cwm Derw and wondered if that was Dic's destination. Then he shrugged, remembering that Lowri would be at work until one o'clock so he had no need to feel alarm. As Marion, he was worried about the closeness between Lowri and Dic Morris, and thought it strange in the circumstances. How could she even be pleasant to the man who had led the police investigation to her father? Perhaps because he was the only one who didn't coax her to give up hope? Marion was right, Dic was the one who encouraged her to – what was it? – drag the tragedy with her like a loose anchor.

If he and Lowri became a couple, could he forget the man condemned to prison for fraud? He admitted the most serious worry was the unproven suspicion of murder. The sensible thing would be to end it now, before one or other of them was hurt. He had reluctantly decided to do what Marion had asked, but his feelings for Lowri were real and it didn't feel right to play with her feelings even if that did make him sound vain. 'Damn Jimmy Vaughan and his greed and temper,' he said aloud.

On impulse, he telephoned the post office in Cwm Derw and was alarmed to hear that Lowri was not there.

'Gone to Maes Hir she has, with Dic Morris. He's got some old stock to sell at the market and thought she'd enjoy a day out,' Stella explained.

'It isn't urgent,' Ken said casually. 'My parents wondered if she'd like to come for dinner on Sunday. I'll ring again tomorrow.'

'I'll tell her and she'll probably ring you,' Stella said. 'There's glad I am that she's making a few friends. Terrible thing to deal with, her father and all that.'

'She's coping,' he replied, and rang off. It seemed unlikely he'd be able to forget Jimmy Vaughan while the name cropped up in even the most casual conversations. She's coping, he had said, but the question was, would he?

The market at Maes Hir, being out of doors, was dependent on good weather to attract the largest crowds, and today the sky was overcast with the threat of rain. But with the temptation of fresh produce, as well as stalls selling china, pots and pans, kitchen equipment and farm implements, there were always plenty of regular customers. As they began to set out their display, every stall was hedged around by prospective buyers.

Greetings were called from one stall to another and people shouted across to report any bargains they had found. Laughter and reminiscences, the unexpected appearance of friends and the temptation of the tea stall and improvised cafe set up in a tent, mean the hubbub of noise was loud and the atmosphere pleasant.

Dic sold about half of his offerings in the first hour and as the interest flagged, Lowri was free to walk around the rest of the market and make a few purchases of her own. Nothing exciting, but rooted clumps of Welsh onions, the everlasting supply of small salad onions, were popped into her bag, knowing Bob and Colin needed more. A freshly baked loaf and a few off-ration duck eggs, and last of all a couple of meat and potato pies for her and Dic to enjoy for lunch. When she returned to the stall he was serving Ken.

'Ken? What are you doing here?' She raised her face to receive his kiss, although slightly embarrassed by the presence of Dic.

'I phoned the post office to ask if you'd like to come to Sunday dinner and meet the family. Stella told me where you were. It wasn't far out of my route so here I am.'

She didn't know what to say, with Dic watching her she was unable to respond to the invitation, although she wasn't sure why. So, rather foolishly, she said, 'Wait there, I've bought pies for our lunch, I'll go and get another.'

'Don't,' Ken laughed. 'I can do better than a pie! Come to the tea tent and see what they have to offer, they must have something more interesting. You as well, Dic?' he asked as an afterthought.

'No thanks. I'd better stay and sell off the last of these.' He gestured towards the few remaining carvings, the more expensive, which had been admired but had not tempted people to open their purses.

'Sorry Ken,' Lowri said. 'But I'm here to help Dic and it's his turn to look around. He wants something to take back for Sarah-Jane and Katie.'

Amiably, Ken agreed and while Dic wandered off, he and Lowri ate the pies, Ken showing exaggerated amusement, as though his standards were far above a simple snack wrapped in greaseproof paper.

Lowri was undecided. She wanted to go back with Dic as she still hadn't told him about Gaynor Dallow and her young baby, but she didn't want to refuse to go back with Ken, presuming he would ask her. The decision was made for her. After making arrangements to visit his family on the following Sunday, Ken left, explaining that he had calls to make.

Ken put his arms around her and kissed her as he was leaving, and seeing Dic watching them she again felt confusion. Why should she worry about Dic seeing her kissing Ken? Dic was hardly a rival for her affections. She smiled at him and asked, 'Did you find a present for the girls?'

He showed her a couple of hand-sewn purses made from dark blue velvet and covered with embroidery, and she nodded approval. She slipped some coins into each one. 'It's unlucky to give a purse with no money inside,' she said. 'I want Sarah-Jane and Katie to have all the luck in the world.'

Packing the last of his stock into the car didn't take long, and they followed the trail of vehicles departing slowly from the field. The cars and vans were interspersed with hand carts and even a few wheelbarrows in which produce had been brought. Weary pedestrians were plodding towards the bus stop some carrying empty baskets with white cloths folded inside.

'I enjoyed today,' Lowri said as Dic negotiated the rutted entrance. 'Can we do it again, d'you think?'

'You'd have to persuade Bob and Colin to sell some of their vegetables,' he said. 'I hope I don't have too many items to sell as cheaply as today.'

'But it was fun, though?'

'Great fun,' he agreed, 'and good company. Thanks for coming.'

'Strange Ken turning up like that.'

'Hardly. He wants to make it clear how much he likes you.' After a pause he asked, 'How d'you feel about him?'

'I think he's trying to accept the situation regarding Dad. I know the shock of finding out was difficult for him. Maybe he'll be more understanding now, about the hope I have for proving his innocence.'

'I'm sure he will.' He wondered whether Ken's family had been told and if *they* would be understanding, but said nothing. A niggle of jealously wormed inside him and he hoped the visit would be cancelled.

It wasn't until they were almost back at Badgers Brook that Lowri told Dic about Gaynor Dallow. Her heart was racing as she waited for his reaction. If Dic discarded the possibility of a lead, then all was lost. He listened intently then agreed to make a few enquires.

'It should be easy to find out how she manages, whether there's a man in the picture, secretly or openly. Although I don't think it will get us far.'

'But you do think it's a possibility?'

'I think we have to check on everything, even the slightest incident. The most doubtful could be the one to guide us to the truth.'

'Thank you.' She was almost tearful at his supporting words. There was no one else who even pretended to believe in her father.

—

On Sunday, Ken arrived at ten o'clock and refused to stay for coffee. 'My parents are longing to meet you,' he said. 'I've told them so much about you. And my brothers are waiting in specially. Giving up their rugby practice would you believe!'

He talked about his family as they drove, explaining that his father was a fireman, his mother a part time canteen assistant, while his younger brother was at college doing English and Drama and the older one worked in a pub. 'A right old mixture the Hardy brothers,' he said with a laugh.

'Very impressive,' she said.

'Not really. Your father owning a business, that's impressive.'

Putting her father in business in the present tense puzzled her. Surely Ken had told his parents her father was in prison, no longer involved in the business? She shrugged the worry aside. Of course he had. Today she was meeting his parents and that lifted a relationship on to a different level. Today was to be enjoyed.

Mr and Mrs Hardy came out to greet them as soon as the car stopped outside the modest terraced house in Barry. They were formally dressed, Mr Hardy in a suit and tie, and Mrs Hardy wearing a pretty summer dress, an apron in her hand that she had quickly removed, Lowri guessed. Lowri was ushered inside to where a fire roared a welcome and the smell of cooking filled the air.

Introductions were made and the two brothers, Geoff eighteen, and Raymond twenty, drifted off to the garden to kick a ball about while they waited for the meal. Conversation was stilted at first, each participant trying to avoid too many questions.

Ken fielded any comments about her family, implying that both of her parents ran a guest house, while her father was also a partner in the clothing factory.

'Mrs Vaughan runs the guest house,' he told them. 'And there's the clothing factory of course. Busy people.'

She felt her colour rise. He hadn't told them and, rather shamefully, her first instinct was to follow the same line. Since facing up to the gossip in Cwm Derw and seeing it die down, she had sworn never to lie about it again, but the prospect of losing Ken made that decision difficult. She thought about it, as conversation drifted around her weighing up the risk of saying goodbye to Ken, against denying her father, pretending their troubles were non-existent, that life was exactly the same as before the death of Ellis Owen.

Conversation increased as the meal was served and she tried to put her serious thoughts aside. She was sitting between Ken and his father and when Mr Hardy asked a question about the clothes the factory produced, the problem re-emerged and she was torn between what she wanted to do and her need to be honest. Ken nudged her, teasing her for being lost in her daydreams. Her mind in turmoil, she had allowed too much time to elapse after the question was asked. She apologized and tried to smile, but the smile was stiff and she felt her cheeks protesting at the artificial attempt.

Her heart began thumping painfully as she knew what she had to do. Surely they would understand? As soon as an opportunity offered, she turned to Ken's father and said, 'Of course, you know about my father being in prison, don't you?'

In the silence that followed, the echo of her voice sounded completely unlike her own. Trembling, anxious, she turned to look at Ken's mother, who had dropped her fork and was staring at her husband. Hastily stifled, nervous sniggering came from Geoff and Raymond.

'We did wonder – the name – it isn't that common… we did wonder,' Mr Hardy muttered.

'Ken didn't tell you?' She looked at Ken who was staring down at the table, unable to meet her eyes. 'Obviously not. Well, should I leave?'

This was a chance for them to tell her they understood she wasn't responsible for her father's situation. She waited as the stony silence continued, her fork laden with food, glaring first at one then the other. When Mr Hardy finally spoke, he lowered his head and stared at the table as Ken was doing, 'You can finish your meal first.'

'I seem to have lost my appetite,' she said, pushing back her chair and rising. 'Ken, if you'll take me to the bus stop? Or would you prefer I walk? After all, the daughter of a man wrongly accused of theft isn't a suitable companion for you, is she?'

Silently she was handed her coat and gloves and she left without another word.

'I'm sorry,' Ken said as he opened the car door for her. 'I thought it was the best way of dealing with this and expected you to follow my lead.'

'Shut up! Just shut up and drive me home!' Anger was stronger than the humiliation, and tears were held back until she walked into her bedroom, closed the door and collapsed on to the bed. Then they fell as though they would never stop. False Friend, her mind shouted, repeating the words until she thought she would go crazy. She had never felt such loneliness. How she longed to see her mother and listen to her reassuring voice.

When Marion came home that evening she came across Lowri huddled up in a chair in front of the fire. She threw on a couple of small logs and stood near her.

'Did Ken meet you?' she asked Lowri as she removed her coat. 'How did the visit with his parents go?'

Lowri shrugged in answer to Marion's questioning.

'Why didn't Ken come in?' Marion asked after putting a plate of sandwiches in front of Lowri.

'Ken is no longer around.'

'What happened?'

'The usual. He hadn't told his parents about Dad and when I did, well, I didn't stay any longer than it took for them to hand me my coat.'

'Ken's an idiot if he allows what happened to your father to get between you.'

'Will it always be like this? Friends until they find out about Dad? False friends?'

'No, not everyone is a false friend.'

'Thank goodness for you,' Lowri said as she smiled weakly. 'I don't know what I'd do if I didn't have you for a friend.'

'I'm not going anywhere,' Marion assured her. Then she smiled. 'At least, not until that man of mine divorces his wife, eh?'

—

On the following Wednesday, with summer flowers giving a heartening display in many gardens, Lowri set off for a walk. She went straight from the post office, a pack of sandwiches brought from home in her bag. She was miserable and unaware of the summer day, with the trees displaying their summer greenery and the ever present daisies and buttercups spreading their beautiful covering over the fields; wild pansies showed their shy faces amid the grasses and she saw none of it.

She went to a corner of a field and sat near the gate to eat her sandwiches, wishing she'd thought to bring a flask of coffee, smiling as she thought of Connie Tanner, who never went anywhere without a picnic.

Packing the wrappings into her pocket she hurried on to where she knew Gaynor Dallow lived. She had since realized that a small baby could hardly be Ellis Owen's, his death had been too long ago. How stupid she had been. Dic would have realized at once if she had mentioned the child's age. But she still wanted to talk to her. Simply by knowing the man, Gaynor might have something to add to the little she knew about him. She wasn't sure what she would say, but she hoped that during a conversation she might glean a few clues. Any contact, however fragile, must be worth investigating.

She knocked on the door of the rather smart semi in a village called Nant Mel-Honeybrook, named she was told, from the colour of the water as it flowed over the yellow stones.

'Hello, Lowri! It's a very long time since I saw you. Come in.'

Relieved that she was remembered, and that didn't have to make an excuse to be invited in, Lowri went inside the attractive living room and took the chair she was offered.

'How is your father? So sorry I was to hear about his troubles. And is your Mam coping all right?'

'Dad apparently looks like an old man. He's accepted his sentence, given up hope of his innocence being proved, although I haven't. And Mam, she's amazing. So very brave. She's bought a house and has paying guests to help pay the mortgage. Lucky to get one, they aren't keen to give mortgages to single women. It was because it was a business, I believe.'

'What a tragedy it all was. To think that Ellis Owen died in the sea! So ironic. He was a strong swimmer and an expert in small boats and canoes. He'd always been so confident in his ability to take the sea on under any circumstances.'

'Dad tried to save him you know.'

'I believe that too.'

'Thank you. Can we talk about Ellis Owen and my father for a while? There might be something that will help my father. Some small, unimportant memory.'

'Of course. This must be very hard for you.'

'Worse for my parents. As for me, the people in Cwm Derw are very kind and understanding, but others are not. Almost everyone I once knew shunned me after my father's arrest. And even recently I'm reminded that in the eyes of the world he's guilty. I had a friend, Ken Hardy, we were getting on so well, but he took me to meet his parents, and when they realized who I was, well, you can imagine.'

'Why do you want to know about Ellis?'

'I don't know. I just hope that something will come to light that will clear my father. And I know it's crazy,' she added defensively, 'but I can't let it drop.'

'I wouldn't either in your circumstances. Now let me think.' She frowned as she tried to bring the man to mind. 'Ellis was a flirt, but I expect you know that. He took me out a couple of times, until I realized he was married. There were others too, although I doubt whether that helps.'

'Anyone more serious?'

Gaynor frowned. 'I seem to remember some gossip, but I'd left your father's firm by then and I can't remember what happened. He was fond of adventurous sport, did some climbing, but it was the sea he loved. He was either in it, or on it, or at its edge, on the beach or balanced on the craggy cliffs dangling fishing lines into it.'

A baby began to cry and Gaynor pointed upwards. 'My son is awake, I'll have to see to him.'

'Of course. If you think of anything more, will you let me know?' Lowri said, as she stood to leave. 'But before I go, can I meet your son?'

The chubby six-weeks-old Thomas settled in her lap while his mother prepared to change and feed him. As she left, Lowri looked back at the beautiful cameo of the young mother nursing her child, afraid that unless she could forget her dream of rescuing her father, it was something she was unlikely to know.

On the bus heading back to Cwm Derw she passed a school and thought of Dic waiting, as other parents waited, to greet his daughter, holding hands with Katie. She was again overwhelmed with a feeling of loss for something she would never know. Ken had given her hope of living a normal life, but the spectre of her father's sentence lay over every prospect of that.

Gaynor was another hope dashed and despite her belief in justice and in her father's innocence, there was nowhere else to look. She had to give up and try to live a life without this foolish dream. Ken was lost to her and how many others would she turn away before she faced the inescapable truth? Perhaps if she told him of her visit to Gaynor and the feeling of futility she now felt, he might ignore his parents' attitude and come back to her. The tiny flicker of hope failed to excite her. He had turned away from her and she didn't think it could ever be the same as it had once been.

She rang Dic to tell him the result of her visit to Gaynor Dallow. 'At least things are still coming up, hopes and ideas we haven't known about – one day we'll be lucky,' he said.

She was determined not to feel depressed and drag others into her gloom, so she straightened her shoulders and increased her speed, and walked along the lane after leaving the phone box, head high. So high, that she didn't see a fallen branch on the ground. She caught her foot in it and, unable to recover her balance, fell into the arms of Geoff as he and Connie came around the corner.

'Women are always falling for my husband,' Connie teased, helping Lowri to rise. 'We've just called on you. There's a Bring and Buy sale in two weeks time, in aid of the NSPCC and we wondered if you'd manage one of the stalls.'

'Monday evening,' Geoff added. 'So most people are free to come.'

'Of course, I'd love to help. What if I deal with the "white elephants", if we can find any,' she said, referring to the traditional stall for unwanted items. Her heart lightened and she walked on down the lane beside the wood. At least here, in Cwm Derw, she was among friends, she thought, as she hurried home.

Eight

Betty Connors had recovered from her fall and she often wondered about the man who came to help her and disappeared without further word. Her brother Ed had helped in between dealing with the guests at his and Elsie's bed-and-breakfast establishment and some of the regulars contributed by dealing with the deliveries and restacking the boxes and bottles. Marion had done some of the food preparation as well as her usual cleaning duties. None would accept payment and Betty promised them a special evening as soon as she was well enough to cope.

With Ed she had interviewed several men for the post, and they had chosen a man in his forties with lots of experience called Ernie Bright. He was due to start that day but so far he hadn't arrived, and she was already having doubts about their choice.

Since her brother had left The Ship and Compass to live with his wife Elsie and help her to run the bed-and-breakfast, Betty had had several people to take his place, but none had stayed.

'I think it's partly because most men don't like working for a woman,' she said to Bob Jennings as she handed him his first pint of the day.

'I thought that estate agent, young Teifion Dexter, was keen,' Bob remarked. 'If his father hadn't died he might still be here.'

'And there was Daphne Boyd,' Betty mused sadly. 'Now she was marvellous, until she went to farm in France. If I could get a young woman like her I wouldn't say no. But Daphne was an exception, it's a man I really need, some of the work is quite heavy.'

'There are a few of us who'll help if you're stuck,' Bob reminded her.

'And I'm grateful, Bob. But it's regular help I need, someone who enjoys the work. Isn't there anyone out there who needs work?'

The door opened and a group of builders came in. Betty smiled cheerfully and went to take their order. 'The usual hot pies?' she asked, taking the list they had written. Jokingly, she asked, 'Any of your lot looking for a change and willing to work for a crotchety landlady? I'm looking for someone strong and hard working.'

The new barman suddenly came rushing in, camera and shoulder bag swinging from his shoulder and a few pieces of photographic wizardry dangling from his hand. Colin shouted out, 'No point in running now, boy! It's half an hour late you are.'

'Sorry I am,' the hot and anxious Ernie said, bent almost double in an attempt to get ahead of himself. 'I was photographing a heron and forgot the time. Got a picture of him with a fish in his beak. Marvellous it'll be, if I haven't spoilt it rushing.'

With few words, Betty sent him to take off his multi-pocketed jacket and change into a coat he was pulling out of his bag. He accepted the teasing with good will and soon settled into the rhythm of the work. He was pleasant, and quick and, despite his disastrous beginning, Betty had hopes of him.

Lowri was pleased to have been asked to help at the local fund-raising for the NSPCC. She was accepted here in Cwm Derw and was thankful that not everyone was treating her like a pariah. It would put her father's plight slightly into the background, at least for a while, as well as helping take her mind away from the disappointment of parting from Ken. She had begun to believe they had a future, until his parents made it clear they didn't want to open their door to the daughter of a man who was a thief and suspected of murder.

'When will *my* sentence end?' she asked Marion, as they were going through things at Badgers Brook for the sale.

'Come on, let's go through our stuff and see what we can give to the White Elephant stall. No time to worry about Ken. I'm here and I won't let you down and you have plenty of friends here. Heavens, this place is never empty!' She patted Lowri's shoulder and added encouragingly, 'There'll be others. Someone more deserving of you, remember that.'

They made a pile of a few ornaments and unwanted oddments of china in the back bedroom and added to it as they searched their drawers and wardrobes. As she put down a summer jacket that had a torn pocket and a badly stained lapel to the growing collection, Lowri remembered the key she'd replaced in its pocket and took it out.

From the doorway Marion watched, and asked, 'What have you found?'

Lowri's instinct was to hide it but she was beginning to admit her friends were right and it was time to forget trying to help her father and get on with her life. She held it out on her palm. 'A key. I found it among Dad's things and thought for a while it might lead me to something useful in the search for evidence. Mam doesn't know what it's for so I might as well throw it away.'

Going downstairs with the clothes they needed to launder before offering for sale, she took the key and threw it into the bin among the ashes and other rubbish. Later on, she thought better of it and went to retrieve it. She stared at it, a slightly rusty key, little more than an inch long. What could it be for? A shed? A cupboard in a house they no longer owned? Then she frowned, remembering her father's fishing expeditions with Ellis Owen and Dic's father, Jack Morris. They had once stored their gear in a hut once used on occasions by shepherds during lambing and shearing. Could that be where it fitted?

Used by several people, it was hardly a suitable hiding place for anything of value, but unable to ignore even the faintest of hope, she determined to go there and explore. She had a vague idea of where it was situated, remembering rough grassland rising up to craggy hills with rocks protruding through the green surface here and there. At the lower end, cliffs that Ellis had loved to climb fell sharply to the sea below. She pressed the key into her hand, leaving its indentation clearly marked, and wondered if there would be something to find, or whether it would be yet more hopes dashed. She knew she had to try.

She was surprised a few minutes later, when Marion carried out more unwanted rubbish, to see her friend digging around in the ash bin. Was she trying to retrieve the key?

If so, did it mean she knew its purpose? She opened the door and stepped out. 'Lost something, Marion?'

'Yes, a teaspoon. We have eight and I can only find seven. I must have thrown it out by mistake. Come and help me find it will you?'

They pulled faces as they moved the unpleasant mixture about and when Dic came through the gate and saw them, he laughed. 'What on earth are you two doing? Your faces are a picture!' He found a stick and helped them and the spoon was eventually recovered.

Lowri looked at the key after scrubbing her hands and wondered whether Marion had really been trying to find the spoon, which she could easily have hidden as an excuse. Aware of being neurotic and foolish, she nevertheless said nothing to Marion about having retrieved the key. Closing her bedroom door, she hid the key again in a corner other wardrobe, wrapped in a sock and tucked into a Wellington boot. She felt ashamed of suspecting Marion of... of what? She wasn't at all sure. There was just a feeling that it was too soon to give up, and that the fewer people who shared her thoughts the better.

She didn't believe for a moment that Marion had been implicated in her father's arrest, of course she didn't, that would be nonsense; but Marion would talk to others, who in turn would pass it on, and if there was something to find...? As though to make up for her unwillingness to share confidences with Marion, she was extra nice, insisting on cooking the meal and clearing away afterwards.

Dic stayed and offered to carry anything they couldn't manage to the sale for them. He caught Lowri's eye a few times and guessed there was something she wanted to tell him. It was late; too late to suggest a walk. Whatever it was would have to wait until next time.

Like the rest of Lowri's friends he wished she would stop dwelling on her father's situation. She was young and lovely and shouldn't be wasting her life on this nebulous, fragile dream. However hard she tried, it was bound to end in failure and disappointment. The police had found evidence and a court had found him guilty. Sad but undeniable. He longed to hold her, comfort her and help her through the years ahead, but that was a dream as impossible as hers.

On Sunday morning, Lowri rose early and, packing a few sandwiches and taking a flask of coffee, set off to find the shepherd's hut. She slipped out of the house very early and having previously arranged to borrow Kitty's bicycle, rode along the side of the wood with a picture of the map she had studied in her mind. Getting there from Cwm Derw was different from being taken there from home, by car.

She had often visited the area near the hut with her father and his friends when she was young. She used to go out with them on their boat too, but as she had grown up, she'd found more interesting things to do than watch her father and Uncle Jack Morris messing about with fishing lines. Dic had been there too, treating her like his precious little sister who had to be cared for. She had been so happy then. Ellis Owen had been with them on occasions, but he'd always preferred going out alone. She remembered that much about him, and wished she'd learned more.

She cycled for an hour but when she reached the place she had marked on the map, nothing was familiar. She'd made a mistake. She cycled on for a while and stopped at midday to eat her sandwiches on a ridge high above the coast where the sea glistened in the summer sun. Conscious of aching muscles that had rarely been exercised by cycling, she decided to give up for the day and return home. She would study the map and her memory and try to identify the place then try again.

Thankfully, Marion was out when she returned to Badgers Brook's welcoming comfort, stiff and tired. She would relax in a bath to ease her unexpected aches, then sit and examine the map and prepare for a second attempt to find the hut.

Marion came home at six and Dic followed almost immediately after with Sarah-Jane and Katie. 'Where have you been?' Sarah-Jane demanded. 'I brought a doll to show you and you weren't here.'

Laughing, Lowri hugged the two girls and apologized. 'I borrowed Kitty Jennings's bike and went for a ride. And am I stiff! I haven't ridden a bicycle for ages.'

'Next time, can we bring our bicycles and come with you?' Katie asked.

'That would be lovely.' Lowri agreed, smiling at Dic as she imagined them setting off, with Katie on a three-wheeler. 'Now, who would like a glass of lemonade and who wants tea?'

Frustrated by seeing Dic and still not having the opportunity to talk, Lowri invited him to walk with her to take Kitty's bicycle back.

'Has anything happened?' he asked when they were free of the house.

'Like Ken's parents more or less telling me to leave?'

Dic was angry but tried to make light of it, explaining how confusing it must be to those who had never been in contact with the mildest of criminals. 'Few of us know anyone who's been in trouble with the law so they have

176

nothing to balance what you told them. It would have been a shock for anyone.'

'And Ken? Shouldn't he have talked to them first, made them understand? Instead of allowing me to walk into it without warning?'

'Yes, he should. I just hope that once the memories fade and people find other things to fill their minds, feelings will die down.'

'Memories won't fade. I won't let them.'

'And that's as it should be. But you'll be less inclined to tell everyone you meet.'

'I almost decided to give up but I can't. Not ever. Even though it seems that Mam and Dad have. It's so sad the way they've put aside all hope, accepting the punishment and separation. It's as though they're guilty.'

'Tell me exactly what happened when you went to see Gaynor Dallow.'

'As I said on the phone, it was another disappointment,' she told him, as they were walking back to the house. 'She remembers Ellis Owen, described him as a bit of a flirt, admitted they were close for a while – until she found out he had a wife. But I don't think she has anything to do with him stealing money.'

'It really would be best if you stop expecting a miracle. For your mother's sake as well as your own. Some people wouldn't be as kind as Gaynor Dallow and might complain at your pestering. Be careful, Lowri. Let it go.'

'Dic, how can I?'

–

The sale took place on a warm summer evening and from the moment the doors opened the place was heaving with enthusiastic bargain-hunters. Clothes were particularly in demand; the best quality items were gone in the first half hour. Women had become thrifty during the war years and even after six years the inclination towards frugality was still strong. Many found it impossible to forget the hard lessons on economy they had learned. Coats would be carefully unpicked and would reappear made into clothes for children; knitted garments would be opened up and unwound, the wool washed and reknitted into gloves and hats; mending small tears was something many took a pride in.

Bob and Colin came and bought a number of plant pots and even a damaged wheelbarrow which they planned to repair. Dic came with the girls, who had been allowed a late night with pocket money to spend on toys. Katie ran to Lowri with great excitement to show her each purchase and Sarah-Jane asked her advice about a dress for her doll.

Lowri looked up at one point to see Dic talking to Gaynor Dallow who was carrying her little boy Thomas 'Welsh fashion', in a shawl around her shoulders. She didn't have time to wonder what they talked about, but hoped Dic would tell her when things had calmed down.

People continued to arrive with more items to add to the sale and people would leave what they were looking at and rush over to look at what new bargains were on offer. Lowri and Marion did well on the White Elephant stall and made almost five pounds by the time they were about to pack up. At the last moment, a woman came in and brought some fishing tackle to sell and to Lowri's surprise, this was quickly bought by Dic, who explained he'd bought it for Jake Llewellyn, from the boatyard.

'He hires out rods and reels as well as boats, and I think he'll be pleased with this lot,' Dic explained. 'Why don't you come with me when I take it, you'd enjoy meeting him again.'

He suggested the following Sunday but she declined, having decided to try again to find the shepherd's hut. With Ken no longer a friend, and even Dic warning her to give up dreaming of a miracle, she would tell no one. At least then she wouldn't have to explain another disappointment if the hut proved impossible to find.

On the following day, she closed the post office at five thirty and hurried towards the bus. Alighting at her stop, she walked down the lane aware of being content. Marion was working late so she had Badgers Brook to herself. She loved sharing with Marion, but just sometimes she was grateful for the friendly silence of the old house to relax and put her confusing thoughts into some sort of order.

She prepared a snack of cracker biscuits and had just finished eating when there was a knock at the door. She wiped her mouth and opened the door. Ken stood there with a bunch of roses held towards her.

'I'm so very sorry,' he said. 'And ashamed. Please will you let me come in and try to explain?'

She stood back then went to the gas stove to heat water for tea. He stood just inside the door and, placing the flowers on the table, he asked, 'Can I have one too?'

In silence she reached for a second cup and saucer. When the tea was made and a tray set, he carried it into the living room. She turned to him and asked, 'I don't know what you want me to say, Ken. You let me walk into that situation without warning. How could you do that?'

'I hoped that on the first couple of visits they'd get to know you, then when I explained about your father they'd like you enough to understand.'

'I've tried that tack but it never works. I could have told you that – it didn't work with you, did it? Smiles at first but they fade like snow in the sun as soon as they know who I am.'

'Who you are? But you are Lowri Vaughan, a beautiful and bright young woman. It's your father Jimmy who's in trouble.'

'Try telling most people that and they back away and mutter about being from the same mould, tainted by contact – it never changes. But I don't have to tell you, do I? You saw how your parents reacted.'

'I'm sorry,' he said again. 'I was wrong.'

'Perhaps it would have been different if they'd come here to meet me. This house has a calming effect on people. It's the only place where I feel safe.'

He took a tentative step towards her and held out his arms. 'I want you to feel safe with me. Please, Lowri, can't we start again?'

'And your parents? And your giggling brothers?'

'You have me, and all your friends in Cwm Derw. Won't that be enough for a while? My parents will come round. They'll have to if they want to see something of me in the future.'

Without coming close, he leaned forward and touched her lips with his. 'I'll go now but can we meet, perhaps on Sunday? I don't want to lose you, Lowri.'

'Not Sunday, I'm going… I've made plans.'

'As long as it isn't someone tall, dark and handsome.'

'Just me.'

'Saturday then? Pictures?'

She nodded. Although it had gone terribly wrong, perhaps he'd had the best intentions; and it *had* been her own decision to blurt out the truth about her father.

She sat staring into space after he left. The flowers were in a vase in the hearth where the fire was set but not lit. His arrival and apology and even the chaste kiss had warmed her as the fire would not.

When Marion returned rosy-cheeked from walking home along the lanes, Lowri told her about Ken's visit. 'I still feel hurt by the way he let me face his unprepared family, but I have to admit that it was at least partly my fault for making an announcement of it.'

'Why don't you make a decision to tell no one until they mention it, and then react all casual? Always going in full fuss and expecting them to run away in horror, doesn't that make it happen?'

'Perhaps you're right, but not telling them makes me feel I'm letting Dad down, being ashamed of him.'

'You do talk a lot of nonsense sometimes,' Marion sighed. 'Now, what's to eat? I'm starving.'

'Kitty brought some pies. They were on sale at the bakers and she queued, then pleaded for two extra for us as we were at work.'

'Pies it is, and potatoes mashed with milk – there's no margarine to spare. Really, how they expect people to manage on the rations they give us I don't know. Cheese ration down to one ounce a week in April. I ask you! What can we do with that? It isn't enough for a mousetrap! Thank goodness the meat ration's being increased to one shilling and seven pence a week. That will help a bit. I'm heartily sick of meatless meals, aren't you?'

She chattered on leaving Lowri to her thoughts. When Marion came in singing 'Nice Work if You Can Get it' with the broom as her partner, Lowri jumped up and joined in, her good humour returned.

Saturday night was pleasant, but they parted without arranging another meeting and Lowri had the strong feeling that his parents' behaviour and her failure to show an interest in putting things right, meant their friendship and growing love was over.

On Sunday morning Marion went to see her family and as soon as she had gone, Lowri packed a few sandwiches and found a small crocheted purse which hung around her neck into which she put some money with a handkerchief to stop it rattling. She gathered other necessities including a torch and a small trowel – although she didn't quite know what that was for – and set off again to search for the shepherd's hut.

She had studied the map, marked the place where she thought it was situated and worked out where she had made her earlier error. This time there wouldn't be a mistake. It wasn't until she stopped to push the bicycle up a steep hill that she realized she had already made one: the map was at home in her bedroom.

She had a clear picture of the place in her mind and memories of those earlier visits came back and added to it. Although she guessed that being so small then, and with the years in between, her impressions were bound to be distorted. Yet she felt confident, this second time, of going straight to the spot. The day was more typical of April than June, with clouds chasing across the sky, squally showers that had her struggling in and out of the yellow rain cape Bob had insisted on her bringing, and brief spells of surprisingly warm sunshine.

The road began to climb and she stood on the pedals to add strength to her tiring legs. She felt a surge of confidence as she began to recognize trees, houses, and ahead of her the track leading around the cliffs. She hid the bicycle under some brambles and, gathering her food and tools into her pockets and carrying her waterproof, she walked on.

To her relief the hut was there, leaning slightly but apparently still intact, and she fingered the key and wondered whether it would still turn and open the padlocked door. She glanced around the quiet spot, where only the sound of the distant tide murmured. The wind had either dropped or this side of the headland was in the lee of it. Slowly, she approached the old building.

The door had a wide sill fitted across it to guide the rain away from the base from where it could have entered the building, and this looked new. The window to one side also looked like a replacement. She fingered the rusty old key apprehensively. Would it fit and open the door? And if it did, should she go in to a place where she clearly had no right to be?

There was no padlock. A new lock had been fitted and the key she held was far too small. It might have opened the hut at one time, but not any more. Disappointed, she grasped the doorknob and waggled it and to her surprise the door opened inwardly with ease. She opened it wider and was met by an unpleasant smell of rotting wood and dampness. Feeling for her torch, she stepped inside and with a squeal of alarm, fell over. She had forgotten the steep step down from the door. The earthen floor was twelve inches lower than the step – the reason for the wide sill, now seen to be about twelve inches up from the bottom of the door. She stood up and rubbed her knees ruefully remembering now the steep entrance. Taking a few cautious steps, she gripped the key and in the beam of the torch she looked around the small room.

There was a fireplace and a few mildewed papers on the floor near it. The window was dirty and gave little light and she was glad she'd brought a torch. None of her father's possessions remained. Not even a length of fishing line or the smallest lead weight. Apart from the few logs of wood and kindling, the place was empty.

The floor was hard earth, impacted by feet over many years. With the light behind her through the open door, it took a while for her eyes to become accustomed to the poor light, but even when they were at their clearest, she knew there was nothing here to find. Unless... she knelt down and rubbed a trowel across the surface. Could something have been buried? Foolishly, aware that she was behaving like a character in Enid Blyton's 'Famous Five' books, she began to loosen the soil.

A gust of wind blew the door against the wall then allowed it to swing back and almost close. The reduction in light and the faint sound startled her and she looked around, but was reassured, confident it was only the breeze which swung it gently open and closed as she watched. When she was back on her knees, it happened again, but this time she wasn't alarmed. It was hardly worth trying to prop it open. She was too intent on her task to worry about the semi darkness.

Then a shadow darkened the room and there was movement close by. Someone was there with her. Before she could move something heavy landed on her, the weight frightening and confusing her. Someone was lying across her, holding her down, grasping for the key and the trowel in her hand. She squealed as her hand was forced open and the key taken. Her head was pushed to the ground and as she tried to call for help, her face was pressed into the loosened soil.

The smell and taste of earth was terrifying and there was another smell, unpleasant and suffocating, coming from her assailant – noxious, teasingly familiar but one she couldn't name. More pressure, and she couldn't breathe as earth filled her nostrils and she tried to hold her breath as she feared choking on it. Then, in seconds, the pressure was gone and after a scuffling movement, the door was closed leaving her in almost complete darkness. In utter disbelief she heard the door close and a key turn. She was locked in and no one knew where she was.

She jumped up and banged on the door, twisting and turning the doorknob, pulling to try to open the stout door but it didn't move a fraction. She called and called, outraged at first, thinking it was some stupid joke, then as she began to feel alarm chilling her blood, she pleaded and begged to be freed. But there was no reply. Whoever had locked her in, was gone.

–

Marion was surprised but not worried when darkness fell and Lowri hadn't returned. They usually knew where the other was, but they had no strict rules about sharing their every move with each other. But with the meal almost ready and the hour approaching eight o'clock, she went to see if Lowri was with Kitty and Bob.

'Borrowed the bike she did,' Kitty told her, 'and there's no lights on it, so she should have been back before this.'

'Do you have any idea where she went?' Bob asked. 'Perhaps I'd better go and look for her?'

'Go and see if Colin's home,' Kitty said. 'You can go together. Try some of her friends, she won't be far away for sure.'

'Perhaps she went too far and is walking, afraid of breaking the law by riding without lights?'

At ten o'clock Lowri still hadn't appeared and they phoned Dic and Ken to see if they'd seen her. After contacting everyone she was likely to visit, they then called the police.

–

Lowri's torch was fading. She had examined the room inch by inch but there was no way out. The place she remembered had been falling down but now it looked as though it had recently been repaired. The roof, which she remembered as rusted corrugated iron that rattled in the wind, was now made of thick planks of wood, solidly fastened. The window had no opening. The door opened inward and couldn't be kicked outward; with the earthen step around it, it wouldn't give even an inch. She knew this but still struggled with it, pulling on the knob and twisting it backwards and forwards, shouting from time to time in the futile hope of someone passing.

She was thankful she had brought her sandwiches and flask in with her. Although so far she had been afraid to eat, in case she was left there a long time. She needed to conserve the small amount of food and drink. Rationing had a new meaning for her. She looked at the kindling and wished she'd brought matches. A blaze, even for a little while would have cheered her, and smoke pluming out of the chimney might have attracted attention, even in an isolated spot like this.

Darkness fell and she wrapped herself in Kitty's water-proof cape and tried to sleep. She was hungry but only drank some coffee, promising herself a sandwich for breakfast. Morning seemed a long way off.

–

During the night, while his mother looked after the girls, after trying all Lowri's friends without success, Dic searched the woods and lanes, calling her name. Ken too drove around the roads, stopping to ask everyone he met if they'd seen a solitary young woman with a bicycle – or without one. Betty Connors had organized a search party from her regulars at the pub and Kitty and Stella made food and hot drinks for the helpers. Ernie, the new barman, seemed to enjoy the excitement and he worked hard serving the regulars, learning their names and persuading them to talk about Lowri in the hope of jogging their memory about a place they hadn't yet thought of where she might have gone.

At five in the morning, when the bar was closed, it was still being used as a centre for the searchers. Ernie had regretfully gone home after taking a few photographs of the bar filled with regulars and strangers, interspersed with uniformed police. He promised Betty one to hang on her wall once Lowri was found, safe and sound. He didn't tell her that the pictures might be of interest to the local newspaper if the search ended less happily.

A bit later that morning, when nothing had been reported, a policeman knocked on Lowri's mother's door and asked her if she had seen her daughter or knew where she might be. Alarmed, Emily began to suggest people she might have visited, but they were people who had already been contacted. Patiently the constable waited as she racked her brain, working her way through Lowri's friends. Sadly, she admitted there were very few. 'Most have avoided her since the arrest of Jimmy,' she explained.

'Her friend Marion said something about a key. Would you know anything about that?'

'No, I couldn't think where it belonged.' Emily frowned then added, 'Of course it might have been for the old hut my husband and his friends used to store their fishing gear. But it would have fallen down by now, it was in a precarious state when they used it. A huff and a puff, was all it needed, Jimmy used to joke.'

'Where would it be?'

'I don't remember exactly. I never went with them on their fishing and boating days. The great outdoors never appealed. Lowri would—' she stopped, about to tell the policeman that her daughter might know. 'Silly of me,' she said, hiding her distress with another offer of tea. Then she stared at him. 'She might have remembered and if she did, she might have gone to look. But not overnight. It can't be that far away from Cwm Derw. She's always off some-where chasing daydreams about Jimmy being released,' she added sadly.

'Just where would this place be, Mrs Vaughan?'

'The trouble is, I never went there. Apart from it being near the coast, not far from where Ellis kept his boat, I don't know.'

–

Lowri dozed uneasily, listening for the slightest sound and twice she was woken by a movement against the door, which – after a brief panic – she guessed might be a hedgehog or other small creature hunting for food.

The night seemed endless and she thought of the nights she had so easily slept, with the morning coming too soon and the temptation to stay a minute or two longer in bed was strong. On the uncomfortable floor and wrapped in a waterproof cape, she frequently screwed up her eyes, risked wasting a few seconds of her precious battery, and checked the time. The hands on her watch crawled reluctantly towards five o'clock.

She must have dozed then and she was disturbed by a scratchy sound outside the door. She grabbed her torch, her only weapon, and rose to a kneeling position, tense and frightened as she prepared for her attacker's return. There was no further movement and she sank back into her corner. It was getting light and her watch told her it was six o'clock.

She unpacked the sandwiches and poured herself some coffee. The food warmed and comforted her and even revived her anger a little. She shouted and kicked at the solid door 'Let me out! This has gone far enough!' She rubbed the dirt-encrusted window pane with her sleeve and looked out. The area she could see was empty and as fear returned, she began to sob. She pushed at the door, her shoulder ramming it, even though she knew it wouldn't open that way. Then she shouted some more, at the top of her voice, demanding, pleading, begging, even though she knew there was no one likely to hear her. It was anger and fear, not logic that lead her actions.

There was a knob on the inside and as she shouted again for whoever was there to let her out, she turned it, waggled it to and fro, pulled it, and suddenly the door opened. She stepped out and peered around, afraid there was someone waiting for her to emerge, but there was no one. It was silent apart from birdsong and the gentle, sibilant sound of the distant waves. Her purse was no longer around her neck, the crocheted chain had broken when the man had attacked her and she knew she needed it. She couldn't face going back inside for fear of being locked in again, but if the bicycle was no longer where she'd left it, she'd need money to get back to Cwm Derw.

Hauling a stone from a few yards away took time and she was afraid of the man returning, but she had to go back and before she did, she had to make sure the door couldn't be relocked. The stone rolled down over the step and wedged itself so the door couldn't be shut without moving it. She went inside and gathered her things, and ran out as though a thousand devils were at her heels and headed for where she had left the bicycle. As she had dreaded, it was gone.

She was chilled after the hours spent in the cold, damp place and she put on the cape for extra warmth, but the trowel and torch and the flask were no use to her now and she didn't want to be encumbered by carrying them. She put them under the brambles where she had left the bicycle and hurried on, eating the last of her sandwiches. She ran towards the road hoping to see a bus that would take her at least part of the way home. As she reached the road and turned right, Ken and two policemen came from the left and missed her.

As the hut came into view, Ken and the policemen ran towards it. The door was wide open and they were over-whelmed with disappointment when they looked inside and found it empty. They returned to the path wondering where to look next, when Ken saw her torch and flask. They all went back to look again at the hut.

'She was here, I'm sure of it,' Ken said. 'The floor is disturbed as though someone has been digging, looking for something, and there was a trowel near the torch and flask.' He left the police to continue their search and went back to Badgers Brook to ask Kitty if there was any news.

—

Dic was sitting on a fence looking down at Treweather's old farm that was now a muddy building site with new houses in various stages of completion. He went over the little they had learned: Bob had seen Lowri going up the road towards the bus stop on Kitty's bicycle, but from the corner she could have gone in one of several directions. No one saw her passing the shops and post office so had she turned away from the town? Around the back of the wood? But where had she been going?

His mind was filled with terrifying images. She might have found something that would incriminate someone for the crime for which Jimmy was serving a sentence. If it meant avoiding a prison sentence, then violence was a strong possibility. Even the mildest person was capable of hurting her if that was an alternative to prison. Why hadn't she told him what she was planning? He knew he had let her down. Restlessly he walked back to Badgers Brook, looking around the garden and the nearby woods, then he went to The Ship, where Marion and Betty were making sandwiches and filling flasks for the people searching.

People came and went off again, but there was no news, not even a single sighting to report. He sat near the fire and concentrated on people passing on the road that led to the top of the lane leading to Badgers Brook. He was only half listening to Marion, who was telling Bob and Colin about the rusty old key. Then he had a mental picture of the old hut he had often visited with his father and

Jimmy. Could she be there, searching for something? He was suddenly sure he was right.

'Bob,' he called, 'can you come with me? I have an idea of where she might be. In fact, I'm sure she's there.' Without explaining to the others, he ran from the pub and he and Bob drove to where Lowri had dismounted from Kitty's bicycle. Parking the car, Dic led Bob along the edge of the cliffs and up on to the hill, where, half-hidden in a shallow depression, was the hut.

'There's no sign of the bike,' Bob puffed.

'She's here, I know it.'

They ran to the hut and pushed open the door, calling her name, but there was nothing there and no sign of recent visitors. Dejected and with increasing anxiety, they returned to Badgers Brook. An hour passed and Dic was standing at the gate of Badgers Brook, restless, unable to keep still, when he decided that he would walk up the lane – he couldn't just hang around doing nothing. As he neared the bus stop, he saw her. She was standing, looking right and left to make sure the road was clear before running across. 'Lowri!' he called and ran towards her and hugged her, repeating her name, thanking the heavens she was safe. She clung to him as though she would never let go.

Tearfully she began to tell him what had happened, and as soon as she had explained where she had been, he took her inside, then hurried to The Ship to let everyone know she was safe.

Later, she repeated her story with greater detail as Marion wrapped her in blankets, plying her with hot tea and many hugs. Dic was there, unwilling to leave her even though she was apparently unharmed. The constable who had been one of those present when they searched the hut, looked solemn.

'And you say you didn't see this… er… man? You have no idea who he was?'

'He leaped on me for the doorway, I think. I wasn't aware of him coming inside, The wind was blowing the door a little, opening and closing it and I didn't worry when it grew dark and a shadow passed over me, I presumed it was no more than that. Then he landed on top of me, I was winded and terrified. He pushed my face into the floor and wrestled to get the key from my hand.'

'How did he know the key was in your hand, I wonder?' The policeman's voice was casual but his stare was intense. Lowri frowned. 'I don't know. Perhaps he'd been watching me?'

'But the room was very dark, and the key was what, an inch long? He must have had the eyes of an eagle, this… man.' It was now very clear he didn't believe her story.

'Perhaps he felt it when he pushed me over? Perhaps he grabbed my hand?'

'Well, did he? Grab your hand?'

'I don't remember. I was too terrified, thinking I was going to suffocate in the earth to think about what he was doing and why.'

'Surely you believe her, officer?' Dic asked.

Lowri stared at the policeman in alarm. 'You think I made all this up?'

'You want to bring attention to your father's situation, don't you?'

'Yes, but… that's rubbish! What it means is that someone doesn't like the way I'm searching for new evidence. I must be getting close! So catch him and make him talk! My father didn't steal that money, so someone else

193

must have!' Her voice was edging towards hysterical as the policeman snapped shut his notebook and stood up to leave. As he reached the door, he turned. 'Remember, Miss Vaughan, it's a serious matter to mislead the police and fake evidence.'

Lowri reached out and held Dic's arm. 'Why doesn't he believe me?'

Dic waited until the constable had closed the door behind him. 'I think he was being a bit cautious, that's all. Not jumping to the obvious conclusion. They'll look again at the hut and will see you were telling the truth. But Lowri, you must promise never to do something like that on your own. I'll go with you no matter how slight the hope of learning something.'

'And so will I!' a voice called from the doorway, and Ken walked in. 'Lowri, thank goodness you're safe! My darling girl, I've been so worried.' She stood and hugged him while Dic stood aside. 'I persuaded a man with a small motor boat to take me along the cliffs near that hut, in case you'd fallen. Thank goodness you aren't harmed.'

Later that evening, when she was bathed and fed and comforted and had slipped beneath fresh clean sheets, she went over everything that had happened once again to Marion.

'There was a funny smell about the man who held me down, but I can't think what it reminded me of.'

'Don't worry,' Marion said. 'It'll come back to you. Just sleep and try not to think about it any more tonight.'

Lowri lay there but the sequence of events passed through her mind time and again. It was midnight when she crept downstairs and made a hot drink in the hope it would help her settle.

Marion heard her and followed her down. They looked around the room with its carelessly abandoned items left by the hordes of people involved in the search: gum boots on the doormat; a coat left hanging on the banister; food wrapped and left on the kitchen table; cups and saucers belonging to Kitty, brought as the need arose. A coat belonging to Dic was hanging over the back of a kitchen chair and as Lowri looked at it she began to shake uncontrollably. 'Dic's coat! There on the chair. It reminded me… it's the old one he uses when he goes out into the mud and sand to find pieces of old boats for his carving,' she said, her teeth chattering with shock.

'It's all right, I'll get rid of it tomorrow. Is the filthy smell bothering you?' Marion asked in concern.

'That was what I smelt on the man who attacked me. Mud and seaweed. Marion, it must have been Dic who locked me in.'

'Come on, Lowri, that's crazy. That hut must have smelled of nothing else if it was used by fishermen. Bits of lug worms and dead fish used for bait, they're notorious for their smelly habits, fishermen.'

'It was he who knew where to find me, wasn't it?'

'No, your mother told the police. And it was Ken who found it first, wasn't it?'

'Yes, but he was led there by the police. Mam wouldn't have known exactly where, she'd never been there. Yet he, Dic, went straight there.'

'He knew it well. Didn't you tell me he used to go with his father and yours?'

'That was years ago.'

'But he's older than you and his memories would be stronger,' insisted Marion.

'It was Dic,' Lowri said again with a low groan of despair.

'Sleep!' Marion demanded, taking the cup from her shaking hands. 'Tomorrow you'll be thinking more clearly.' She led her friend back upstairs and gently covered her with the blankets. Tomorrow it would be easy to convince her this was nothing to do with her father, just a prank or someone objecting to her using the place. Perhaps now she'd accept what had happened to Jimmy and let things rest.

Nine

When Lowri woke the morning after her alarming adventure it took only seconds for her to remember it. 'Dic,' she muttered in growing dismay. Dic, who had always been her trusted friend. He'd locked her in and made sure she didn't find what she was looking for.

'Nonsense,' Marion said when she tried to discuss her conclusions with her over breakfast. 'How could it have been Dic? What, chance you seeing him and recognizing him? Of course it wasn't Dic. A smell of fishing on a man's clothes? The place was used by fishermen for heaven's sake! What else would you expect to smell except mud and seaweed and rotten fish? Roses and lavender? Come on, Lowri, this is all built up from nothing more than your imagination.'

'There had to be something to find, or why did someone search through my belongings? And why did someone follow me and lock me in the hut?'

'Perhaps no one did.'

'What do you mean, don't you believe me either?' Lowri looked stricken with the shock of her friend doubting her.

'I believe you couldn't open the door, Lowri. I really do. But you said the wind almost closed it several times and it wasn't locked when you tried it in the morning, was it? Don't you think that the wind might have blown it a bit fiercely and it got jammed? It's in a place where it gets the worst of the weather, and these things do happen. My mother has a lot of trouble with her back gate in the winter.'

'It was locked. The man – who I *couldn't* have imagined – lay over me and forced the key from my hand. I couldn't see him, only smell him. He pushed my face into the earth and ran out, locking the door.' She pointed to the grazes on her face. 'And these aren't imaginary, are they?'

'You did say you fell.' Marion sounded apologetic.

'I fell on to my knees, *these* happened when my face was pressed into the ground.' Tearfully, she looked at her friend. 'Please, Marion, don't say I'm making this up.'

'Sorry. I do believe you, I was just trying to see it as the police did. A man came in, attacked you, stole the key from you and locked the door. But why believe it's anything to do with your father? It could have been boys, planning to sneak in and have a sly smoke. Perhaps it was a tramp who used the place for time to time? He would have been alarmed to find someone there and perhaps he panicked. You said it's been repaired, and there's a fireplace, so it would make a comfortable place for someone who hasn't a home to rest a while. There are plenty of explanations, so why automatically presume it's connected with your father?'

The word obsession wasn't spoken but it hovered in the air and made Lowri even more convinced. 'I want to go back and look again,' she said.

'No! You have to keep away from there, and you must stop fantasizing about being your father's saviour, riding to the rescue on a white stallion!'

That made Lowri smile. 'Is that what I've been imagining?' she said with a wry smile. 'Then heaven help my poor father. I can't even ride.'

'Promise me you won't go there again.' Seeing the determination on Lowri's face, she added weakly, 'At least, not on your own.'

'I can't get there without a long walk. On top of everything else, I've lost Kitty's bicycle.'

Kitty called to see how she was after her ordeal and she had news. 'The police found my bike,' she told them. 'Down by Treweather's old farmhouse it was. They think someone was walking home and couldn't resist the chance of a ride.'

'Thank goodness for that,' Lowri said. 'I'm so sorry I lost it.'

'Don't worry. And if you want to borrow it again, you know where it is. But not for anything dangerous, mind.'

'I've been warning her about going off on her own,' Marion said, pouring tea for Kitty. 'She has to forget trying to do better than the police, and get on with her life.'

'Sorry I am, but she's right,' Kitty said. 'Now in future, if you want to go off exploring, tell Bob and he'll go with you if you can't persuade that handsome young man of yours.'

'Which handsome young man would that be?' Lowri asked. 'Ken's parents weren't exactly welcoming when I met them, so I doubt whether Ken will be around much longer. Another false friend,' she added with a sigh.

–

Betty Connors was less than pleased with her new barman but was hesitant to ask him to leave in case she couldn't find a replacement. When Ernie was there he worked fast and efficiently and was good with the customers, but he was almost always late and regularly asked to leave early as he had an 'occasion' to attend. On most days she had to do most of the clearing up and setting up and Ernie would run in, bending double in his haste to get there and clutching his camera and the various leather bags containing equipment, apologizing and promising to make up the time.

It was Colin who finally alerted her to what these 'occasions' were.

'Have you seen the way he's always taking snaps of us in the bar and around the streets?' he asked her one day.

'I know he's keen on photography, he never moves without his camera.'

'Then he finds out who the people are and knocks on doors and tries to sell copies,' Colin said. 'Pesters a bit he does.'

'What a cheek.' Then she laughed. 'I think he hopes to earn a living from his photographs and he's using us to get himself started. So these "occasions" of his are weddings?'

'And coach parties setting off on a day trip. And even funerals,' Bob added.

'That seems a bit tactless to me,' commented Betty.

'I don't think he gets bookings, even for weddings. He just goes along and snaps away, taking less formal shots that the professionals don't bother to take, then offers them for sale. Bit of an embarrassment for some of the grieving families,' Bob said.

'I'll have a word, but only about his bad timekeeping. What he does outside The Ship is nothing to do with me.'

'Someone came to see you one day while you were out, Ernie took a photograph of him. Want to see it?'

Betty looked at the black and white study of the man she only knew as Alun. He was standing at the bar, a glass in his hand and he was talking to Colin.

'He's the man who helped me when I fell down in the cellar,' she said.

'Thought it was him. There aren't many men that big and with such a wild beard. D'you know who he is? He dealt with the lunchtime crowd like an expert. Pity he doesn't want a job as your barman, eh?'

Ernie was apologetic when Betty spoke to him about his unreliability. 'Sorry I am, but I want to get myself known to the local papers. The photographer they have now is getting old and I want to be his replacement.'

'That's fine, but while you work for me, you have to work the hours I pay you for, right?'

'I'll do my best,' he promised half-heartedly. 'But these wedding and funerals are rarely in the afternoon. And I'm thinking of doing the dinner dances and the like. They're popular and most people like a memento of the occasion.'

'Fine,' Betty said again. 'But not if you're working at The Ship.'

'What if I work on a casual basis, come when I can?'

Betty went to the till and counted out his wages. 'All or nothing,' she said and he took the money and his insurance forms and left. What she had intended to be a reprimand had ended with her being once again without a barman.

–

Marion went to see Dic at the shop, where he sat working on a model of a small rowing boat. 'I suppose you know Lowri believed it was you who locked her in the hut?' she said at once.

Dic put down the half-finished boat and stared at her. 'Surely not! I'd never do anything to hurt her, she must know that?'

'I'm worried,' she told him. 'You know how I feel about this crusade of hers. It's time Lowri gave up hoping for a reprieve for her father, it's distorted her thinking for too long. I've always believed it better that Lowri kept away from you and your family, to start again and make new friends, but it isn't happening. She's obviously in distress and there's no sign of it ending. Because of her determination to tell everyone she meets that he's innocent, she isn't making friends. Can't you help her?'

'When she believes it was me who locked her in that hut? That I attacked her and frightened her? No, Marion. Sadly, Lowri will have to come to an understanding in her own time.'

She could see he was distressed. 'You won't even try?'

'When she needs me I'll be here, but I think she will have to come looking for me. Perhaps Ken's the one to help her?'

'She won't see him, either. His mother made it clear that she didn't want the family mixing with "criminals". He's apologized but she's incapable of forgiveness, she thinks the whole world is against her.'

'I'm very fond of Lowri and it makes me sad to see her unhappy, but at present I can't do anything. If I try to see her I'll make everything worse and I have to think of the children. I don't want Katie and Sarah-Jane upset by arguments and accusations. So I'm keeping away.'

Aware that was his final word, Marion went to see Ken, who didn't offer much hope either.

–

On a sudden whim that Wednesday, her half-day, Lowri borrowed Kitty's bicycle and went back to the lonely shepherd's hut. Leaving the bicycle as before, under the bramble bush, now covered with hard green fruit, promising a good harvest. With a torch and spare battery, not knowing what she intended to do, she walked towards the spot from where she would have her first view of the building. She was afraid but knew she had to face her devils and go back.

From the chimney, which was built of stone on the outside of the walls, a thin column of smoke rose up into the sky. She stopped, filled with fear that made it impossible to run. Slowly she calmed down. What should she do? She dared not go inside and neither did she want to meet anyone who was using it. But she had come to confront her fear and standing here wouldn't achieve that.

Showing courage on her face that she didn't feel, she walked towards the door. She knocked, and in a loud voice, called, 'Who's there?' The door opened she was suddenly face to face with Dic.

'What are you doing here?' she demanded, backing away from the door.

'The same as you presumably. Looking for whatever made someone lock you in.'

'There's smoke coming from the chimney.'

'That's nothing to do with me. I think someone stayed here last night. Not a shepherd though,' he said, smiling. 'There's a box of fishing bait and a few hooks here, so it's most likely to have been a fisherman, just like your father and mine.' He stared at her pointedly and added, 'There's a strong smell in here of mud and dead fish, but not from me.' He stepped out and walked a few paces towards her. 'I'll leave if you want to look inside.'

A memory of the man leaping at her and holding her face into the earth overwhelmed her and she backed further away. He was so familiar and she wanted to run to him, be comforted, but she mustn't succumb to those feelings. She was no longer a child and he was no longer a friend. Turning away, she hurried off.

'Wait, Lowri. Come back and talk to me.'

'Go inside you mean? So you can lock me in again?' She began to run. When she was brave enough to look back, he was standing by the doorway, a look of such disappointment on his face that she almost turned back. The bicycle was where she had left it and she rode to Badgers Brook and locked herself in. This was where she felt safe and brave and defiant. Comfort oozed from its walls, its constant gentle warmth relaxed her, knowing the house was keeping all dangers at bay.

Ken called at the post office the following morning where Lowri was serving the regular Thursday customers, and stood talking to Stella until the shop emptied. Then he came across, reached for her hands that were busy restoring order after the busy hour, and held them. 'Come out with me tonight. I want to get a few things clear,' he said.

'I'll make some tea, and there's a few cakes and Colin's got to get ready for work and Scamp will want his walk…' Stella babbled in the background as she disappeared into the living room behind the shop leaving them alone.

'We keep getting distracted,' Ken said, 'and I know we can be friends, loving friends, if only we can clear our way though the tangle of other people's problems.'

'Like my father's, you mean?'

'Like your father's,' he agreed. 'I'm sympathetic, but I know that you can do nothing to help. You just have to deal with it and, quite honestly, I believe that's the best way of helping him too.' Without waiting for agreement, he left, promising to be at Badgers Brook at seven.

'Good friends you've got here in Cwm Derw,' Stella gently warned Lowri, 'don't push them away. Meet Ken and don't try to untangle the tangles, just treat him as a friend, enjoy his company and be happy. It's what we all want for you.'

'Untangle the tangles?' Lowri gave a crooked smile. 'You were listening, weren't you?'

'Of course I was. Can't miss the chance of a bit of romance, can I?'

So when Ken called that evening, they went for a walk. After a talk in which they were both honest, they returned to Badgers Brook more relaxed. She wanted to see him again and he had made it clear it was what he wanted too, despite the attitude of his parents.

'I can't give up on my father,' she told him. 'And how can I cope with your parents' attitude?'

'I don't pretend to believe your father's case,' he said, 'but I'll help with any enquires you want to make.'

She wondered if she could settle for that. 'Do you believe that I was locked in that hut?'

'Of course I do. But like Marion, I don't see that the incident is anything to do with your father.' With an arm around her shoulders holding her close, he went on, 'Let your father serve his sentence and then *he* can search for the truth.'

They learned a lot about each other during their discussion and were surprised to realize they both enjoyed dancing. So, over the next few weeks, they saw much of each other and had great fun out dancing. It seemed that Lowri's life was improving.

Although there was no second invitation to visit Ken's parents, Lowri asked how they were, and he talked about them naturally. Gradually she began to unwind the tensions she had suffered for so long. Being more relaxed in Ken's company helped her to open up to others, and made it easier for others to treat her normally. She was aware of being happy and she glowed.

They went to a big dressy dance in a ballroom one evening and she wore a new dress: red, fairly low cut and with a skirt that clung to her hips before flaring out at the hem. It had been expensive, one of Nerys Bowen's top of the range. That night she and Ken won a spot prize. In the middle of a quick step the music stopped and the dancers stood still. The room was darkened apart from a spotlight that was shining on their excited faces. The compère led the applause as the lights came back and he walked towards them with a bottle of wine for Ken and a bouquet of roses for Lowri.

It had been a wonderful evening. She and Ken had walked out of the hall with congratulations following them and when they reached the car their kiss was like no other. It cemented their relationship and as summer rolled on they became inseparable. Ken would be waiting for her each Wednesday and on Sunday they would spend the day together.

She managed to tear herself away from him to visit her mother twice. She saw nothing of Dic and his absence carried sadness too. She missed him and wished things hadn't gone so terribly wrong between them. Like her father, she had to accept there was no chance of a reprieve there either.

One Sunday afternoon, when Marion was visiting her family, Ken came to Badgers Brook for lunch. He was less animated than usual. Instead of sharing incidents at work, making her laugh at some of the things he and his staff had dealt with, he was formal and over-polite, so much so that her heart began to fill with dread. He was going to tell her it was over, he didn't want to see her again.

In reaction her own attitude became less easy. She served the coffee and took the dishes into the kitchen, filled the sink with hot water from the large kettle that stood beside the fire, implying that he had outstayed his welcome, that she was impatient for him to leave.

'Is something wrong?' he asked, carrying the coffee back and putting it on the big kitchen table. He took her arm and coaxed her to sit beside him. 'Has something happened?'

'Like what for example?'

'Have you and Dic renewed your friendship?'

'Hardly. In fact, I've been wondering if you had something on *your* mind. Is everything all right?'

'I hope so.'

The vagueness of his reply didn't reassure her. 'Perhaps we should forgo the walk we'd planned and make it another day.'

'Do you want to?' Then he gave an exasperated sigh. 'Come on, Lowri, we can talk around each other in circles like this all afternoon! Let's go on that walk!' He helped clear the dishes and they set off across the lane and through the wood.

Lowri was still uneasy, expecting him to explain why he didn't want to see her again. She went through the past week in her mind, remembering the fun they'd had at the community hall where they had danced to records, and on the Saturday at the more dressy affair where they had been a rather fine band playing. Had she said something he might have misunderstood? She had worn her beautiful red dress and knew it had been wrong for the local dance at the small church hall. Had she embarrassed him? Shown a lack of taste? Surely he'd have told her, not decided to leave her? Preparing a response in her mind, determined not to show her hurt, wondering what he would say, how he would tell her 'goodbye'. As though the words had already been said, she walked a distance away from him, stopping to look at the berries beginning to swell on the hawthorn and the ripening sloes on the blackthorn.

'This way,' he called, changing direction. She followed him to the spot above the hill, looking down on the building site that was once Treweather's farm. 'There are some small bungalows for sale,' he told her. 'Shall we go and look?'

Surprised, but curious enough to want to see for herself what was being built, she walked with him down the hill to where the old farmhouse still stood. Beside it was the tumbled remains of a farmworker's cottage, now without a roof and about to be demolished. The bungalows were across a field and Ken went over and spoke to the watchman. He was expecting Ken and invited them to go inside the most complete bungalow, while he stood outside the door.

They admired the neat, two-bedroom property while trying to imagine it complete and without the chaos of mud and rubble and piles of materials in what would one day be the garden.

'It's beautiful,' Lowri said. 'So modern and, once it's cleaned up, it will be so easy to run.'

'Could you imagine living here?'

'Oh yes. Anyone would be thrilled to own a home like this.'

'Marry me,' Ken said.

'What did you say?'

'I said marry me. I have the option to buy this, I only have to get your approval and it's ours.'

'I thought you were going to tell me "goodbye".'

'Lowri, I'll never say goodbye. I want us to raise a family and grow old together.'

'And your parents? Are they happy about this?'

'They don't matter. Your parents, my parents, they don't have to be consulted. It's what you and I want. I love you, Lowri. Marry me and we'll have a family of our own.' He smiled and stepped towards her, about to take her in his arms. He was shocked when she stepped back and shook her head.

'I can't marry you.'

'But I thought… Don't you feel the same way as me?'

'What about your parents? I can't marry you without their approval. At least their acceptance of me. Can you imagine what a wedding it would be? My father in prison, my mother in tears wishing he were there, and your parents refusing to turn up? It would be a farce.'

'All right, then what about a register office wedding with all our friends there to wish us luck? What's wrong with that?'

'I'm sorry, Ken. But until we can do it properly, with everyone important to us wishing us well, it wouldn't seem like a wedding at all.'

'By "doing it properly" I hope you don't mean when your father has served his time?'

She didn't reply, reeling with the unexpected proposal. Ken sighed and led her towards the doorway where the security guard was waiting. He thanked the man and hurried back up the hill towards the wood, striding fast and ignoring her attempts to keep up. He didn't speak to her until they were at the edge of the wood. 'I see. You're determined to serve your father's sentence with him, are you?'

'No, of course not.'

'Then you're letting my parents ruin everything for us?'

'Not that either.'

'Then you obviously don't love me enough to trust me with your life.'

She dared not admit that her first thought when he had proposed, was how Dic would take the news. 'It's too soon,' she said. 'We haven't known each other long enough,' she said.

'It's long enough for me,' he said. 'And I thought it was the same for you. I just didn't realize how badly you've allowed your father's situation to twist your mind.'

They walked the rest of the way in silence and he muttered a brief goodbye and left.

'Surely it wasn't a permanent goodbye?' Lowri asked Marion later that evening. 'I was asking for time, but I didn't make that clear.'

'It seems to me you aren't sure of your feelings for him.'

'I'm not completely sure, no. And I am worried about his parents' attitude. It would be difficult to live with their continuing disapproval.'

'Forget about his parents and think about how you feel about Ken. Love is a strong emotion, it makes you give up on things you might once have thought important. People do things in the name of love they wouldn't normally dream of doing. Loving someone, really loving them, is all consuming.'

She spoke so emotionally that Lowri asked, 'Is this how you feel about your married man?'

'I'd do absolutely anything for him. But this is about you. Lowri, if you don't feel like that you were right to say no. But,' Marion added firmly, 'that doesn't mean love won't grow. Give it time, and see how you feel in a month or so.'

Lowri knew that unless she could remove Dic from her thoughts, the guilty feeling that she was letting him down and owed him some sort of loyalty, an all consuming love for Ken would never happen. She couldn't tell Marion that. She couldn't even understand it herself.

Stella was blatantly curious to know what happened when Lowri and Ken met. When Lowri told her of Ken's proposal she began to cheer but stopped when she saw the seriousness of Lowri's expression. 'You didn't say yes? Why not, don't you love him?'

'I don't know, Stella. His parents would never agree to meet mine, would they? And his mother made it clear she wouldn't welcome me into the family. I don't think I could live with her disapproval.'

'Go on, marry the man, just to spite her, miserable old bat!'

Lowri laughed. 'That would teach her to be rude to Lowri Vaughan, wouldn't it?' Then more soberly she added, 'There can't be a worse reason to marry someone, than that.'

'There's no hurry, let the weeks pass and see how you feel later. Nice young man he is, mind. And he can afford a brand new bungalow an' all.'

'He is very nice. He's kind and caring and all those things, but—'

'Ah, it's the "but" that counts, isn't it? Wait till you're sure, girl. Best to wait till you're sure.'

Lowri wrote to her mother and explained what had happened, making light of it, as though it was amusing and not serious. Putting her thoughts down helped, but she was aware of having no one with whom she could talk it through. She missed Dic's parents and Dic himself, although she could hardly discuss her feelings for another man with him. Dic's mother, her once loved Auntie Cathy, would have understood and helped her to make sense of her jumbled emotions.

She left the post office at five thirty and saw a woman standing outside. The woman turned and said softly, 'Hello Lowri, my dear. How are you?'

It was Dic's mother and for a moment it seemed Auntie Cathy had appeared out of Lowri's longing to see her. She wanted to run to her and be enveloped in a loving hug as she had so many times before. In fact she actually ran a couple of steps, but then she stopped, tightened her mouth that was beginning a smile and replied, 'I'm well, but no thanks to you and Uncle Jack.'

'Would you spare me a little time? Please, dear. I so much want to talk to you. I have the car and I can either drive you home or we could go somewhere and eat. I remember you were always hungry. Or has that changed with so many other things?'

Lowri was confused. The confrontation was without warning, but she knew she didn't want to take this woman into Badgers Brook. The house was only for friends. Auntie Cathy was no longer one of those.

'The café is open until six,' she said ungraciously.

'That doesn't give us much time, would you come to a restaurant I know?'

Lowri nodded, trying to show disapproval in the minute gesture.

They drove a few miles and Cathy stopped near a restaurant in the village of Cowbridge. They ordered their meal without attempting to start a conversation. Lowri didn't know what to say to this once loved person, and Cathy was afraid of saying something that would make her guest walk out.

Finally, as they waited for their meal to be served, Cathy said, 'Uncle Jack has been going through every book, every piece of paper since your father's imprisonment, searching for some evidence that points to someone else.'

'So now he's satisfied he was right and my father robbed him?' Still on the defensive, she started to rise as the waitress approached with their meal. Cathy put a hand on her arm and gently persuaded her to sit.

Still holding her arm, stroking it affectionately, she said, 'Hear me out and then I'll take you home,' she promised. She turned Lowri's arm over and touched the scar on her inner arm. 'D'you remember when you did this? It was when Dic was teaching you to play cricket and you ran, tripped, and caught it on the garden fence.'

Lowri said nothing. Remembering Dic's concern made her unexpectedly weepy: the way he had bathed and bandaged her and given her sweets to make her feel better. Like a big brother, always there to protect her. Life had been so perfect then.

'You were his bridesmaid when he married Rosemary,' Cathy reminded her. 'When you were very small and he started going out with his first girlfriend you cried because you wanted to marry him yourself, even though you were only about seven or eight.'

'I loved Rosemary and remember the excitement when Sarah-Jane and then Katie were born. I was broken-hearted when she died. Influenza. It seemed so unreal.'

Reminiscences followed one after the other and barriers broke down as they talked. Cathy told her that Jack hadn't given up searching for the truth. 'At the time of your father's arrest the evidence was so clear, the police were convinced, and anger made him accept what everyone else believed. When the anger and hurt had cooled he began to think more clearly. He knew your father so well; they had gone through three dangerous years together in the Navy. He knew then Jimmy couldn't have damaged the business he'd helped to build. They were both so proud of what they'd achieved. Once he decided the evidence was false he began to look through every detail, going back to the beginning.

'Whoever had stolen the money was clever. Leaving evidence pointing to your father gave him a chance to get away. Perhaps that was all he'd intended, to be given enough time to get away. He had us all fooled.'

'You're talking about Ellis Owen, aren't you?'

'Maybe, but now we'll never know.'

'I think he's still alive. I've see him twice.'

Expecting the usual sympathetic mutterings she was startled when Cathy nodded and said, 'If anyone could defeat the sea Ellis Owen could.' Hope swelled in Lowri and the months of anger towards this gentle, loving woman drifted away.

It was such a relief for Lowri to be able to talk to Cathy that hours passed, firstly in the restaurant, then walking around the small, elegant town. They exchanged news, Lowri telling Cathy about the friends she had made since coming to Cwm Derw. She made only a brief mention of Ken Hardy who, Cathy remarked, 'Sounds nice.'

They drove back to Cwm Derw and passed the post office as Lowri gave directions to Badgers Brook. Lowri pointed across the road to where a woman was pushing a child in a pushchair. 'Look! That's Marion, the girl who shares the house with me. She's walking very purposefully. I wonder where she's going? She's an ideal person to share the house, but very secretive about her family.'

Cathy looked and frowned. 'That's funny, she looks familiar. What did you say her name was?'

'Marion. Marion Davies.'

'What does she do? I'm sure I've seen her somewhere. A shop, maybe?'

'She cleans for several people, but no one outside Cwm Derw.'

'I've got it! Marion Davies, yes, that's her. She cleaned for us for a while but your Uncle Jack had to let her go. There was some trouble and she only stayed a week, but I can't remember what happened. Jack will remember. I'll ask him – that's if *I* remember. With all we've talked about this evening, and so many bridges crossed, I doubt I will. It can't be important anyway. It was years ago.'

Parking in the lane outside Badgers Brook, Cathy said, 'There's one more thing I have to tell you. Our little Katie is not well. She has a touch of tonsillitis and she keeps asking for you. Dic thought it better not to ask you to call.' She looked at Lowri adding, 'He explained about you being shut in that old hut your father and your Uncle Jack used and thinking it was him.'

'It was the smell. It was the same as that old jacket of his.'

'Dic loves you, Lowri, you know that, surely? He's never do anything to hurt you.'

Loves me? she mused. Love is such an overused word with so many meanings.

'Ellis Owen used the place too, didn't he?'

'Yes. He was a keen fisherman, in fact he loved all out-of-doors activities. Climbing, walking, camping, boats, swimming. D'you know he wanted to try to swim the Channel? And to sail across the Atlantic to America?'

'Perhaps it was some such grand idea that made him steal from us.'

'If he did, dear. Jack no longer believes in your father's involvement, but he hasn't found evidence pointing to anyone else. Even if he suspects Ellis, we have no proof and I doubt we ever will now, despite Jack's efforts.'

'If Ellis hadn't died on that stormy day there'd be a chance for Dad. Do you think he could have survived?'

'Possible but unlikely, dear. If he had, you wouldn't have been the only one to have seen him. He was well known around the hunting, shooting, fishing paternity, wasn't he?' She hugged Lowri and said briskly, 'Now, will you come and see us?'

'If you're sure Uncle Jack believes Dad is innocent.'

'He's absolutely certain and like me, he misses you dreadfully. And little Katie?'

'I'll go to the shop and see her there.'

'Thank you.'

'Can we meet again, before I come to see Uncle Jack?'

'Of course. Shall I write to you?'

'Phone me just after the post office closes. It takes me quite a few minutes to get my coat on and get ready to leave.'

They parted with emotional regrets and promises and Lowri was tearful when she went inside. The place was empty as she expected, having seen Marion with her little sister. So when Marion returned and told her she'd been at the pictures, she was surprised. 'I saw you less than an hour ago, with Sandra,' she said.

'Where did you see me?'

'We were passing the post office and you were walking past with Sandra in a pushchair. You were in a hurry. Meeting someone, were you?'

'Who were you with, Ken?'

'No. Oh Marion, so much has happened.' She told her about the surprising evening and how happy she was at the prospect of having Auntie Cathy and Uncle Jack back in her life.

'And Dic too?'

'I was wrong, you were right. He wouldn't hurt or frighten me.' It wasn't until much later that she remembered Marion's evasiveness when she asked where she had been and why she had lied.

At breakfast, Lowri was unable to resist asking who it was Marion had been meeting. 'Your secret love, was it?'

'Hardly, with a two-year-old in tow.'

'Then who?' Lowi stood and waited for Marion to explain, her determination to be answered clear on her face. She was increasingly irritated by the fact that she opened up almost completely to Marion, but her friend was reluctant to do the same.

Marion sat down and looked away from her. In a low voice she asked, 'If I tell you something will you promise not to repeat it?'

'Of course I promise.'

'Sandra isn't my mother's youngest child. She's mine.'

'Yours? But I don't understand? Is she the child of this married man who's supposed to be getting a divorce?'

'Yes. And he *is* getting a divorce.'

'Come on, Marion. Sandra is two years old. How long are you going on believing that?'

'Typical! The less you know the more you have to say! If you knew more you'd be too busy phoning the… the… his wife, rather than worrying about me!'

Lowri frowned. 'For a moment there, I thought you were going to say I'd be phoning the police. Is he in trouble, this secret lover?'

'No, of course not. I was afraid I'd mention his wife's name, that's all. Keep out of it, Lowri. You and your overactive imagination! It's none of your business.'

'Who is he, this ardent lover who is promising you everything and giving nothing?'

'You don't know him.'

'Why are you protecting him? What can you hope to get out of this? Two, three years or more, and you still believe him? How many more years are you going to waste?'

'Shut up! Just shut up! Stop poking your nose into my affairs. You and I share this house and that's all. Stay out of the rest of my life, it's nothing to do with you! Now, I'm going out to meet my future husband. And here's something to keep that inquisitive mind of yours busy – I'm leaving Badgers Brook at the end of this month and I can't wait to get away from you.'

Hiding her dismay at the appalling way the morning had begun, Lowri spoke quietly and calmly, 'You have to tell Connie and Geoff, they are your landlords, not me. I'm only a friend.'

'Yes, and you're a fine one to talk about false friends, because that's what you are, Lowri Vaughan, a false friend!'

Ten

Lowri stared at the door through which Marion had just left. She was devastated by the speed at which her curiosity had developed into such an angry scene. Was she expecting too much of a friendship by asking – no – by demanding to know about Marion's private life? She hadn't the right. Marion was not a friend of many years, in fact, she hadn't been a very important part of her life until the trouble with her father had alienated so many people she'd previously considered friends. Marion had supported her when no one else had, and agreed to share the cost of Badgers Brook which she could not have otherwise considered. Now she had ruined it by her unreasonable curiosity.

It was as she sat there surrounded by the detritus of breakfast that she remembered Dic's mother recognizing Marion and explaining that she had once worked for them. Another of Marion's secrets. She thought back over the months they had shared the house, remembering odd things, small and unimportant at the time, but building a picture that was puzzling. It's no wonder curiosity got the better of me, she thought.

Marion seemed to know more about Ellis Owen that she should, remarking on his love for boats and climbing and the great outdoors. Where would she have learned that? And why hadn't she told her that she had once worked for Auntie Cathy and Uncle Jack? She knew Jack Morris had been her father's partner and the cause of her father's imprisonment, so why hadn't she mentioned knowing him? Also, if she had cleaned for them, why hadn't Dic recognized Marion? Again she was swamped with doubts about Dic. She had revised her doubts after her meeting with his mother, but the suspicions wouldn't go away. As soon as one puzzle was cleared up another appeared.

Auntie Cathy had seemed genuinely glad to see her but had said very little about Uncle Jack. Had she been pretending when she said he no longer believed her father had stolen from him? Did he still believe her father was dishonest? She was surrounded by false friends and they all had one thing in common: complicity in the arrest of her father, and that had to include Auntie Cathy.

Leaving the dishes on the kitchen table, she set off for the bus at the end of the lane, edgy and deeply unhappy. No Ken, certainly no Dic, and after an evening of hope, no Auntie Cathy and Uncle Jack either. There was no one she could trust except her mother, and she had given up, accepted her father's imprisonment.

She had to find out who had taken the money her father was accused of stealing. No one else believed in him and although she was completely alone she refused to give up. The hut. It had to be something to do with the hut. Frightening as the thought was, she knew she had to go there again, and this time, dig up the whole floor if necessary to find out why the key had been so important.

—

Marion watched from the wood opposite Badgers Brook and listened until the bus arrived and the sound of it had faded as it headed for the main road of Cwm Derw with Lowri on board; then she went back inside the house. It was fifteen minutes to nine o'clock and she had half an hour to kill. She cleared the dishes, brought in a few logs for the fire and filled the coal scuttle; automatic tasks that needed little thought. At fifteen minutes past the hour there was a gentle tap on the door overlooking the garden and she opened it and fell into the man's arms.

'I think it's time to move on,' she said a few moments later. 'Lowri is beginning to ask too many questions. Gossip flies like a whirlwind in a place like Cwm Derw and Lowri working at the post office gives it the best start. Your wife could easily pick up on a few suspicions.'

'We need a while longer. Just a few weeks and everything will be sorted and we can leave.'

'I've told her I'm leaving Badgers Brook.'

'Where will you go?'

'With you. Won't we be leaving soon?'

'Not yet. There are still some arrangements to make. But very soon.'

'Back to Mam's then, I suppose.'

'It won't be for long,' he promised, holding her tight, kissing her cheek, her chin, her lips. 'Just a few things to sort out and we'll be together without having to hide.'

Breathlessly, she asked, 'Have you bought the boat?'

'Not yet, but I think I've found the right one. She's in good condition and the owner has died. His widow wants a quick sale and she's no idea of the real value. I think I'll have a bargain. That means more money to get us started when we reach Spain. You'll have to buy her though, just in case I'm seen and word gets back to "she who must be obeyed". She'd take everything if she found out I was leaving.'

'I'm so excited. I only hope Sandra will be happy and won't miss Mam and the others too much.'

'You're her mother, of course she'll be happy.'

Before he left, she handed him some money. 'This is the money from cashing in my savings certificates.' He hugged her. 'It's going to be so wonderful, my darling, just you and me, and our lovely daughter.'

'Soon?'

'Very soon,' he promised.

—

True to her promise, Lowri planned to go and see Katie as soon as the post office closed. She bought a pair of slippers for each child and also some sweets and two small, locally made floppy dolls. As well as wanting to please Katie and Sarah-Jane, she knew she would be glad of the distraction before facing Dic and apologizing for mistrusting him. She had to tell him she was sorry, and hide that uneasiness, that niggle of doubt about his honesty. She wished she could be so sure of him that pretending would be easy, but she wasn't. She mistrusted him and at the same time, grieved for the loss of his support.

She stepped outside as Stella locked the door behind her and from a car at the kerb, Ken stepped out with flowers in his arms. 'These are for you. I'm sorry I behaved like a spoilt child the other evening – I'm truly sorry. Will you come out and let me show you just how much?'

'Ken, I can't. I've promised to go and see Katie, she's ill and I… I promised,' she ended lamely.

'I see. Dic is more important that the man who loves you and wants to spend all his life with you.' He laughed then and thrust the flowers towards her. 'There I go again.

I have to confess it, I'm jealous of your affection for Dic and his little brood.'

'There's no need. I've known Dic Morris all my life, and he's like a big brother. That's all.'

'As long as you're sure. Shall I meet you tomorrow? Pictures maybe? No more talk about marriage until you are ready. All right?'

'Please, Ken. I'd like that.'

She refused a lift, trying to keep Dic and Ken as separate parts of her life and he waited until her bus arrived. The bus seemed unusually slow, rumbling through the streets and along the country roads, anxious as she was to arrive before Katie had been put to bed. The second part of her journey seemed to last for ever but eventually she knocked on the side door of the shop. It was opened to the sound of laughter, as the two girls listened to a record of 'The Laughing Policeman' – an old one but still one of their favourites.

Dic's eyes lit up when he saw her and he stood back to allow her to enter. She had no time to make her apologies. 'Katie, Sarah-Jane, look who's here,' he called and the girls ran to hug her while the infectious laughter of the policeman continued in the background. Dic hugged her briefly. 'I'm so pleased you could come.'

'I'm sorry about—' she began but he hushed her and shook his head.

'There's no need for explanations. I understand,' he said.

There was no time for more. As the record ended, she took the presents from her basket, one at a time, and laughed at the pleasure they brought to the little girls. The slippers fitted perfectly and the dolls were taken to the toy box where clothes were selected for them. Lowri was not a good needlewoman but she managed to alter a few dresses to fit the floppy dolls. It was late before everything settled and the girls were in bed, their slippers tucked under the bed, the new dolls on their pillows beside them.

Instead of another attempt at an apology, Lowri said, 'Marion and I have had a terrible row. She's leaving Badgers Brook at the end of the month, in fact, I don't know whether she'll be there when I get home.'

'Will you be all right on your own, if she isn't?'

'Of course. I feel completely safe and happy there. Even after someone searched my room, I've never felt a moment's unease. The walls seem to wrap themselves around me and cushion me against any fears I might have.'

'What was the quarrel about? You and Marion seem so compatible.'

'We are, as long as I tell her everything and ask her nothing. She's so secretive and I thought we'd been friends long enough for her to trust me.'

'Is she embarrassed abut her family? There are eight children there and perhaps she finds that people criticize her parents in some way? You know better than most how children suffer because of their parents. Maybe having a two-year-old sister is embarrassing?'

'Well, actually, Marion told me in confidence that Sandra is her child. The father being this mysterious man who is married and promising to leave his wife for her.'

'You doubt that?'

'Dic, I'm in such a miserable state that I doubt everyone.'

'I can understand that, but why me?'

'You smell of the mud and dead fish I smelt in the hut when I was attacked and locked in.'

He laughed and she reluctantly joined in. 'Whatever happens don't doubt me. I care for you very much and would never do anything to harm you in the slightest way. I promise you.'

She felt a blush colouring her cheeks. Was this what she wanted to hear? That he cared? Auntie Cathy said he loved her. What an overused word. Love was offered on many levels and didn't necessarily mean a thing.

'I'm going to see Jake again on Wednesday,' he told her. 'Will you come? He has some wood that I might be able to use. He's an interesting man, we can have a cup of tea and a chat.'

'Only if we take a flask!' she replied with a smile. 'I've seen the way he "washes" those filthy mugs of his.'

He couldn't drive her home as the children were in bed and he watched from the doorway until she climbed on to the bus, carrying Ken's flowers, waving until the bus was out of sight.

He felt light-hearted, thankful that she had faced him after her unfounded fears and he lay awake for a long time wishing futile wishes, dreaming impossible dreams. Eleven years difference and a marriage and two children. It was hopeless to dream of more than being her big brother, but dreams are impossible to control and he slept and dreamed some more.

–

The house was empty and dark when she reached Badgers Brook. It seemed Marion had moved out already – not even giving it until the end of the week. Using her torch to guide her in, she lit the gas light in the kitchen and then the living room. Despite her assurances to Dic, it was strange knowing there was no one there but herself, and the darkness was a little intimidating. She turned on the wireless and felt better when the sound of dance music filled the room.

She prepared for bed, hugging her dressing gown around her, then made her usual cocoa. Forgetfully, she took down two cups and felt a deep sadness as she returned one to its shelf. She would have to find another lodger but until then she would manage on her own and treat it like a challenge. She told herself that she must never refuse a challenge.

She used a candle to light her way to bed and couldn't resist glancing into Marion's room. In the flickering candlelight she saw the bed was made, the wardrobe doors were flung wide and the rails and shelves were empty. All the personal knick-knacks that Marion had brought to make the room her own, were gone. It was the lack of them that brought it home to her how absolutely on her own she now was.

Ken's proposal looked momentarily tempting, but she just didn't know if she loved him in the way Marion had described love, as an all consuming emotion, that would make you do things you wouldn't normally dream of doing. She didn't have such feelings, certainly not strong enough to marry him. She decided that this was another turning point in her life and tomorrow she would tell him how she felt. As for Dic, he was just a protective big brother. Wasn't he?

Ken was waiting the next afternoon as she closed the post office and they went to Stella's country cottage, an arrangement made between Ken and the mysteriously absent Stella without telling her. Tea and sandwiches served in the peaceful gardens relaxed her and afterwards they went to the pictures, then on to a restaurant for an evening meal. Back at Badgers Brook they put on records and danced. When it was time to leave, Ken didn't want to leave, and she was reluctant to let him.

Was he her future? She was never more content than when they were together. They laughed a lot and seemed in accord with practically everything they did. So what was holding her back? It couldn't be a misplaced loyalty to Dic – he was love of a different kind and even that had been lessened by suspicion. Perhaps Stella was right and love needed to grow, to be nourished by the passing days. She had to give it time.

–

Next Wednesday, as planned, Dic arrived early and they set off for the seaside town of Barry and Jake's boatyard. Jake came to meet them and offered them tea, which they smilingly declined, instead offering him a drink from their flask and a share of their packed lunch.

'No better news of your father, then?' Jake asked Lowri.

'No, and there won't be, unless Ellis Owen miraculously turns up.' She was unaware of the scruffy, bearded man pausing and turning to look at her, before getting on with his work. He brushed more slowly, dragging the task out and listening to what was being said, but no one noticed.

'Lowri thought she saw him and it's hard to accept she was wrong,' Dic explained.

'Where did you think you saw him?' Jake asked and Lowri explained, but briefly, light-heartedly, as though convinced now that she had been mistaken and it had been nothing more than wishful thinking.

Dic selected the wood he could use and there were a few minutes of jocular haggling before he promised to buy Jake a drink later and they left. Lowri waved to the young apprentice and to the old man whom Jake had casually introduced as Alun Harris. Alun was now leaning on a yard broom, watching them from the door of Jake's office. As they drove away, with the boot filled with odd-shaped, old and new timber, he came down to talk to Jake.

'Did I hear that girl mention Ellis Owen?' he asked, his voice surprisingly well modulated.

'The man who died after fighting on Mumbles pier, yes. She's Jimmy Vaughan's daughter, Lowri. Jimmy and Owen were fighting, Jimmy accused Ellis of stealing from the firm, but no one believed him. The evidence pointed at Jimmy and with Ellis dead, there's no way of proving otherwise. Jimmy was almost charged with killing the man, but there wasn't sufficient evidence for that. The suspicion still hangs over him though.'

'Ellis Owen robbed from this Jimmy Vaughan's business?'

Jake shrugged. 'No one could prove that and it's Jimmy who's serving a sentence for fraud. All the evidence pointed at Jimmy, not Ellis Owen.'

'And Ellis Owen is really dead?'

'Drowned when he fell into the sea while he and Jimmy were fighting. Although the body was never recovered. Young Lowri's so upset by her father's imprisonment. She can't believe he's guilty, and thinking she's seen Ellis Owen, who's supposed to be dead, well… as she admitted, it must have been wishful thinking.'

'Tell me about it, will you? I knew Ellis Owen and I didn't know he was dead until a few months ago when

I came back from France. If he's alive I want to kill him myself!'

'What d'you mean?'

'A man called Ellis Owen worked for me. A brilliant accountant he was, even though he wasn't fully qualified. He took over every aspect of the financial side of things, leaving me free to concentrate on the business. I was very pleased. Until the day I received a letter from the bank to tell me the account was empty and there were serious debts.'

'That's more or less what happened to Jimmy Vaughan and his partner Jack Morris.'

'I had to sell everything I owned and still work for six months to clear the debts he'd left. He disappeared and there was nothing the police could do. In fact, he'd covered his tracks so well they didn't believe me.' He looked away into a distant place, reliving despair and sadness. 'My fiancée left me, and I was rudderless, without an aim or a hope of starting again.'

'What did you do?'

'Once all my debts were paid I went to France and stayed there until a few months ago. I had no heart to try and rebuild my business.'

'What business was that?' Jake asked.

'I had a restaurant. I trained as a chef and with my fiancée, planned to go for the upper class clientele. Specialize in top-class French cuisine. But everything was ruined by that man. I tried to find someone to back me but the suspicion that I stole from my own business in the hope of an insurance claim, meant no one trusted me.'

'Did you claim?'

'No. There was no chance of a successful claim. He'd made sure of that. The evidence showed that I was the culprit. Then Rachel left me and I gave up. So you can understand why I'd love to think Lowri Vaughan is right and the man is still alive.'

'Not much chance of that.'

'Where can I find her? I'd like to talk to her anyway. Perhaps if I go back to the police and remind them of what happened to me, they might look again – sympathetically – at her father's case, maybe mine too.'

Jake hesitated. Although Alun Harris had worked for him for a few months, he didn't know much about him. He didn't want to send someone to find Lowri without being sure she wasn't at risk. The man could be unbalanced, the story a nonsense.

'I think you'd better talk to Dic Morris,' he decided. 'Dic's father was Jimmy's partner and he knows as much as anyone about what happened.'

Alun left the boatyard with Jake after making sure everything was securely locked. Then, promising to talk to Dic at the address Jake had given him, he left. A tall, powerful figure, his eyes clear and far-seeing, the clothes giving a false impression of an ageing, dispirited man. He thumbed a lift from a passing lorry driver and was soon knocking on Dic's door.

Jake had forewarned his friend by telephone, and Dic had taken the girls to stay with his mother until he called for them at bed time. Lowri was sitting beside the fire having insisted on staying. They greeted their visitor and waved him to a seat. Then they waited for the man to explain the reason for his visit. Alun went over the same ground he had covered with Jake, and then Dic, and occasionally Lowri, filled in their details.

'Your father believed Jimmy Vaughan was guilty?' Alun asked Dic.

'At first, but when the anger cooled and he began to think more clearly he had doubts. My mother never believed it,' he added, glancing at Lowri. 'Ellis had been given full access to every part of the business and, well, he could easily have altered the books to implicate Jimmy.'

'That's what he did to me. Fortunately, I didn't have a partner so I couldn't be charged with fraud. There was only the accusation that I was intending to cheat on the insurance. But even that was stretching the evidence too far. So I was left with nothing but debts and a name no one would trust.'

He questioned Lowri about the times she had believed she'd seen Ellis and he also heard about the time she had been locked in the hut.

As Alun stood to leave, he wrote his address on a piece of paper. 'Can I ask you to let me know if you think of anything else?'

'Such as what? There is nothing to find. The truth died with Ellis Owen.'

'If he's dead,' Lowri added defiantly, glaring at Dic.

Dic gave Lowri a lift home before collecting his daughters but first he offered Alun a lift to the railway station where he could get a train to Cardiff, where he had a room.

Lowri was so excited she thought she'd never sleep again. Could this be the miracle she had hoped for? She wrote to her mother to tell her Alun Harris's story, warning her not to say anything to encourage her father to hope, until she had learned more.

–

Alun found out from Jake that Lowri worked at the post office in Cwm Derw and as he was paid for the time he worked rather than regular hours, it was easy to absent himself from the boatyard and wait for Lowri outside her work. So at one o'clock the next day, he was waiting outside the post office wearing his best suit and a trilby hat, a pair of shiny shoes on his feet.

She didn't recognize him at first and he smiled and reminded her, 'Alun Harris from Jake's boatyard?'

'Of course. You look different today.'

'Miss Vaughan, please excuse me approaching you like this, but if you're willing, I'd like to talk to you a bit more about what happened to your father.'

'I only have an hour,' she began. 'I have to be back here at two o'clock and I need to eat.'

'That café should be able to provide a sandwich without too much delay. Will that do?'

'That will be fine.'

As they ate, they went over all Lowri knew and Alun added details of what had happened to him. The similarities were compelling.

'Surely the police will re-examine the case against your father when we face them with this?' Alun said.

Lowri shook her head. 'I don't think they'll listen unless the money turns up and with Ellis dead that isn't going to happen, is it?'

'Why did you think the isolated hut was where you'd find some answers?'

'I found a key to which there was no lock which someone else tried to find. At least, someone searched my room and I happened to have had it in my handbag. Then there was the man who locked me in there. Oh, I know Dic doesn't quite believe me,' she added quickly, 'but I didn't imagine having my face pushed into the earth.' She stared at him, his blue eyes so clear and honest. 'Do you believe me?' she demanded.

'I have no reason not to,' he replied, looking straight at her, a reassuring expression in those remarkable eyes. 'You don't strike me as an over-fanciful person. If you say it happened, I believe it did.'

'Thank you.'

'What happened to the key?'

'It was taken by the man who attacked me.'

'D'you think your father would see me if I applied for permission? The more facts I have before talking to the police the better.'

'Mam might not be too keen. Her visits are too special to share, and besides she's decided that to encourage him to keep on hoping for a pardon unsettles him. Better he should concentrate on getting through the sentence. I think she's right.'

'Then it's just you and me.'

She stared at him and then smiled. 'That's right. You and me against the rest.' She took the hand he offered and they shook solemnly.

'First, I want you to tell me where I'll find this hut.'

'That's easy. I'll take you there. Dic will come as well. He used to go there with my father and his, when they used it to store fishing gear. They'd sleep there sometimes when they were planning to fish a very early or a late tide.'

When Alun contacted him and suggested the three of them went to look again at the hut, Dic agreed to take Alun but he insisted they went without Lowri.

'I want to cool down the idea of Jimmy Vaughan being freed and encourage her to concentrate on today and tomorrow instead of yesterday.'

'That makes sense to me. I would like to see the place if you'll come with me.'

'We'll go when Lowri is at work.'

They set off early the following morning, Dic leaving a friend in charge of the shop, and parked near the cliff path that would lead them to the area. They walked quietly and approached the hut warily, keeping undercover of the surrounding trees and bushes until the small building came into view. Neither had discussed a need for caution but they both crouched under a covering of bushes and watched the door as though expecting someone to appear.

Minutes passed and there was no movement and with a self-deprecating grin, they moved forward towards the door. Dic had no key but, depending on what they saw inside, he was prepared to kick the door in if necessary. The door had been protected with a metal bar and padlock; there was no chance of that.

Peering through the window, the grime still showing the clear patch Lowri had made with her hand during her imprisonment, they saw that the place contained fishing equipment.

'There's an awful lot of it,' Dic said.

'More than you'd need for a short fishing trip,' Alun agreed. 'Someone is preparing for a long voyage. There are water carriers and a paraffin stove and boxes of stores.'

'I don't know what I was hoping to find, but this is clearly nothing to help us.'

'Curious though. Will the owner tell us who is using it, and why?'

'Several people have used the place over the years – it's a long time since it was used by shepherds.' Alun walked around, kicking at the stones and rubble that had collected near the walls and he bent to pick up a small key. 'This isn't the one Lowri lost, is it?' Dic shook her head. 'Unlikely, but you should show it to her anyway.'

As they walked away, Dic asked, 'Fancy a run into Mumbles and a coffee? We might get some oysters, they used to be very good there.'

They parked the car and walked towards the beach, then continued along the road towards the pier. At the slip, where boats went out into the bay, Dic saw Marion. She was walking along holding her little girl's hand. He pulled on Alun's arm and stopped him. A brief explanation and they watched as the couple went on to the sand and sat down to play.

As they began building a sandcastle, Dic chuckled. 'Talk about Lowri being obsessed! I'm as bad as she is! Marion and Sandra playing sand castles. What can I find suspicious in that?'

'The way she's looking around as though she's expecting someone?' Alun observed.

A few minutes later, a rowing boat came towards the shore and Marion and the child waded out amid much laughter and climbed on board. The rower kept his head turned away as he helped them on board and as he was heavily dressed, it was impossible to see his face. The boat was brought around and rowed out to where a sleek, cabin cruiser was anchored. The group was too far away to be recognized. They wouldn't even have known it was Marion if they hadn't seen her earlier, the distance was too great and the man was wearing a padded coat with a hood over his head. With the boat towed behind, the powerful twin-engined boat took off towards Gower.

'I wonder who it was?'

'I don't know but I do know that boat,' Alun said. 'She's *The Sunflower* and she's been in Jake's yard for maintenance.'

'Can you find out who owns her?'

'I know who owned her when Jake worked on her – a man called James Harry, but he died a few weeks ago. I could ask if his widow still owns it.'

'We're being stupid, aren't we?'

'Almost certainly. Marion is being given a little treat by a wealthy friend. And we're a couple of old women! No harm in finding out a bit more though.'

Instead of stopping for coffee, they went to Cwm Derw in time to meet Lowri at lunchtime.

'What are you two doing here?' she asked, smiling as they walked towards her.

'We've come to take you out to lunch.'

'Something really exciting, like chips in the café?'

'Better than that. Fish and chips from Gwennie Flint's chip shop. I'll go and get them, you get the table set. OK?'

As they ate, they explained where they had been and told her about Marion's boat trip. Alun showed her the key which she recognized as the one she had lost. She slipped it into her handbag.

'So much for encouraging her to forget it,' Alun teased, when Lowri went to make more tea.

'So, you couldn't get into the hut?' She frowned as she returned to her seat. 'Why did you want to if you didn't believe someone attacked me?'

'We do believe you,' Dic assured her.

'I wanted to see the place and Dic came with me,' Alun explained. 'We both thought it wiser for you to stay away. If someone is looking for something you might have, it's best you avoid being in the wrong place again.'

'Please, Lowri, stay well away from there,' Dic added. 'Anyway, it's padlocked and being used by someone to store boat equipment.'

'Ellis loved boats.'

'Don't, Lowri,' Dic pleaded. 'There's nothing to be done except support your parents and help them through this.'

Later that day, Alun went to see the widow of James Harry and learned that she had sold the boat, *The Sunflower*, to Marion Lewis. Could it be linked with Ellis? Had he survived the sea on that day, to enjoy his wealth with Marion and her child? That, he decided with a wry smile, was truly fantastic. He talked to Dic and although they were both unconvinced, they admitted to being curious.

'Where could someone who does a bit of house-work get the money to buy such a beautiful boat?' Dic wondered. 'If only we could watch Marion and follow her for a while, we might find out who this man of hers actually is. But we're probably no better than nosy old women looking for a bit of gossip.'

'You can't follow her, you have the children and the business, but I can,' Alun said. 'I'm only casually employed by Jake to keep the yard clear and the office relatively clean. It's probably a waste of time and, as you say, we'd be accused of being inexcusably nosy if we were caught, but I want to try.'

'If we find out he's a cowardly little man who's leaving a wife for a younger woman, that will be gossip and we'll let it go, but even the slender chance of finding some connection with Ellis Owen at the end of it makes it worth trying, doesn't it?'

'And helping Lowri.'

'Yes,' Dic admitted, 'that most of all.'

'Someone must have the money and from what you tell me, it doesn't appear to be his widow. There has to be someone else.'

'Marion couldn't get the money to buy that grand cabin cruiser.'

'She obviously bought it in her name but for someone else. Someone who wants his name kept out of it? At least that's a starting point, and after all this time that's more than we could have expected.'

–

Lowri and Ken went to the pictures the next evening, and with his arm around her shoulders and the romantic story unfolding before her, Lowri was seduced into believing that for her, love and future happiness lay with this kind and considerate companion. But, as they walked out of the warm cosy darkness into the light, hand in hand, leaving behind the artificial romance depicted on the screen, she admitted to herself that kind and considerate were not adjectives compatible with a deep and lasting love. Marion's words returned: 'an all consuming love, a love that makes you do things you wouldn't normally do'. With deep regret and the frightening feeling that she was alone, she knew she had to tell him she would never love him enough to become his wife.

He took her home and stayed for coffee and toast, which she spread with a mixture of margarine and the top of the milk to make pretend butter. She felt her heart racing with anxiety as she prepared to tell him, first as they made their snack, then when they were eating it, each time failing to find the words and the moment. Then as she hesitated, she decided to wait for another day. They'd had such a good evening it was a shame to spoil it.

She admitted her cowardice and finally faced it. When he'd put on his coat and was reaching for her for a good night kiss she blurted out, 'Ken, I've grown very fond of you, but I can't marry you. I don't think I love you. It isn't fair to pretend it might grow. You deserve better than that. I'm very sorry.'

He was shocked, his face stunned by the unexpected end to what had been a pleasant evening.

'Is it because of my parents?'

'No, of course not.'

'And you don't love someone else?' She shook her head.

'Then can we go on being friends? You never know, your feelings for me might change.'

'I want you as a friend, but I don't want to stop you meeting someone else, someone who loves you as you deserve to be loved.'

He didn't know what more to say and the kiss that had lingered in the air faded and he gave her a brief hug and, promising to see her soon, he left.

The house seemed more empty than she'd ever known. The low hiss of the gas light the only sound. She was too alert to sleep and she slipped a coat over her shoulders against the late evening chill and sat for a long time, thinking about Ken, and Dic and her parents and wondering if she would ever find happiness.

How much of her decision to turn Ken away was down to her foolish dream of finding the answer to her father's problems? Being the devoted daughter and becoming a heroine? Had she become so obsessed with an impossible dream that it was ruining her life? She knew she had been stupid to believe even for a moment that Ellis was alive. No one believed her, even though Dic and Ken pretended to out of kindness. Now, in the quiet comfort of the old house, she didn't believe it either. Was that all she could expect? Kindness? She knew it wasn't enough. Something had to change, but what?

She touched a match to the candle to light her way upstairs when she heard a sound. A faint tapping on the glass of a window or door. She lowered the gas light to the smallest glimmer and went to the kitchen. It was impossible to see anything. Then the small white shape of a hand appeared on the glass pane and a voice called, 'Lowri, it's me, Marion. Can I come in?'

'What on earth are you doing here at this time of night?' Lowri asked as she opened the door.

'I hurt my ankle and I can't walk. Can I stay till morning? Then I'll go straight to the doctor.'

Lowri couldn't resist saying, 'Only if you'll tell me what's going on.'

'I can't. Does that mean you won't help me?'

'Of course not.' Lowri turned away, irritation rising and Marion came in and locked the door.

'I fell off a bike.'

'Come on, Marion, let's have the truth for once.' She was tempted to tell her Dic had seen her getting into a luxurious boat with her daughter, a boat she had bought, longing to face her with what she knew, but held back. She stood waiting for her to speak.

'I don't want my mother to see me like this.' She turned her head and exposed her arm and Lowri gasped to see the skin on her face and upper arm grazed and red and angry, and her limbs shaking. When the light was turned up Lowri could see the unmistakable sight of blood in Marion's hair.

'Marion! It looks very painful. How did it happen?'

'I fell off a bike.'

'Come on, Marion, falling off a bike wouldn't give you those cuts and bruises. Tell me the truth!'

'Please, Lowri, don't ask questions.'

'You look as though someone pushed you over a cliff!' To her alarm, Marion burst into tears and at once Lowri was ashamed of her persistence and stepped back from her wrath. 'I'll help you bathe the cuts and make you a hot drink.'

'Thank you,' Marion said, trying to hold back her sobs.

'Your bed's made up. I'd better fill a hot water bottle for you, it will help you sleep.' She bathed the extensive wounds and treated them with salve then helped her friend to undress and settle into bed, leaving a candle burning on the landing in case Marion woke in the night. Then she went to her room, confused thoughts rattling around in her head. The dangerous cliffs dropping sheer down to the sea near the hut were where rescue organizations sometimes trained for mountain and sea rescues. How could she have fallen there? She'd never mentioned an interest in rock climbing and was too sensible to risk going close to the edge.

When sleep eventually claimed her she dreamed a confusing montage of Ken chasing Ellis, Dic supporting Ken's parents in their dislike of her, and Marion falling off a bicycle into the sea. At midnight she awoke and remembering what had happened, she looked in on Marion and went downstairs to make another hot drink. After returning to bed she slept easily and awoke refreshed.

She went down without disturbing Marion and made tea but when she knocked and went in to give Marion hers, the bed was empty. Marion had gone.

Eleven

Alun sat in a pub and quietly sipped his pint. He exchanged a few remarks with other customers but watched the doorway. The man he was waiting for didn't know him, but Alun thought he'd be interested in what he had to say.

Finding Harold Saunders had been easy. He'd used his usual process of finding out where the policeman involved with Jimmy Vaughan's arrest lived, guessing which of the local pubs he would use, then a few more casual questions had led him here to The Red Lion.

Harold came in at eight o'clock and by good fortune sat near Alun where he could watch the game of darts taking place. To comment on the course of the game began a conversation and soon the two men were chatting like friends. Then Alun introduced the subject of Ellis Owen.

'Isn't it near here that Jimmy Vaughan lived?'

'Not any more. He's in prison, for fraud.'

'Yes, he was cheated by Ellis Owen the same as I was, yet the law allowed him to get away with it. Doesn't that make you angry?'

'Sorry, I don't know what you mean?'

'I owned a restaurant and Ellis was my accountant. He disappeared and I was left with huge debts and a reputation for robbing my own firm in the hope of claiming on insurance. Sound familiar?'

'You have proof of this?'

'No, but I don't believe in coincidences like that one, do you?'

'If you have evidence of a miscarriage of justice, why don't you go to the police?'

'Oh, I have, and just like Jimmy Vaughan, I begged them to believe me, but Ellis Owen is clever.'

'Was, you mean, he drowned.'

'Dead men don't walk!'

It took a while but gradually his words were more and more convincing and Harold agreed to go with Alun and take his story to the police station. If it were true the coincidence was remarkable. He'd met a few nutters in his years as a constable, but Harold was tempted to believe the man partly because he wanted to. He'd always been half convinced of Jimmy's innocence anyway. They arranged a time and Alun left, pleased with his progress.

The young constable on the desk took details but doubted there would be any action taken. 'With the suspect dead,' he said reasonably, 'what do you expect us to do?'

Alun could hardly try to convince him that Ellis was alive. He would be instantly classed as a 'nutter' as Harold had already warned. At least the subject had been noted, he thought, and that was all he could expect at present.

Harold Saunders watched the big man walk off, still unconvinced, but already doubts were growing. He went to call on Terri, Ellis's wife.

Terri looked hot and flustered and he said, 'If this is an awkward time… I was just passing and thought I might scrounge a cuppa.'

'No, it's fine, come in. In fact I'll be glad of your help.'

He walked into the living room and wondered what was going on. Most of her possessions were set out on tables and chairs so it looked like a bazaar. Everything from bales of bedding and household linen, to cutlery tied into bundles, ornaments and china, glassware and kitchen items. 'What's going on? Is this an unseasonal spring clean?' he joked.

'I'm selling everything,' she told him.

'But, won't you want these things? It'll cost a fortune to start all over again, unless these are all spares?'

'After the way Ellis behaved I can't bear to see them. I've bought new bedding and everything,' she sobbed, and turned away to recover. 'Harold, he was leaving me, abandoning me like an unwanted shirt. Something he'd outgrown.'

'I'm sorry, but I think you need to think about this.'

'I have. The neighbours and friends are coming this afternoon to see if there's anything they want.'

'You've found a flat, then?'

'Sort of. It's vacant and for rent. I'll move in and later on I'll buy something more permanent, when I know where I want to live.'

'Here might be the best,' he said. 'Where your friends are, where you're comfortable. Don't let Ellis drive you away.'

'Friendships are frail, you ask poor Lowri about that. My so-called loyal friends thought it a joke that I was being abandoned, secure in their own families, certain it would never happen to them, convinced that I must be to blame.'

He saw a label on the armchairs and asked, 'You aren't selling the furniture too?'

'Everything. I don't want a single thing left to remind me of my loving husband.' She cried then, unable to hold back the tears any longer and he sat near her soothing her with words of comfort, persuading her to look to the future and let the past go. There was nothing else he could say. He could hardly tell her about Lowri and Alun's belief that Ellis was alive and hadn't come back to her. How could she cope with that added insult? He made a cup of tea and sat with her while she drank it, then he left.

Whether or not Ellis had survived that storm all those months ago, it was clear that Terri knew nothing about it. He decided to go back during the afternoon and keep an eye on her while her goods were sold. She was certain to be upset. Leaving the past behind sounded easy, but in her circumstances, the pain would be hard for her to bear.

–

Lowri was restless, aware of the emptiness of her hours after leaving the post office each evening. Seeing Marion again had reminded her of how much she missed having her around. If only she hadn't tried to pry. Marion's secrecy was odd, but everyone has some part of themselves they're unwilling to share. For Marion this was greater than most, but in other ways she had been a perfect companion.

She wanted to find out if she was all right. The ankle must have been painful for her to knock on the door of Badgers Brook and ask her for help. And the wounds where she had fallen off a bike, or – more likely scraped herself on rocks needed medical attention if they weren't to leave scars. Was this a good enough reason to call at her parents' house and enquire? Or would that make things worse between them? She thought the latter.

The problem of the house feeling empty was easily solved; she would invite a few friends for Sunday lunch. About fifteen, she mused, plus, as always, a few who 'just happened to call'. She knew she could rely on most of them bringing something to swell the feast, and it should be warm enough to eat outside. That always made it special. She was able to put aside her thoughts about her father and Ellis Owen, and Marion's strange behaviour, and concentrate on making sure she would have sufficient food and drink.

When she had taken the tenancy of Badgers Brook she had been amused at the number of chairs that were there. She soon realized that the reason was because the house enticed visitors in an almost magical way, with people arriving unannounced and creating a party-like atmosphere that left good memories for everyone who came. The house was always welcoming and always warm and needed the chairs to accommodate the guests.

—

Alun Harris went to The Ship and Compass that lunch-time an ordered a pint at the bar. 'Hey, you're the man who helped me when I fell, aren't you?' Betty exclaimed. Alun smiled, his pink mouth showing through the new neatly trimmed beard. 'Oh, so you recognize me today, do you?'

'What d'you mean, you haven't been in here before, have you?'

He nodded. 'Very busy you were with a young man supposedly helping, but leaning on the bar as though he didn't have the strength to stand without its support.'

'Oh, that would have been Ernie or Roger. Useless, the pair of them. He's late again. Typical!'

Alun sipped his beer, talking to Betty whenever she was free, helping with the glasses when they piled up. 'Where's that barman? He's very late, if he's coming.' He looked around the room as he put the glasses he'd collected on to the bar.

Betty shrugged. 'No sign of him and no word either, lazy man that he is. I've got a coach party coming tomorrow and I've promised them lunch. Only sandwiches and pasties, but if he doesn't appear I'll have difficulty coping.' She shrugged. 'But there, I've managed this place on my own since my brother Ed married Elsie Clements and I dare say I'll cope with tomorrow.'

'I can help, if you'll allow me,' Alun offered. 'I know the trade, although from a different angle. I owned a restaurant, and drinks were a part of my daily routine. More wines and spirits than beer, but I do know how to pull a pint without producing a glass of foam.'

'You mean it?' There was no hiding her relief.

'Of course. I do a bit of cleaning at the boatyard but nothing that will stop me having another day off.'

'Been on holiday?' she asked, as she made a shandy.

'No, I was just chasing a wild goose, or something.' He laughed, his clear blue eyes meeting hers giving him a friendly honest look. 'No secrets. Just a boring tale that I'll tell you one day.'

'Don't worry, I don't want to know the ins and outs. Just help me tomorrow and I'll be satisfied. If you could come early I'll show you where everything is kept and talk about how I like things done.'

'I look forward to it,' Alun said, wondering how he could get hold of some decent clothes by morning.

The next morning, he arrived early and Betty was startled at the change in his appearance – he had shaved off his beard. 'I know,' he said ruefully, 'a face that's pale and unfamiliar. But I'm not an impostor, it's me, Alun. I thought I needed to look the part before working beside the famous landlady of The Ship and Compass. Will I do?'

'That was a shock. Until you spoke I didn't recognize you without that wool on your face,' she teased.

After a brief tour of the cellars and bar, Alun took over the cooking, making the pasties in half the time it would have taken Betty, who marvelled at his skill. She was curious to know what had happened to the restaurant but she didn't ask. He would tell her when he was ready, if he wanted to, and until then she was grateful for his professional assistance. He was just as capable behind the bar as in the kitchen, and after a few of the regulars had joked about his previous appearance being like 'a rat peeping through a ball of oakum', they accepted him.

When the bar closed that evening, he would sit and drink the cup of tea Betty promised, and tell her the full story.

Meanwhile the bar was full and he was going to earn his pay.

–

Lowri got on with her preparations for the Sunday lunch still wondering if Marion was in some sort of trouble. If only she could persuade her to talk. It might be something she could help her with, and privacy shouldn't go so far as to cause harm. The idea followed that if she went to Marion's parents' house carrying an invitation for her to come to Badgers Brook on Sunday, it would seem less like prying and she might be able to talk to her. However she had received those injuries, it was not from falling off a bike!

Straight from work, she scribbled a note and set off. The back door of the house was open and several children were riding bicycles across what had once been a rockery with deep concentration. They ignored her after an initial friendly wave and she tapped on the door. Marion came with Sandra in her arms and for a moment she glared, then her expression softened as Lowri held out the invitation.

'There'll be the usual crowd, I thought you'd like to see them again,' Lowri explained, feeling like a traitor, knowing that was not the true reason. 'Dic is coming with the girls, and Ken, and Betty Connors and her friend Gwennie Flint. We'll eat in the garden if the weather is suitable. Will you come?' She was aware she was gabbling and she turned to leave. 'No need to let me know. Just come if you can,' she said, waving goodbye.

She stopped and glanced back and saw Marion put the little girl down and hurry inside. Curious, and feeling like an idiot, Lowri pushed into a hedge and waited. Moments later Marion rushed out of the gate and ran down the road. Cautiously Lowri followed. She led Lowri through narrow lanes where she had to stay well back then hurry to catch up afraid of losing sight of her. To her disappointment Marion knocked on a door and disappeared inside. The voices that reached her suggested she had called on a friend and would stay for a while.

Unwilling to stand and wait for what could be hours, she walked past the house while hidden by the bushes, then on past a row of small cottages. Without any plan in mind she walked on, and eventually found herself in the narrow road that led to the cliffs on which the hut stood. She sat on a bank, hidden from the road and tried to tell herself she had been mistaken all along, that the times she had seen Ellis had been foolish fantasies brought on by her determination to help her father.

She had almost convinced herself that it was time to stop chasing dreams and get on with her life, when she heard someone approaching. Not wanting to be seen sitting in such a lonely spot, feeling foolish and ashamed of all the trouble she had caused for her friends, she pulled herself a little higher, out of sight from the road.

She took a sharp intake of breath as she saw the person passing her hiding place. It was Marion. All promises to herself vanished into the air. Where was Marion going? Had she seen her sheltering in the hedge and called on a friend to avoid being followed? She carefully slipped down the bank, the suspicions she had tried to put aside were back in place, her awareness heightened.

Unbelievably Marion went towards the hut. What was it about the place that attracted so much attention? Instinctively she grasped the key in her pocket, like a talisman; a connection with her father keeping her safe.

The boat equipment could hardly be anything to do with Marion, so what secret did it hold? In the same place where she had hidden before, she pushed herself into the prickly branches of a bramble and saw her friend rap on the window. The door opened and there, without any doubt, stood the man who was supposed to be dead, the man who had caused her family so much anguish: Ellis Owen.

With her heart racing madly she watched as Ellis stepped outside, taking Marion in his arms. Their laughter could be heard on the still evening air as they hugged each other. Ellis stepped backwards down into the hut and lifting Marion, carried her inside and the door closed behind them.

Lowri began to tremble, her legs seemed unable to hold her and she sank to the ground. She had been right all along. She looked around hoping someone was near – anyone, just a second person to face the man and help strengthen her case when she told the police he was alive. Ellis and Marion: so many things were explained, but why did this have to happen when she was far from home? And in a place where there wasn't a telephone box for miles. Dic! She needed to find Dic! But by the time he reached the place both would have left and sadly she knew that again he wouldn't believe her. The euphoria of seeing the man again, and so clearly, left her feeling cold as she realized that once again she wouldn't be believed by anyone.

It was already getting dark and she had a long walk back to Marion's home from where she could catch a bus. She hesitated, realizing that the chance of being seen made the shorter route too risky. She hadn't a choice; she had to walk the long way back along the route she had previously cycled. Then what would she do? No one would believe her. She groaned in despair. Pulling herself together, she began to walk, practising what she would say, trying out different versions of the events in an effort to sound more convincing, each time accepting that Dic would be kind, sympathetic, but certain she had been mistaken. Dic wasn't at home when she telephoned and wearily she walked on. She finally caught a bus that took her to the main road of Cwm Derw and on impulse she went into The Ship, where to her surprise, Alun was serving.

'Is Betty here?' she asked, after greeting him.

'In the back room having a ten minute breather.'

Lowri went through, calling as she knocked on the door of the living room. 'It's only me, Betty. You don't know where Dic is, do you?'

'I haven't seen him, dear.' Catching sight of Lowri's anxious face she asked, 'What is it? What's happened?'

'I know you won't believe me, but I've just see Ellis Owen. He was meeting my friend Marion up there at the hut. Betty, I swear I saw him as plainly as I'm seeing you now!'

Betty jumped out of her chair and went to the bar. 'Alun,' she called. 'Come here and listen to this.'

Surprised at the reaction when she'd expected only platitudes and soothing disbelief, Lowri repeated her story to Alun. 'It's too late to catch him,' she said sadly. 'I was stuck there too far from anyone who'd listen. Dic was out and anyway, by the time I reached the phone box it would have already been too late.'

Betty tried Dic's number again and this time he answered. He spoke to Alun and although Lowri gathered from the one-sided conversation that he was still unsure, he agreed to make a few enquiries. 'And I,' Alun said, 'plan to watch that hut day and night until I find out what's going on.' He smiled at Betty. 'There are advantages in being a casual worker.'

When Lowri reached Badgers Brook, there was a bowl of blackberries on the step, a present from Kitty and Bob, and on the doormat, a letter addressed to Marion. As another excuse to call on her again, Lowri was tempted, but instead she would wait until Sunday in the hope her friend would come. Too many vague excuses to knock on her mother's door might make her suspicious and with a lump in her throat for the implications of what she had witnessed at the hut, she knew that Marion – once considered a friend – was almost certainly involved in Ellis's supposed death and the imprisonment of her father.

The thought that Marion was yet another false friend didn't keep her awake for long; she went to sleep as the old house settled around her with its comforting sounds, relaxed in the knowledge that someone believed her. Alun Harris, who had also suffered at the hands of Ellis Owen, believed her and was helping to find him.

–

The following day, Dic called at the farmhouse and asked Tommy Treweather who was using the hut. He pretended he'd seen lights there and it had made him curious as he'd supposed it to be almost derelict and unused.

Tommy offered tea, which he called on Rachel to provide, then led Dic into the large, cosy living room. 'Several people have used it. I don't need it any more, no sheep, so no shepherd, so no need of a shelter.' There was sadness in his voice as he talked about the loss of the farm that had been in his family for several generations. 'We only have a few hens which Rachel can't part with. It's tractors and lorries on the land now. So I don't mind if fishermen or bird-watchers use it occasionally. I go up to check it now and then and a fishing club paid for it to be repaired before the group disbanded.'

'D'you know who's using it at present?'

'A young woman called and asked if a neighbour could store some fishing gear in there. I didn't bother to ask his name. He fixed a padlock, I believe, although who he thinks will pinch his rods and stuff I don't know.'

'You don't know his name?'

'Didn't get hers either.'

'Someone looked through the window and thought they saw boating equipment.'

'Boats? That doesn't make sense. It's a long way from the sea – except down!'

'I went to look, just out of idle curiosity, but there's something covering the window.'

Tommy sighed. 'Look, the fact is, I'm no longer interested. Since the farm was sold and my animals taken away, I've had to put it all out of my mind. I'll go crazy if I don't. It was our sons, see. Neither Ryan nor Gareth wanted to take it on. And the wife wasn't sorry to give it up. It's a hard life. Without the boys there's never a chance to get away for a holiday. Days, weeks and months have a predictability about them. Not to me, mind. There were never two days the same, but that's how it was for Rachel. Loved it I did, but Rachel was glad to retire.'

Dic sat and listened to Tommy, aware of the man's unhappiness, then made his excuses and left. He had learned very little but the one thing that made him curious was Tommy saying it had been a girl who had asked permission to use the hut. Why had the man not gone himself?

He got into the car and sat for a moment, trying to convince himself that Lowri had been correct, and she had seen Ellis. Then he shook his head. It was impossible and she must have been mistaken. Perhaps she ought to get away for a while. Perhaps she would consider coming on a holiday with himself and Sarah-Jane and Katie, if his mother came too? It was time Lowri renewed her friendship with her Auntie Cathy. He would talk to her when they met on Sunday, although Badgers Brook always attracted a lot of people, too many to hope for a private discussion.

Up on the hill above the cliffs dropping down to the sea, Alun stood. A calm, quiet, patient man. Showers soaked him and the sun dried him and still he waited. He'd decided on twenty-four hours, sitting to eat the food he'd brought and resting for a few hours during the darkest hours of the night. He'd continue coming back until the hut had been emptied and he had lost his chance, or he faced the person who had ruined his life. On Sunday he'd go to the luncheon party Lowri had arranged. If Marion went too, he'd listen with great care to everything she said.

Sunday morning was showery but towards eleven the showers drifted away and the sun strengthened. Lowri and Kitty decided to risk taking tables and chairs into the garden. Stella arrived soon after they began, bringing baskets of food and flowers for the tables. Lowri had cut the grass the previous day and the geraniums and fuschia bushes, the rambling roses and passion flowers that hid the old fences, gave colour and perfume to the setting that sparkled after the recent rain.

Dic came early with his daughters, who ran at once to the swing Bob had fixed in an old apple tree, and Colin followed them to make sure they didn't fall. Kitty was pouring teas from one of the three teapots they were using and Betty Connors was walking around with a plate of food, introducing Alun to those who hadn't already met him.

Everywhere he looked people were talking and laughing, contentment on every face. The pleasant garden hummed with murmuring voices, a place where everyone felt at home. 'Badgers Brook is a wonderful house,' Lowri said to Dic. 'It's impossible to be unhappy here.'

'Perhaps,' he surprised her by saying. 'But I think you need to accept your father's situation and let it go, or even in a beautiful house like Badgers Brook, you could make yourself ill.'

'Rubbish!' she stared at him in disbelief. 'How can you think it? Of course I can't push my father's injustice aside. He should be here enjoying this wonderful place. If it weren't for your father, he would be free!' Leaving him, she busied herself among her guests and avoided him as though he were poison.

As more friends arrived and the conversation swelled, Lowri looked around to see whether the large platters on the tables needed replenishing, forcing herself to ignore Dic's stupid remarks. She piled up some plates and emptied others and took the dishes into the kitchen. Glancing out of the window she was surprised to see Marion walking up the path hand in hand with her daughter, Sandra.

She opened the door and smiled a welcome but her heart was racing. How could she pretend she didn't know about Ellis when she had seen them together? Avoiding looking at Marion, afraid her friend would see the deception in her eyes, she concentrated on the little girl. She led her down the garden to join Dic's two girls who were sweet in the care they gave the newcomer. Leaving Marion and the girls, she hurried back to the kitchen.

She didn't see the glance exchanged between Dic and Alun and was surprised when Alun made his excuses and left. 'I have an errand, but I'll be back before you leave,' he explained. 'I borrowed a car from Jake so I won't be long.' He took another sandwich, as he left with a wave at Betty.

With Marion well within hearing distance, Dic said, 'I called on Farmer Tommy Treweather the other day. Did you know he owned the old hut where your father and mine sometimes stayed when they went fishing?' he said to Lowri. 'A bit of a wreck as I remembered it, but someone has repaired it, strengthened the roof that was in danger of being blown away. I walked up there last week to revive a few memories.'

Marion began to straighten her daughter's coat, fidgeting with the buttons, Sandra protesting as she struggled to get back to the swing.

'Someone was using it, birdwatchers perhaps. They'd lit the fire,' Dic went on, 'and the place was filled with smoke. Something blocking the chimney, no doubt. I think I'll go up and have a closer look, it might be treasure,' he said jokingly, making Sarah-Jane's eyes widen.

'A bird's nest more like,' Bob said. 'Well, I'll be off in a while. I want to get my front borders dug over if the ground isn't too wet.' He and Colin discussed the weather and which seeds they planned to buy for the following season and after a further ten minutes they left. As they were shouting their goodbyes, Marion hurried to the phone box at the top of the lane, dragging a protesting Sandra, and after an impatient wait, observed by Alun, went by taxi back to her mother's home.

Alun had borrowed Jake's van and was soon standing in the place where he had spent many hours in recent days, staring at the door of the hut. He hadn't dared look inside. If Ellis were there he hadn't wanted to risk warning him. Ten minutes later he was joined by Bob Jennings. They stood in silence for more than twenty minutes, then they saw Marion approaching. The little girl was no longer with her.

She went to the hut and, using a key to open the padlock, she went inside. Still they waited but she didn't come back out and no one else arrived. After a couple of minutes the smoke from the chimney faltered and soon there was only the smallest wisp in the air.

'She's put the fire out,' Bob whispered. 'She must think the blocked chimney is where whatever she's looking for is hidden.'

'But where's Ellis Owen?' Alun muttered.

After half an hour Marion came out again, looking all around her before locking the door again. Alun raised his binoculars and reported, 'She has a lot of soot on her arms and face.'

'She's fastening the padlock, so he isn't inside,' Bob muttered. 'Damn it, we've missed our chance.'

'There'll be another.' Alun spoke confidently. 'He still doesn't know we're on to him.'

'I still think we should go to the police,' Bob said.

'I've tried and they don't believe a word of it. Anyway, better we don't. Things have a habit of getting out so why risk warning him? He must be on the point of getting away and we can't take that chance.'

They waited for several hours, Bob sitting on the ground to rest his aching legs, Alun continuing to stand as still as a statue.

—

On Monday morning, Alun was back in his usual position on the hill, his binoculars near him, a pack of sandwiches prepared by Betty in an ex-army shoulder bag, together with a flask of coffee. He showed no sign of boredom, content to sit and watch the wildlife around him. Birds became accustomed to him as he was so still, apart from an occasional change of position, and they went about their business, flying to and fro with flying insects or with struggling beetles and worms in their beaks. An adder slowly slithered over his boots once as he stood with binoculars trained on the hut soon after he had arrived.

At five o'clock on the evening after Lowri's party, Marion approached, and Alun watched through the binoculars as she unlocked the padlock and went inside. He was tense and expectant but as minutes passed and nothing further happened, he began to relax. His concentration remained focused and he didn't take his eyes away from the door. It was seven o'clock and dusk was shrouding the scene before he was rewarded.

A man walked up the hill, casually, stopping to look out to sea just as any walker might do. Alun prepared for disappointment, but suddenly the man changed direction and hurried to the hut, opening the door with a push and stepping down inside. With a speed that would have surprised anyone knowing him, Alun ran to the hut and tried to relock the padlock. His fingers fumbled and it fell to the floor. Pulling with all his strength to hold it closed, he tried again. The door was forced open and with a grunt the man inside pushed him aside and ran off.

Alun chased after him while Marion screamed. Down the hill, slipping on patches of loose gravel, the two men headed for the road. Alun caught up and threw himself on top of the man. 'Ellis Owen! At last,' he panted. Ellis pushed him aside, grasped his wrist and twisted it painfully and in that moment of weakness dug his elbow into Alun's solar plexus. As Alun, weakened momentarily, tried to hold him, Ellis wriggled out of his grasp and made his escape.

Alun ran to find Marion. He would have no qualms about holding her and making her talk. The hut was empty, the hearth a mess of ashes and piles of soot, where they had again searched the chimney for Dic's imaginary object.

Not only had he allowed Ellis to get away, but Ellis was now warned that his secret was out. With a boat and the supplies he had gathered, he would get right out of the area where no one would find him. Alun had had a second chance and failed, not only himself, but a man he didn't even know: Jimmy Vaughan.

He hurried back to the car and drove to tell Bob of his failure. He stared at Badgers Brook. Was it his imagination, or was the old house with its dark windows glaring disapproval? 'Now what do we do?' he asked, as though it could tell him.

'I'll go and tell the police the name of the boat that Marion bought,' he told Bob. 'It could have been changed, but boat owners often don't bother, unless it's to rename it after their wife or their mother. We need to find it and watch it every minute. If, as I suspect, he's leaving by sea, he's bound to leave soon now.'

'In the meantime,' Bob promised, 'I'll keep a close eye on Marion.'

-

Ellis Owen stood on Mumbles pier, looking down at the water. He was laughing. He had defied the sea, had beaten it at its worst. Nothing would stop him now. Certainly not a man as stupid as Alun Harris. The money was all there now, including what Marion had given him, and it was time to go.

Even if Lowri stumbled on the diaries in which Jimmy had kept his own records, it would be too late. He'd be out of reach of the police, with a different name and nothing to connect him to his crimes. Besides, no one would be looking for him. 'Presumed dead' he mused. It had a fascinating ring to it.

As the waves moved hypnotically below him, and children's voices filled the air, he wondered if there was anywhere else he might try to find the incriminating diaries. Then even if the law caught up with him he would be able to swear he'd suffered amnesia since his near-drowning, and he'd be in the clear.

He turned as a little boy began to cry, begging his mother to give him one more turn on the ride, and he handed him a handful of coins, smiling at the woman's bemused thanks. 'My pleasure,' he said, patting the boy's curly hair. 'I've got none of my own, more's the pity.' Whistling contentedly, he strolled along the promenade and back to his room.

–

Marion ran home and began packing her things into a suitcase. Now they would have to leave. Ellis couldn't risk staying a moment longer. He had told her not to bring too much. Just a few clothes and whatever Sandra would need. They would buy all they needed when they reached their destination in Spain, he promised her.

She was a bit tearful, knowing she wouldn't be able to say a proper goodbye to her mother and brothers and sisters. But when they left it would have to be without anyone waving them off. She carried the suitcase down to where the boat was anchored and rowed out in the small boat, her efficiency with the oars due to hours of practice.

Ellis was such a lover of sport and she was determined to enjoy them with him. Practice at rowing, and swimming, climbing the rocks near the hut, it was all a part of loving him, wanting to share every moment with him. The times she'd slipped and fallen down the rocks had been frightening. The second time his hand hadn't been there to hold her and for a moment she'd thought she would die in the swirling waters below. He'd been so apologetic, almost tearful, and so ashamed of his carelessness. But for one terrifying moment she had doubted him. The delay had been deliberate, she knew that. The memory still made her shiver.

–

From the beach Ellis watched the sea gradually moving up towards the land. Later, when the place was quiet, he rowed out with the boat full of fuel cans which he stored neatly and securely. A couple of hours later he went out again, this time with water and food. Dragging it across from the hut was tiring and he wished he'd persuaded Marion to help. But the less she knew now, the better. He looked at the suitcase she had left on board, then stabbed holes in it and threw it overboard. As he rowed back to shore in the twilight, he was whistling contentedly.

Twelve

Police Constable Harold Saunders heard about the report of a suspected body being tipped overboard from a boat in the bay and went to where the search was taking place. It was sheer good fortune that the incident was seen and if it weren't for a man walking his dog on the cliffs, it might have gone undetected.

Saunders, wearing civvies, stood with a small group of people including police officers and divers and various onlookers, including a newspaper reporter who had been notified by the man who had informed the police.

The divers came to the surface a few times and shook their heads, then there was a shout and all focus was on the area where two men in the water were signalling to the boat.

Some people drifted away slowly, glancing back from time to time as though afraid of the sight they expected to emerge yet unable to ignore it. Others drew as close to the landing area as the police would allow. Saunders stood and waited, binoculars to his eyes. A diver emerged and a conversation ensued before he went back down with a line.

Harold guessed from the signals and the lack of excitement that there was no body, and he wasn't as surprised as the rest when a suitcase arose, dripping, to the surface and was transferred to the boat.

News spread, conjecture interspersed with fact, and by evening the whole town knew of the recovery of the suitcase, each person adding their own opinion for its discovery as the news went from one to another.

It was Lowri who told Marion, who had come to the post office to send off some letters. 'There were clothes belonging to a woman and a little girl,' she said, having been told this by the police. Ashen-faced, Marion ran from the shop. With a nod of agreement from Stella, Lowri ran after her.

'Marion, please wait, if you know something about Ellis Owen, please, please tell me.' She grabbed Marion's arm and held her back, turning her to face her. 'Marion, my father's in prison for a theft he didn't commit and is suspected of murdering that man you're protecting.'

'I don't know Ellis Owen. Why do you think I'm protecting him?'

'Alun Harris saw you together. You were searching the hut for something after he'd hinted that there was a blockage in the chimney. He tricked you and you fell for it, you and Ellis.'

'Fell for what? I don't know what you're talking about. Someone's been telling you a lot of lies and *you* fell for *them*!'

'Please, Marion. If you've any compassion, please help me find him.'

'All right, I'll make you believe me. I'll bring my secret lover, as you call him, to Badgers Brook tonight. Then will you accept that I don't know anything about this Ellis Owen?' She pushed angrily against Lowri and ran off. Lowri watched her jump on a bus and find a seat but she didn't look back. The bus would take Marion back to her mother's house and Lowri hoped that was where she was going.

Lowri ran to The Ship and Compass and asked to use the phone, not wanting Stella's customers to overhear her conversation. Trembling and confused by Marion's promise to reveal her mysterious friend, she had to tell Dic of the latest developments.

'I'll get my occasional help Jessie to stay in the shop, arrange with my mother to look after the girls and then I'll come down,' he promised.

'Where's Alun, at the boatyard?' Lowri asked Betty, after explaining what had happened.

'No, he's watching the hut. He's convinced that whatever happens next, it will be somewhere in that vicinity. After losing everything to that man and being given a second chance of catching him, he's furious that he allowed him to get away. He's determined not to let him escape another time.'

'An interesting man, isn't he? When I first saw him at Jake's yard I found him a bit frightening, so large and silent, and with his face hidden by that unruly grey beard, but when he spoke, and I looked at him properly, I saw a gentle, kindly man.'

'He's a great help to me here. I know he's capable of being much more than a barman, but I admit I wish he'd stay. Over the past year I've had many assistants, but each seemed worse than the last, except Daphne Boyd, who went to live in France, and Teifion Dexter, who runs the estate agents on the high street. It's a wonderful job running this place, it's all I've ever wanted out of life, but I do need reliable help.'

'Perhaps he'll stay.'

'Unlikely. He's a fine chef apparently, and he owned his own restaurant, until Ellis stole it from him. How can he be expected to stay here and help in the bar? Lovely if he did, mind,' she sighed.

-

Marion was upset but she couldn't see Ellis and demand an explanation. He must have thrown her clothes overboard. He was leaving without her. She went to some of the places she knew he frequented but there was no sign of him. Calming down, needing to believe in him, she began to imagine other reasons for the case with her belongings being dropped from the boat. None of them were convincing, but they made her want to believe in whatever story he told. If only she could see him, talk to him, allow herself to be reassured. She didn't know what she'd do if he let her down. Gradually she convinced herself he would not.

-

Alun was on the cliffs, crawling towards the edge and trying to look at the sea below. Because of the inward curve of the rocks and the impossibility of stretching out without risk of falling, he couldn't see where the sea touched the land. What he did see were some marks that mystified him. In several places there were indentations and scrapes in the turf near his hands and similar marks in the sparse greenery on ledges a little below him, as though ropes had been sliding over them. Something was happening here and it was here he had to stay.

It was tempting to run to where Marion's family lived and hopefully see her and follow her. He had no doubt that she was helping Ellis Owen. But if they were in this together, and preparing to leave, why had the man discarded her suitcase? The witness had said it had been thrown over, not dropped by accident – he had been quite clear about that, and to Alun, that only meant one thing. Ellis was planning to leave without Marion and very soon.

He left the cliff edge and walked back to where he could see the hut without being seen. He hoped he had made the right decision. If he stood here while the man made his escape he'd be so furious with himself. Might it be better to search for the boat? It must be anchored somewhere close by, but he had to make a decision, one man, one position, trusting others to do what he could not. He calmed himself and settled to watch the door of the hut and the surrounding area.

–

Harold Saunders spoke to his boss and together they went to see Terri Owen. He said nothing about the possibility of her husband being alive, he didn't want to upset her unnecessarily. She'd been through enough.

The living room, in what had once been a beautiful home, was practically empty. One couch, which appeared to be used as a bed, one small table, one wireless, and one tearful, lonely woman. They invited her out for a meal and listened as she told them she had booked into a guest house until she could find a place where she could settle down and begin a new life.

'I agree about starting again, but wouldn't it be better to start again here, where you have friends?'

'No, I think I need to get right away.'

Below where Alun was watching the hut on the cliffs, tucked well into the foot of the cliffs, Ellis sat in the cabin of the cruiser. He stared at the rocks around him. He had manoeuvred the boat cautiously in through a narrow gap and around a curved entrance which was a tight fit but which, once negotiated, gave him shelter that was out of sight from above and from the sea. It was a gully he and Jimmy and Jack had found years before when they were fishing. They used to put a night line across at low tide and come back in the morning to see what they'd caught. A fine bass he remembered once. That was a treat. Thank goodness Jimmy was in prison, he was the only one likely to remember this place.

He reached for a notepad and started a letter to Marion. He felt guilty leaving her behind, but she wasn't the one he wanted to spend his new life with, even though it meant leaving little Sandra as well. He would leave Marion a brief note, promising to come back once he'd found a place in Spain, and that would keep her happy for a while. By the time she realized she'd seen the last of him, it would be too late for her to try and find him.

It was getting dark and he climbed into the dingy, cautiously left his hiding place and began to row himself back to the small, little-used beach. It had no access from the road and it meant another climb but he was used to it and could manage it in the dark, his hands and feet finding the familiar places with hardly a thought. Time now to find something to eat and, without her realizing it, say his silent goodbyes to Marion. Tomorrow, when the last of the money had been transferred, he would leave. It had taken a long time, gathering the money and searching unsuccessfully for those damned diaries, but at last he would be free.

Alun heard someone approach and pressed more deeply into the bramble bush, gritting his teeth against the pain of sharp thorns.

'Alun, it's me, Harold Saunders. Have you seen anything yet?'

'No one has used the hut, and as it gets darker I'll move closer. If I see him I don't want to lose him like last time.'

'Is there anything in the hut?'

'A few ropes, and crampons and the like.'

'They don't mean anything, he still might not be back.'

'I don't know where else to look. The boat could be anywhere. There are dozens of small coves where a small boat could be hidden.'

'Then we'll wait here,' Harold said.

But Alun became restless. He accepted that two people watching was a good idea – after all, if he'd had someone with him when he'd cornered Ellis in the hut, the man wouldn't have got away – yet as minutes passed he knew he should be elsewhere.

'If you'll wait here, Harold, I want to go and search along these rocks below. I have a feeling that's where he'd have hidden the boat. I'm told he knows these cliffs well and if there's a small place where he could be out of sight, I might find it.'

'It's getting dark,' Harold said doubtfully.

'Eyes like a cat,' Alun assured him.

–

At Badgers Brook, Lowri sat waiting for Marion to come and introduce her secret love. If the man was Ellis Owen,

271

he most certainly wouldn't come. If he were a stranger, then where would that leave their investigation? The clock moved with agonizing slowness and she checked it against her watch, more than once, convinced it had stopped. Dic arrived early and he suggested they look again through the papers and books belonging to her father.

'All right, but it's a waste of time. I've been through them so many times, I don't see what I'm looking at any more, they're just a blur. If there was something to find I'd have found it before now. Dad couldn't help. He only knew that he'd put them somewhere safe but he didn't remember enough for us to find them, or Ellis knew about them and destroyed them.' Dic didn't expect to find anything either, he just wanted to give her something to do to take her mind off the search for Ellis Owen.

Kitty and Bob called and seeing the books spread across the carpet, asked if there was something they could do. Bob left almost straightaway, taking sandwiches and a flask of coffee to Harold who was still standing near the hut. Kitty helped them sort out the books into more orderly piles and watched as Dic and Lowri went through them once again. 'This one's a cookery book,' she said with a laugh. 'Your father into cookery, was he, Lowri?'

'Couldn't boil an egg,' Lowri replied. 'That must be one of Mam's put with the rest by mistake.'

'I'll borrow that later,' Dic said, putting it on one side. 'Sarah-Jane wants to help me make vegetable soup as a surprise for my mother tomorrow.'

'A recipe? You take a handful of every vegetable you can find, that's the best way to make soup. Macaroni, or rice, and some lentils too. Easy it is.'

'Sounds good, but I think I'll need the recipe,' Dic said ruefully. '"Chuck and chance it" might be all right for you experts, but not for me. Besides, Sarah-Jane likes reading out the instructions. Cooking helps with reading and arithmetic.'

When Kitty had gone, promising to come back later, they pushed the books aside and Lowri went back to staring at the clock.

Dic tried to reassure her. 'If it isn't Ellis, and I don't think for a moment it will be, it just means she's trying to trick us into giving up,' he said. 'Perhaps it's best we pretend she's convinced us.'

'When I was the only one to see Ellis, I felt utter despair, but Alun knows him and he wrestled with him. He wouldn't be mistaken.'

'Neither were you. I believed you; after all, Ellis Owen was a man you'd known well, but I didn't want to build up your hopes when there was so little chance of him being caught.'

The knock at the door made them start and Dic hurriedly disappeared up the stairs to stop on the landing and listen as Marion came in and cheerfully introduced her supposed boyfriend, Eric.

'Lowi, this is Eric. The reason he hasn't introduced himself before is because of his wife,' she said brightly. 'So considerate he is, doesn't want me involved in the embarrassment of his divorce.' She turned to the tall, young man at her side. 'Eric, love, meet Lowri who's put you in the role of a criminal, and a dead one at that.' She laughed and the young man stepped forward offering a hand. Bemused, doubtful, Lowri shook it.

The couple sat down close together, hand in hand, and began to discuss their plans and Lowri was almost beginning to believe she had been mistaken.

'I married too young,' Eric explained. 'I knew that, as soon as I met Marion. Made for each other we are, and as soon as the divorce is underway, we'll tell everyone how we feel.'

Dic came down the stairs and smilingly offered his hand to Eric. They sat for a while, Marion eagerly informing them of their plans and Lowri sinking more deeply into depression by the minute. Her belief that Marion was helping Ellis had been pure fancy, dredged up by her desperate need for it to be true.

Typically, there were other callers and with growing confidence, Marion told Kitty and Bob and Stella and Colin about how soon she and Eric would be together with their child. Eric said very little; nervous, Lowri presumed. When questions were asked he generally deferred to Marion for the answers. It was as Marion and Eric were about to leave that the third knock announced another visitor. This time it was a policeman, who made both Marion and Eric tense nervously.

The constable showed them some of the clothes found in the submerged suitcase.

'Can you tell me if you sold any of these in the post office?' he asked Lowri. 'Mrs Stella Jones told me earlier she thought so but couldn't be sure.' He gave Stella a smile. 'You deal with the buying, she explained, so we're hoping you'll be able to tell us who bought them.'

As he revealed the first cellophane package, Lowri gasped and looked at Marion, who was white with shock. The policeman held it in front of her and asked again, 'Recognize this do you, Miss Vaughan? Or can you tell us who it might belong to?'

Lowri was silent, she knew it was one she had chosen from Ken's warehouse and also that it had been Marion who had bought it. After a brief hesitation, Marion said, 'Sandra has one like it. I bought it for her when she went to a birthday party. This isn't hers though, got jelly all down the front, she did, and it's hanging on the line. I washed it this morning.'

Lowri stared at her friend. The party had been weeks ago, surely the dress had been washed sooner than this? The uneasiness increased after the constable had gone and Marion forced the conversation onto more cheerful things, like children's parties. Eric seemed to be getting more nervous and as he stood to leave, reaching for Marion's coat from the chair where she had thrown it, there was yet another knock at the door.

'Busy place this is,' he said helping Marion on with her coat. 'No wonder you've got so many chairs.'

Ken walked in and smiled, having overheard Eric's comment. 'I've never known such a place as Badgers Brook for attracting visitors,' he said, then he turned to Eric and offered his hand as introductions were made. 'Hello, Eric.' It was clear that Ken made Eric even more nervous and he walked to the door in a hurry to depart.

Ken stared at him curiously, trying to place him as Marion went through her story yet again. Then he said, 'I've got it! I knew you, but couldn't remember from where. You work in Cardiff, don't you, a salesman in a small bespoke tailors? But what's all this about a divorce? You're still living at home with your mother and sisters, no wife that I've heard of. I know your sisters quite well, one of them worked for me for a while.'

Dic stood up and asked, 'How much did Marion pay you to take part in this charade, Eric?'

Eric ran from the house and white-faced, Marion followed.

'Ellis is going without you, Marion,' Lowri called after her, following her towards the gate. 'Can't you see it yet? He's used you to cover his tracks and now he's going without you.'

Marion ran up the road and Lowri, followed by Dic, went after her, determined to make her listen. 'He threw the case overboard. Ellis did that and he's laughing as he leaves you behind.'

'Tell us where we can find him, please,' Dic pleaded. 'Come on, get out of this with some dignity left. Marion, face facts before it's too late.'

Marion screamed at them as she and Eric ran off, 'Shut up! Shut up, you're talking rubbish.'

Confusion was followed by relief after a puzzled Ken listened to the explanations from the others of what had gone on before he arrived.

'Thank goodness you came, Ken,' Dic said. 'How did you know our impostor?'

'I actually bought a suit there recently. It was as simple as that!'

–

Ellis sat near the beach and watched as Alun dragged the small boat up on to the gravelly shore above the high tide mark. He had watched and listened as Alun had rowed slowly along the edge of the cliffs as the tide was at its highest and was hindering Ellis's plans. 'Damn the man,' he muttered. 'Now I'll have to wait.' It was almost dawn and the chances of being seen were surprisingly great. Not many people were about, but the few who were would be certain to notice anything unusual. Fishermen, bird-watchers and dog walkers and those who couldn't sleep.

They all looked around observing, noting stories to tell when they got back home to convince others of the great time they had had.

He waited with growing irritation while Alun stood, staring out across an empty sea for what seemed hours, then heard him crunch his way up to the road. A car started and moved away and only then did Ellis move. He was laughing – the dangerous situation excited him. He moved through the slowly wakening day and made his way to Marion's home, preparing his story as he went.

A few stones thrown against her window brought her running out of the house to where they usually met, in a small stand of trees not far away.

'Darling,' he said holding her close. 'Did you hear what happened? Some one got into the boat and stole the food and threw your case into the water. I haven't been able to get near you since then with so many people searching for me. How did they find out about me?'

There was reproach in his question and she forgot her suspicions and held him tight. 'Lowri won't give up on finding you. And now she's convinced Dic and Alun and everyone else, it seems. Even the police called to show Lowri the contents of the case and asked if I recognized Sandra's little party dress.' She began to sob. 'They looked at me suspiciously.'

'You were imagining it.'

'I'm not, they know something. I could see it in their eyes. I went with Eric as you suggested, to put them off the scent and it was working, but then Ken Hardy came and he recognized him. Ellis, when can we leave? I'm so afraid.'

'Give it a couple more days. You can cope with that, can't you? I have to restock the boat with food and with most things rationed I have to find the right people and pay a lot of cash.'

'I've still got about thirty pounds. I was saving it to keep us as we travelled through France.'

'Thirty pounds, that will help replenish the food. Where did you get that?'

'I sold a few things and worked extra days over the past months.'

He laughed and looked at her with pride. 'You are a remarkable young woman, Marion, and I'm so lucky to have found you.'

'I'll bring it to you tonight,' she promised, her eyes glowing.

'Don't forget your clothes,' he reminded her. 'Just a few things, mind. We can buy all we need when we get there.' He hugged her and added, 'Just a few more days, three maybe, four at the most, then we'll be together without the need for secrecy, never being parted again.'

–

Lowri was at the post office the following day but she was finding it difficult to keep her mind on her work. Where was Dic? He had decided to go to the boatyard and ask Jake for help finding the boat on which Ellis was apparently making his escape. He knew all the small recesses along the cliffs and they needed his expert help. And where was Alun? With Stella's permission she phoned The Ship to be told Alun was resting but would be out searching again in a couple of hours. More importantly, where was Marion? Had she joined Ellis and ignored the suspicions they had tried to engender?

At four thirty, Stella came into the shop and told her to go. 'No use at all this afternoon, Lowri, love. Best you go home and find out what's happening.'

'There's no phone there. How will I know anything?'

'If I hear some news I'll send one of the boys to tell you, there are always a few hanging around the street. And, I'll tell Betty Connors to do the same. Now go.'

Lowri knew Stella was talking sense but she couldn't go back to Badgers Brook and wait. There had to be something better she could do. The day wasn't one to entice her to walk. It was dreary, cold and damp with occasional drizzle making the ground slippery. She jumped off the bus at the top of the lane and, despite the lack of appeal, instead of going down the lane to the house, she turned and walked along the overgrown path alongside the wood.

Mosses and struggling grasses and weed made the path hazardous and once she slipped and grabbed a tree to prevent herself from falling. With smart court shoes on her feet this wasn't a good idea. She went into the wood, pushing her way through the hedge and headed in the direction of the cliffs and that hut. It was still slippery underfoot but she moved with care, avoiding the worst areas. It was a long walk but at least the strenuous exercise had helped her mood. At six thirty, filled with regret for her stupidity, she was standing a few yards away from the hut in the gloom of the evening, wondering why she hadn't gone home.

She was surprised to find no one watching the place. From the few discussions they'd had it was decided that someone should be there at all times. Harold Saunders had taken annual leave to contribute his time to the watch and Alun was free to help whenever he wished. Dic had to go home to the children but even he had agreed on the hours he would spend there. So where was everyone?

She went towards the hut. It was already getting dark and a nervousness settled in the vulnerable spot between her shoulder blades as though a target had been drawn and somewhere an arrow was being lined up ready to shoot. So when a low voice called her name she almost screamed.

'It's me, Marion.'

'Marion, what are you doing here?' Recovering, she added, 'Waiting for Ellis, the man you don't know?'

'I had to come to collect a few things he'd left behind. Don't think you can stop me, we have it all planned. Sandra and I will be leaving tomorrow night to start a new life with him in Spain.'

'You won't get away. The police believe me now and there are so many people looking for him. Give him up, Marion. He'll let you down. If you help the police now they'll be lenient.'

The movement behind her was so sudden she didn't have a chance to run. Someone grabbed her from behind and held her. A hand covered her mouth and she saw Marion react, her hands covering the lower part of her face, her eyes staring and filled with shame. 'I'm sorry, Lowri, I really am. But we have to do this.'

There was momentary relief as the hand across her face slipped and she shouted, 'Marion. You can't let him harm me. You're the one who'll take the punishment. He's leaving you behind!' She was shouting and then the hand was back and another held her wrist and pulled her around. A knee pressed behind her own and she fell to the ground. It happened so fast she had no chance to break free. She heard Marion wailing for him to stop and then the pressure was gone and Marion and her assailant were gone. There were voices then, and feet running towards her and before she could stand, arms lifted her and Dic was holding her and uttering soothing sounds as though she were a child.

Harold helped her up and Dic set off to where he had left the car, half supporting her in a way she found comforting. Alun was in pursuit of Marion and Ellis but he came back after a few minutes disgusted with himself for failing to catch the man yet again.

'I didn't see them go. One minute they were running across the grass and the next there was no sign of them.'

'Take her back to The Ship, will you?' Dic asked Harold. 'Take my car and I'll stay here with Alun. It's time you had a rest.'

'No, I'll stay, Dic. You take her home and wait with her until someone comes. She shouldn't be on her own, not for one minute. Besides keeping her safe, someone needs to make sure she doesn't go wandering off again,' he said, shaking his head with disapproval.

Back at Badgers Brook, where Lowri insisted on being taken, Dic made tea and a sandwich and then admitted that he had to leave. 'I have to be back for Sarah-Jane and Katie or they'll wonder what's happening,' he told her. 'Will you be all right here alone?'

'Of course. You go and see to the girls.'

'I shouldn't leave you here, really. Won't you come with me? Or I could take you to The Ship? Betty will look after you.'

'I don't need looking after, Dic. You go and see to the girls. I'll be perfectly safe here.'

'You'll keep the doors locked and you won't go out?'

'Just go, Dic, I'll be fine. Someone is sure to come soon. As you know this isn't a house that's empty for long.'

He went out and waited until he heard the key turn and the bolt being pushed across, then he drove back to the shop. Barry was only about seven miles away but it seemed like double that as he left her further and further behind.

Back in Badgers Brook Lowri picked up the cookery book that she had forgotten to give Dic. She propped it up on the mantelpiece, hoping that Sarah-Jane wouldn't be too disappointed not to have it as promised. Lowri sat with the wireless off, listening to the small creaks and sighs of the old house settling for the night. She wished Dic had stayed. Her confidence was fading fast and she was tempted to leave and spend the evening hours with Stella, where there was a phone. Or with Betty Connors at The Ship.

–

The police were still unconvinced about Ellis Owen. After all, they had only a few sightings of the man and with nothing else to back them up they could hardly organize a full-strength manhunt for a man believed to be dead. It was only Harold Saunders's determination that persuaded a few to help, and that was in their own time. One watched Marion's house, another stood near the hut; no one watched Badgers Brook as nobody knew Lowri was there on her own, the presumption was that Dic had stayed.

Alun served in the bar of The Ship for a few hours that evening, hoping that if Ellis heard of him being there he would be persuaded that they had given up their search. He had contacted Jake, who had agreed to row quietly along the stretch of beach where the cliffs rose straight out of the sea. He knew of the many small inlets capable of hiding a boat.

Jake moved slowly across the dark water, oars moving in the rowlocks with hardly a sound. The tide was high and calm. He checked the rocks and went into every inlet large enough to conceal a small boat. An hour passed without success, but he didn't give up. His eyes were accustomed to the low light of a thin moon, and the shapes of the rocks were sufficient for memory to fill in the rest. As a boy, he had spent hours around the coast, hours that would have terrified his parents if they had known.

It was as he reached the area below the place where the hut stood, where the rocks curved in, he was about to pass by when a straight line caught his eye – a straight line where there were only rough irregular shapes. He moved cautiously until he was certain, then moved slowly back before turning and making his way back to the beach from where he had begun. He was impatient now and, once he was far enough away from being heard by anyone on board, he increased speed, beached the boat and hurried to where he could telephone The Ship.

-

At Badgers Brook Lowri was relieved to hear a knock at the door. Kitty, Stella, or perhaps Dic was back. Oh, how she hoped it was Dic.

'Lowri, dear, it's me, Terri.'

In haste Lowri unlocked the door and threw herself at Ellis's wife. 'Oh, thank goodness. I'm so glad to see you, I've been so scared.'

'What's happened?' Terri asked hugging her. 'Tell me everything.'

'Ellis is alive.'

'He can't be. You're imagining it, love.'

'Someone else has seen him, someone he knows very well.'

'Who, dear?'

'You wouldn't know him. His name is Alun Harris.' Lowri felt a tightening of Terri's grip but it was momentary and she didn't give it a thought.

'Alun Harris?'

'He says your husband cheated him too. You've had a lucky escape, you might have been accused with him once he's caught.'

'There can't be any evidence or all this would have come out at your father's trial.'

'You're right, we've searched for Dad's diaries but they aren't among his things. They must have been destroyed by your husband when he left, taking the money with him. I'm sorry, but you must prepare for more trouble. You have to face the fact that he was a real criminal and he faked his death somehow.'

'So many people saw him drown, how can you believe he's alive?'

'I've seen him. He attacked me earlier today. He's alive, and planning to run out on you and the gullible, besotted girl who's been helping him.'

'Marion Lewis you mean?'

'Come with me and find her. Between us we can persuade her to tell the police where to find him. This could all be over in hours if you'll help. My father could be free and your husband behind bars where he deserves to be. Cheating on you in the worst possible way, you must want him caught?'

'Oh no, dear. I don't want him caught. He and I are leaving tomorrow on the early morning tide.'

Lowri was alarmed to see a glint in Terri's eyes, a tightening of her lips. 'What do you mean? You can't think of forgiving him?'

'Why not? I planned the whole thing.' Lowri made a dash for the door and when she reached it, the key was missing and the door firmly locked.

'Sorry, but you can't leave. Not yet.' A man's voice. She turned and stared at the man who had put her father in prison.

'Ellis Owen.'

She wondered later why she hadn't struggled. Being faced with a woman whom she had trusted and the man she hated above all others, she had just surrendered. Terri's hand on her arm, Ellis holding her wrists behind her, she went with them like a lamb.

It wasn't until they tried to push her into the car that she recovered from the almost trance-like acceptance. Then she shouted and screamed and pushed against them. But Ellis held her tight, kicked her legs from under her and within moments she was lying across the back seat with Ellis on top of her and Terri was driving down the lane like a maniac.

\-

At The Ship and Compass, Betty watched Alun, who was trying to behave normally, yet was obviously on edge. 'Alun, why don't you take a break,' she said loudly, then as she beckoned him towards the door into her back room, she whispered, 'Please, Alun, go and find Jake and catch this man. I have an awful feeling about this. I'll pretend you're still here taking a break.'

285

Without arguing Alun grabbed a coat; Betty handed him some sandwiches and made him wait until she had filled a coffee flask, then he hurried out by the side door. Betty picked up the phone to ring Dic, but put it down again. He would be at Badgers Brook looking after Lowri.

Ken called in soon after Alun had left. 'Where's Lowri?' he asked at once. Betty gave him blow by blow details of what had happened. 'Where's Lowri?' he asked again.

'Dic's with her at Badgers Brook.'

The telephone rang at that moment and it was Dic. 'I wondered if there was any news,' he asked.

'Where are you?' Betty asked. 'Is Lowri with you?' She listened for a moment, her eyes widening with alarm then put down the phone. 'Lowri is on her own! He left her, without even asking Kitty to stay with her!'

'How could he do that?' Ken ran from the pub and drove to the old house where a light shone from the kitchen window, the door was wide open and the place was empty.

–

Alun rowed to the spot Jake had described and found Jake there, his boat a short distance from where he had seen the bows of the cruiser. He tied up his boat by fastening a rope around a convenient rock and they waited.

Ellis had climbed a few yards above where the now loaded boat stood. If they didn't leave soon, he'd miss the darkness. Not knowing exactly where Terri was added to the problems. After all these months on the run, to have messed up so close to departure was frustrating. That damned Lowri Vaughan. Why had she been so stubborn? And to have come to Cwm Derw to live was fate playing a cruel joke. In the calm movement of the water below, he remembered the night of the storm. He had been struggling in the wild sea for several minutes, then remembered the safest way to deal with the life-threatening situation. He relaxed and allowed the waves to take him where they chose. He concentrated on breathing and staying afloat by spread-eagling and floating. He hit against something and clung to one of the supports of the pier for a few moments, but the escape was illusory and he was wrenched away from it and sent further away from the shore.

Fate was generous that day and he had hit his head against an anchored boat, turned upside down but still afloat and managed to get underneath it and clung to the seat, pushing his arms under to get better purchase, and there he stayed until the tide relented and he was able to make the shore.

He smiled to himself. Being given those two chances that night had been an augury. A sign that he was going to succeed in getting away with the money. The confidence he'd had from that moment had never wavered. All he had to do now was stay calm and be patient. It was so easy.

Then suddenly there were shouts from above…

–

Seven miles and Dic drove them faster than ever before. He'd been so stupid to leave Lowri on her own. But there was always the children. They would come first with him whatever happened. He wondered how much of his feelings for Lowri was because of them, a dream of having a mother for them as they grew up and needed a woman's care.

Guilt overcame him and he lost concentration, swirling to avoid a car coming from the opposite direction. He quickly picked up speed again and was soon running up the path to Badgers Brook. Like Ken before him, he found it empty apart from Kitty, who sat on the step wondering when someone would tell her what was going on.

'I told Ken, Bob and I heard screams and shouts and when we went out there was a car driving off and that's all I know. Bob's gone to phone the police,' she wailed. 'Poor Lowri, something awful happened, I know it.'

Without waiting for anything more, Dic drove to the cliffs. It had to be something to do with that area, although he couldn't imagine anyone expecting it to hold any secrets any more.

Ken was there when he reached the hut, kicking at the padlock and shouting in frustration. He turned on Dic and began calling him every name he could think of, then said, 'Wait here, I'll go back to the car and get some tools.' He put a hand between the bars and held it against the window, and inside, a ghostly pale hand pressed against his behind the glass. 'No,' he said, changing his mind. 'You go and *I'll* wait with Lowri.' He handed his keys to Dic who ran off instantly.

The padlock was eventually broken under Ken's frantic efforts and Lowri ran out. She was going to Dic to be hugged but Ken stopped her and turned her towards him. His arms held her and his voice was emotional as he said, 'No, Lowri. It's my arms you need. I'm your future, Dic is from the past. A big brother who's always been there. But everything changes, I'm here now and I'll never leave you.'

In a moment of clarity, a sense of relief and happiness overwhelmed her and Lowri knew he was right. She raised her head awaiting the kiss that would confirm their love and their future.

They moved away after Lowri had told Harold Saunders all she knew and the information had been passed to the policemen. In the distance, a police launch would soon be on its way to the rocky anchorage below.

–

Ellis knew he had to get away, but how? The boat he had was far more powerful than those waiting outside the inlet, but once he started the engine whoever was in them would have plenty of opportunity to leap aboard and overpower him. He looked up apprehensively. He had made the climb several times just for fun, but he had been fully equipped then and precautions had been in place and he'd had a friend with him. Could he do it alone? It had to be soon, before the police were here in force. Taking the risk of there being someone waiting for him above, he tried to remember a point where he could change direction and reach the top, out of sight of the hut. Memorizing the places higher up where there were loose pebbles and soft soil where his feet might slip, he began to climb.

–

When the police found Terri sitting calmly in a small hotel a few miles away she pretended surprise at their questions and denied any rumour about her husband being alive. Then they brought Lowri into the room and Terri's face betrayed the truth and they took her away for questioning.

–

In her mother's house, Marion sat waiting for the night to pass so she could go with her new suitcase to where Ellis had promised to be waiting. Less than twenty-four hours now and they'd be on their way. Excitement filled her and made her heart race. To have such an adventure was unbelievable. Imagine the story she'd be able to tell Sandra when she was old enough to understand. It's better than a story book, but unlike the best stories, the ending was not what she had so often dreamed.

The police came and after a very brief interview with her mother and stepfather present, she was taken to the same police station as Ellis's wife, where she learned the painful truth that she had been used and had been helping a criminal evade justice. A criminal who all along had planned to leave her behind.

–

Ken didn't leave Lowri. 'I'm not leaving until the police tell us Ellis has been arrested,' he said. 'Even then, I don't want you to be on your own.'

Lowri stared at him as though seeing him for the first time. 'Why have I been so wrong about you?'

'You had no brothers and Dic filled the gap so well, you convinced yourself you couldn't manage without him. And you probably thought he needed you, too.'

She snuggled closer. 'D'you think your parents will accept me now they know my father isn't a criminal?'

'Lowri, don't build up your hopes. Ellis being alive is one thing, but proving he was responsible for the fraud is another. It will probably mean another trial.'

'But they'll have to admit they were wrong!'

'I hope so. As for my mother and father and giggling brothers, forget them. I'm marrying you whether they come to the wedding or not. Besides, I haven't met your father, and he might not approve of me!'

Lowri frowned. 'All this and we still haven't any proof of my father's innocence?'

'I'm hoping that will follow, but don't expect everything to be perfect straightaway. It must justify further investigation and surely that will be enough.'

'If only we could have found Dad's diaries.' She rose to make some tea. 'Will a sandwich do?' she asked.

'A sandwich? And what's the cookery book doing on the mantelpiece? Don't tell me I'm marrying a woman who can't cook!'

'Fish and chips from Gwennie Flint's?'

'No, a sandwich will be perfect.' He picked up the cookery book and opened it at random. 'Lowri?' he called thumbing through it. 'What sort of cookery book is this? It's full of figures.' The covers were loose and inside them, instead of recipes there was a notebook filled with her father's writing with dates and figures to show he was noting Ellis's thieving.

'Ken! It's my father's diary. It's been in front of us all along.' Then she frowned. 'But why didn't Dad tell anyone? He must have put it there for safe keeping, so why didn't he show the police?'

'I don't understand either. What did he say about it?'

'That the evidence was in a notebook somewhere.' She looked at the cover with it's picture of a picnic table set in a vegetable garden. 'He must have used an old cover so it looked like a harmless recipe book. And that's just what I presumed it was.'

'This is what Ellis must have been searching for.'

It was two days before Ellis was found. He had slipped as he reached up for a hand hold yards away from the rope marks Alun had found on the cliff top. His fall had ended on sharp rocks not far above the waves he had cheated once before. His injuries hadn't been fatal, but a night on the cold rocks with broken bones, suffering from shock, had resulted in hypothermia, which had been. Ken was with Lowri when they heard the news she had dreamed of for so long, Ellis Owen's body had been identified, the evidence against him in the form of the notebooks handed in and Jimmy Vaughan would soon be free.

It was Harold Saunders who went to tell Terri the news of her husband's death and to arrest her. The real reason she had sold everything was undoubtedly to help fund a fresh start. But it was in France – not Spain as Marion had believed – with the man whose survival she had helped to conceal.

Love has its dark side, he thought. Marion Davies had been duped by its tender folds into breaking the law and cheating on a friend before being let down in the most humiliating way.

Lowri and her mother as well as Dic and his parents were interviewed and told all they knew. Jack Morris, Dic's father, was inconsolable.

'Knowing I doubted Jimmy is bad enough, but the way I behaved towards Lowri is inexcusable,' he said to Cathy. 'How can I face her after this?'

'I've spoken to her,' she said. 'It was difficult at first but she listened and I think, given time, she'll understand and forgive us both.'

'I'm not sure I can forgive myself,' Jack said sadly.

'We have to go and see her. She's living in Cwm Derw not far away.'

'Just walk in and tell her I'm sorry? It won't be that easy.'

'We have to try. Perhaps Dic will go with us.'

'She might not want to see any of us. Even Dic let her down, leaving her alone, knowing Ellis was looking for her.'

'Don't underestimate Lowri.'

He smiled then. 'Ellis Owen and Terri did that, and look what happened to them.'

–

Ken's parents too were uneasy about how Lowri would behave towards them. They had acted badly when she had told them of her father's imprisonment. They both wrote to her and explained their reaction and ended with the hope that as their prospective daughter-in-law, she might forgive them. In answer, Lowri, with her mother's full agreement, invited them to come on the day her father was being released, knowing that his intention to face everything immediately had to be her way too.

–

While investigations were beginning, there were celebrations at The Ship. Alun was helping in the bar and he had stayed on after lunchtime session on Saturday to deal with the cellar ready for the following week's deliveries. After brushing the walls, washing the floor, cleaning the copper and brass, he went up to the ground floor where Betty was making tea. She had been to the bakery for cakes and they sat in the quiet of the room behind the bar and Alun felt utterly content.

'Glad it's over, even though you might not get your money back?' Betty asked.

'It was more than money he took from me. I lost interest in everything. To have worked for years learning my trade, then struggling to get the property and build up a reputation, for those things there's no compensation.'

'What will you do now?' she asked. 'Are you ready to start again?'

He turned to look at her. 'Yes, I am.'

Betty tried to hide her disappointment. He was leaving and there was nothing to offer, except a job helping run The Ship, to persuade him to stay. 'Good on you,' she replied knowing the words sounded less that genuine.

'What I'd really like to do,' he began, then he looked at her, his clear eyes staring at her, lighting up his sometimes solemn features, 'really like to do, is stay here and help you run this place.'

'You mean it?'

'Betty, I've never been this happy since I lost the restaurant. I like the variety, the visitors passing through, the locals, who have made me so welcome, and I like the way you work. Will you consider taking me on? I might not give as much amusement as 'Willing-But-Won't' and the rest, but I'm sure I can avoid being boring.'

Betty didn't know what to say. Ever since Ed had moved out, she had dreamed of finding someone who cared about The Ship and Compass as much as she did, and unbelievably, she had found him. 'Alun Harris, get off that chair, there's work to be done. Tonight we're having a celebration.'

It was a few weeks before Jimmy was freed. Leaving the house in the hands of a regular guest, Emily met him outside the prison and took him straight to the railway station. She hardly spoke, tears were so close to the surface. He seemed content to look around him, feasting his eyes on the towns and countryside they passed, and was fascinated just watching people go about their normal routines. It was as though he'd been on a journey to a far distant planet.

She had suggested they went away somewhere where they were unknown for a few days, before meeting everyone, to give him a chance to adjust to the freedom, but he had refused.

'I want to go to Badgers Brook,' he'd insisted. 'I want to face everyone straightaway and from what Lowri has told me, Badgers Brook is the best place to do that.'

When their taxi arrived at Badgers Brook that evening, he stepped out and straightened his back as though about to march into battle, which, in a way he was. Knowing who would be there, facing everyone for the first time since before his arrest, took all the courage he could muster.

Lowri had been looking out of the kitchen window and she ran out and took the suitcase her mother had brought, plus the pathetic bundle that represented Jimmy's life over the past months. She chattered as they walked up the path to the back door, giving him time to prepare.

It was his partner Jack he saw first and hesitantly Jack offered his hand. A moment then as Jimmy's pale face tightened, then he took the hand and shook it. Cathy came forward and kissed his cheek. Lowri, standing beside

Ken, introduced him and Ken offered his congratulations, remarking on his wonderful daughter.

Lowri didn't know whether to take charge and lead him in to face the others at once or allow him to sit in the kitchen for a while talking to Jack and Cathy. Jimmy made up his own mind: Putting aside his wife's supporting arm he walked into the living room of Badgers Brook, where a fire burned brightly. The windows shone and reflected the people inside so the outside was an extension of the group of friends. There were a few he knew and some were strangers but all were smiling. He looked at Dic, sitting in an armchair with his daughters on his lap and said, 'Hello everyone. Hello Dic. My word, Sarah-Jane and Katie, haven't you grown.'

Then the peace of the place settled on them and conversations began until laughter and the murmuring of friendly voices filled the air. An hour later the neighbours started to arrive.

Lowri and Ken looked around them and smiled contentedly. 'I know you had your doubts, but look at everyone,' Lowri said to her mother. 'No one can be unhappy here.'

Ken's parents found friendliness; Lowri's parents seemed to hold them no grudge for their earlier behaviour and his brothers enjoyed comparing experiences with Bob about their prowess on the rugby field.

Dic sat there feeling like an interloper, only occasionally joining in with the conversation. His father, Jack, was still uneasy too, only his mother seemed relaxed. Then she whispered something to Jack who went back to his car and brought in a package.

'I have another apology to make,' he said handing it to Jimmy. 'You gave me this to look after for a few days and I'm sorry, but with all that's gone on, I forgot it.'

Jimmy took it from him but didn't open it, he handed it to his wife. 'Emily, love, this was your birthday present, but you might have difficulty opening it.' The paper was removed to reveal a small tin box with a lock on one side. 'I'm afraid I've lost the key,' he admitted. 'We'll have to break it open.'

With a gasp, Lowri stood up. 'No you won't, I think I have the key.' She ran up to her room and rescued the key from the toe of her Wellington and brought it down. It turned sweetly and inside was the necklace Jimmy had bought for Emily's birthday, many months before.

'So all the mysteries have been solved,' Dic said. 'Life will be quite dull after all the excitement.'

'I hope so,' Ken and Lowri chorused.

Later, when her parents were asleep and everyone else had gone, Ken brought out a small box. 'I hope it fits,' he said as she opened it. 'And I hope we'll buy the wedding ring to go with it before the spring. The bungalow is ours and will be ready in April.'

'A perfect month for a wedding.'

'And the ring? Does it fit?'

'It's just perfect, like you, and everything else on this wonderful day.'